Roly's Rules

By

Rob Legg

Published by New Generation Publishing in 2023
Copyright © Rob Legg 2023
First Edition

ISBN

Paperback	978-1-8356-3003-7
Hardback	978-1-8356-3004-4
eBook	978-1-8356-3005-1

www.newgeneration-publishing.com

 New Generation Publishing

For Celia, Rowan & David
Without their love and Support
I would be a different person.

Chapters

Chapter 1

Anything but a Fill-in

If he had been asked to describe himself, Roland would have said that he was thirty-six years old, no children, but happily married to Hayley. That was because Roland lied. He didn't mean to, but he just wanted a safe little message to give out if others wanted to question him. He was thirty-six and he had no children, but he was not happily married. He had known that for some time but had thought that it was his own little secret. Roland could go through life moulded into a rut for a comfortable fit.

It was Sunday evening. Roland Johns lay on the sofa. His eyes were open, the television was on, yet anyone observing him could tell that he was not watching. An old familiar hymn started up as an introduction to a regular religious programme. A hymn Roland remembered from childhood, at least some of the words, and it was as if the television was trying to ring a bell and announce calmly, "Six o'clock and all's well." But all was not well and frankly, Roland was not sure if it would ever be well again.

Yesterday, Hayley had surprised him by announcing that not only was she not happy but, unlike Roland, she had decided to do something about it. She was leaving Roland to move in with Tony, her married boss.

Hayley had an energy for life that when they first met had been a great attraction to Roland. If they went to a nightclub and danced, she would drag him into the centre of the floor, while he would have preferred anonymously to fling a few limb twitches about in the shaded fringe areas.

If they were in a group of friends talking, she always ensured she was in the middle holding forth with her views on the topic of the moment, while Roland tended to listen. They had been married now for over eight years, and his admiration for her energy and her delight in encouraging his shyness had changed. Not overnight but gradually. Now he saw her as an egocentric person. She would respond to a discussion about a possible global flu pandemic with, "I had flu once." During a discussion on tsunamis, she would mention how on their Greek island summer holiday the waves were so strong that they knocked her over. For Hayley, any subject regardless of scale, criticality or seriousness could be used as an introductory segue into an insignificant event in her life. That allowed her to turn everything into something that had her firmly placed in the centre. Roland had held these views for at least two years now. Although Hayley was capable of irritating him, he had developed the ability to switch off from it. He had been so unaware of her feelings for him – but last night she had certainly made him aware of how she felt. It started with a secretive mobile telephone call which she took while running from the lounge into the dining room for obvious privacy. Phone call over, she swaggered back into the room and announced, "Roly, we have to talk."

Roland looked up with raised eyebrows and said nothing.

"Roland, I am leaving you. Tony is leaving Beth and he and I are going to re-start our lives together. Do not try to stop me!"

Roland did not try to stop her. Indeed, his only response was to raise his eyebrows even higher as he tried to match the words to a meaning. This was not the response that Hayley wanted; the actual lack of a response seemed to drive her into a frenzy.

"Oh, that is so bloody typical, you don't even have the energy to fight me or to fight for me." With that, she left the room looking more miserable and upset than Roland had seen her for a very long time.

As she left to pack, Roland started to wrestle with the significance of the moment. Slowly, he followed her to the bedroom, where she was crying on the bed. Roland sat down on the opposite side of the bed and in a quiet voice started to talk.

"How did we get like this? How long have you been seeing Tony? No, don't tell me, that's not my first question. Why are you having an affair in the first place?"

As the question hung in the air, Roland realised he knew the answer. It was about energy, as she had said before. It was all about a lack of energy in their life together. They had the same values, they even had many of the same interests, but it mattered only to emphasize their differences. Hayley had to be in the centre, Roland always expected and wanted to be on the fringes. With Roland, Hayley would always feel that she was missing out.

"My God," said Roland, which didn't really mean anything as it was just the sound that came out as Hayley's announcement started to sink in. Hayley at first simply stared at him as he paused and then after a while the pause became a silence and so she got up and started to pack things. It was probably only seconds and not minutes but Roland was wrestling with all these internal questions.

Did he care? Did the thought of Hayley and Tony

upset him? Did he want more? Did he want more with Hayley? Did he want to fight for Hayley? What should he say? What should he say? What should he say? This last question echoed around his head like a stuck track on a CD. It was provoked not only by his confusion but also because he was aware that he had to do something. He could not sit on the edge of the bed and be quiet while his wife of eight years walked out. He looked up and in despair said to her, "Hayley, is it because I cannot make you happy?"

He looked up and saw Hayley now staring back at him with mouth agape.

"What did you say?"

"Is it because we are not happy together?" he repeated almost apologetically as if he had already taken the blame.

The explosion of malice, disrespect and almost disregard hit him like a wave as Hayley responded, "I am leaving you because you are a nobody; you're going nowhere and dragging me with you. You suck up oxygen that could be better used by others. I want out – from you, with Tony or frankly with anybody or on my own. I want away from you."

If ever there was a statement that crystallised all Roland's thoughts into clarity, Hayley had said it. Looking back, Roland wished that he had simply turned away and left her, but he didn't. He stepped forward intending to hit her, not just a slap but a full-blooded punch into that evil little mouth. A punch that would split her lips, rattle her teeth, knock her down on her backside. But he couldn't. He simply turned and walked out. Hayley was very aware of what had almost happened.

Many hours later when he returned, she was gone, gone for good. Roland had walked the streets, embarrassed that he did not know where to go but after about an hour a nondescript pub appeared and he entered and got drunk. Isn't that what you are supposed to do? He didn't have maudlin conversations with strangers or the bar staff, but he did drink.

He made it back to the flat but could not remember how. He made it to the sofa but not to the bedroom. He slept until about midday and woke up feeling like shit. He had managed to relieve his bladder and drink some coffee but was still queasily laying on the sofa waiting for his body to feel human again. The television programme had changed; now there was an old black and white cowboy film on, the type he would watch as a child. Yes, the town bank had been robbed, the robbers had fled, the sheriff had pulled together a posse and the chase began. As the long camera shot played upon the posse as they rode towards the camera, Roland realised that there were three or four characters in the middle (the sheriff, his young handsome deputy, the local rancher and the town lawyer) surrounded by another six to eight individuals who were anonymous fill-ins.

"Who am I?" asked Roland aloud. He knew what he meant, was he a character in life or a fill-in? He knew the answer, yet almost independently of conscious thought his mind drifted immediately to Mrs Smith's English class in school at the age of thirteen or fourteen. They had been given an essay to do on the subject of Lord of the Flies – if you were one of the boys on the island who would you choose to follow, Jack or Ralph? Thirty kids in the class and twenty-nine wrote: If I was on the island, I would follow Ralph because he is good and Jack is evil. Roland had written: If I had been on the island, I would have followed Jack because he frightens me. And then he proceeded to mention all the various bits of the book where Jack bullied the weak. Mrs Smith thought it was an outstanding essay with such a good understanding of the nuances of the book. He got top marks, a gold star and was asked to step out in front of the class to receive his due praise. For that moment he was a character, for that brief moment he was in the headlights, but it was a false position. After all, his essay had simply said that he preferred to be a fringe nonentity trying to stay out of the way when the big action took place – a fill-in.

As a wave of tiredness flowed over him, Roland wondered about the future and all the changes that would come. He wanted to know what he was going to do with his life but, even more basically, what type of person he was or even, if changes were to come, what type of person he wanted to be.

"Anything but a fill-in," he murmured to himself as he fell asleep.

Chapter 2

On the Way to Work

Roland woke with a start and at first could not work out what he was doing on the sofa. As he lay there, the quietness of the flat told the story and it all came back. Hayley was gone and that was fine. There were changes to be made and that was also fine, but it was 06:15 on a Monday morning and he had to get ready for work.

He headed to the bathroom for a shower and twenty minutes later, clean, shaved and smelling sweet, he stood in the kitchen making coffee. He felt surprisingly good, well-rested and in good spirits. The alcohol of Saturday night was now out of his system. The lost Sunday to hangover and sleep had restored his body. He felt hungry for breakfast and ready for the world.

At 07:20, Roland approached his parked car ready for the forty-minute drive to work. Roland enjoyed his work colleagues but not the job and he loved his car. His car was bought with the money left to him by his father, who on his deathbed had whispered to him, "Enjoy your life, don't waste time and don't put off what you want."

Roland smiled as he remembered. He was left £57,000 and Hayley was so supportive. He should have used £50k to reduce the huge mortgage they had and the rest on a holiday. Instead, he bought a Range Rover Vogue with every option on it and so many dials and knobs that there was probably a three-week residential training course on how to work everything. That was two years ago and there were still buttons he had not pressed but there was never a moment when he sat in it that he did not rub the leather interior, remember his dad and smile. And Hayley had understood and supported him – there had been times when they were close. He started to wonder again – where or when did it start to change? A shiver ran through him, enough to snap him out of that particular train of thought.

Off to work. Roland was a senior product manager for a large medical instruments company. His boss had recently retired leaving him and another senior manager running the department. Frankie and Roland were in competition for the top job and a few weeks ago they had made a pact to split the work and let the best man win with no hard feelings. Roland had already realised that Frankie's concept of an equal work split was that he should go to all the big marketing conferences in exciting places around the world and make all key product presentations to the board while Roland did the work. But Roland did not mind, he was happy working with the staff, working with the factories and generally getting things done. He knew he was well liked and respected by many and all the good feelings were returned from him to them.

The journey to work through the morning traffic was another routine that Roland enjoyed. He prided himself that he knew the roads so well. He knew what lane to be in when there were going to be snarl-ups and how best to avoid them. And as he drove, he drank his coffee from a travel mug and listened to the news on the radio.

On the outside lane of two, approaching the roundabout which gave access to the motorway, the traffic slowed as usual. You can sometimes tell in traffic when something is not right. A driver might hesitate when he shouldn't, or a vehicle might weave a little or just not be positioned as normal. For these reasons, Roland noted the van behind him. It was quite an old van – something like a Ford transit van with a back door, side door and a bench seat in front where three people could sit. For the last 400 yards, it had been jerking forward as the rest of the traffic rolled slowly and it had been weaving towards the inside lane and then back out to the opposite side of the outside lane while the front three peered forward as if searching for something. Roland noted it all but put it down to impatience. He tried to ignore it but found himself constantly glancing in his interior mirror. The traffic in front started to move forward and as Roland started to follow, suddenly, with a surprising roar the van lurched out from behind and started to overtake him. Road rage thought Roland as he braked to stop the van hitting him as it darted back in front, but it got much worse. In absolute horror, Roland saw the side door fling open and two men jump out with automatic guns. Roland simply stopped and watched through the windscreen as if he was in a cinema watching a film. Just in front in the nearside lane was a typical limousine, chauffeur-driven and with all the windows blacked out. This was the men's target. One shot the driver point blank through the driver's side window and then ran around to the other side only to shoot and be shot at by what must have been a bodyguard. They both went down. The second man was tugging and then shouting at the back door before preparing to shoot. Roland did not think, he did not decide to get involved, but seeing the man standing with the machine gun ready to rake the car with bullets just caused a reaction. He accelerated hard and simply ran the man down. Horns had been blaring, gunfire had been crackling but suddenly there was quiet. The limousine's back door opened and out scurried a very old gentleman in Arab dress, pulling behind him a young schoolboy in school uniform. The old man, with a firm grip on the boy, started to move away, half crawling, and looked directly at Roland. Their gaze met and in an instant, he had pulled open the back door and pushed the boy inside.

"Please, please, sir. Help us," the man said.

Roland was dumbfounded. His mouth just hung open and no words came out. But his eyes saw movement and he saw another terrorist (because that is what they must have been) start to exit the side door.

"Get in, get in," Roland shouted.

Roland screamed and as the old man fell into the back of the car on top of the terrified boy, he hit the accelerator and launched forward, hitting the van on the back nearside corner, causing the terrorist to fall out, dropping the gun, and the vehicle to swing into a horizontal position over the nearside lane. Roland hit the van again, pushing it further up the pavement towards a small garden wall and then reversed back and accelerated to the roundabout.

In the time that it took them to travel the hundred yards to the roundabout, Roland was examining what was happening behind. His heart leapt as he saw the van aggressively reverse back and then start to chase them. Oblivious to all that had happened, the traffic on the roundabout coming from all the other directions was patiently rolling forward as if it were a normal day.

"Mustn't stop, mustn't stop!" shouted Roland to no one in particular as he tried to progress at speed while spending more time looking in the mirror at the van coming up fast behind as he tried to negotiate normal morning traffic congestion.

"Please, sir," said the old man, "don't let them kidnap the boy. If they can they will, or they will kill him and us."

Roland's mind was racing, not over anything specific, just racing as if it was in overload mode and couldn't take it all in.

"Mustn't stop, mustn't stop," he repeated and then launched the car across the roundabout traffic over the small dome of grass and flowerbeds, and headed diagonally across to the small exit of a country lane. Cars screeched, one bump to a small car, but within seconds he was away leaving absolute chaos behind.

Within twenty seconds of quiet at an almost leisurely 40 mph, Roland drove through the winding lane almost normally. In a surreal fashion, the old man was picking up the boy and sitting him down and putting the boy's seatbelt on before sitting calmly by his side.

"You must take us to the police, sir," he said quietly to Roland. "There we will be safe until our people come."

"Who are you? What's going on?" Roland asked, trying to keep his voice as low key and calm as the old man.

"We are members of the Saudi royal family, and my grandson's father – my son – is responsible for eradicating terrorism in our country. I came this morning to collect my grandson from boarding school and to return him home because we had intelligence that he was to be kidnapped to pressurise his father to release people who have been imprisoned for terrible wrongdoings. You are a very brave man, sir, and you will be well rewarded for your assistance."

Roland did not feel brave, in fact he was shaking all over.

"My God, look at my car!" he said.

Roland had been glancing in the interior mirror during the conversation and now his heart leapt as he saw the white top of a van above the hedgerows rapidly catching up as the country lane meandered through the Berkshire countryside.

"Shit!" exclaimed Roland and the car shot forward as he hit the accelerator. "They are still behind us." As the car accelerated Roland switched on the hands-free mobile and stabbed in 999.

After a brief ring, it was answered with a calm female voice, "Emergency services. Do you require ambulance, fire or police support?"

"Police, police – get me the police!" shouted Roland.

"Your name please and where are you calling from?" the lady calmly responded.

"I'm Roland Johns, driving a beat-up sage green Range Rover, speeding from Bedley Green down some country lane that I pray to God is going to come out the other side of Welford Town. I have two members of the Saudi royal family in the car, and I am being chased by a big fucking white van that is filled with terrorists that just shot up Bedley Cross roundabout and now want to kill or kidnap us."

There was an explosion in the back of the car as the back window shattered. Roland glanced backwards and as the road had straightened out the van was getting closer with a man leaning out of the passenger side window.

"Oh fuck! Now they are shooting at us," Roland said.

"You've got to help, are you still there?"

Still calm and in control as if she handled such calls every day, the emergency operator said, "Yes I'm here, what is your destination?"

"Destination? Destination? I've got no fucking destination. I am just trying to get away from them."

Roland thought for a moment and had a brainwave. "No, I tell you what, if this road comes out where I think it does, I am heading for Welford Town Police Station. Tell them to get some guns out because they are going to need them – the terrorists have machine guns."

"Yes, Mr Johns, please stay on the line – I will pass your message on and get back to you."

She sounded a little anxious and Roland could not help but smile, albeit just a little, as it was likely that she didn't have a call like this every day. Suddenly, the left side of his seat seemed to disintegrate into bits of leather and seat filling.

"Oh shit, my car. They're destroying my car," squealed Roland and at first he didn't notice that he had lost all control of his left arm and blood was running down his sleeve and rippling over his watch strap.

"Fuck, I've been shot!"

Accelerating even faster one-handed and looking in the mirror, Roland saw the white van about fifty or sixty yards behind.

The old man (now again on the floor behind trying to cover his grandson with his body, who was crying silent tears but with no sound), pushed his head, shoulder and arm through the gap in the front seats and tugged at Roland's jacket.

"Sir, sir, are you alright? Can I help you?"

It made Roland smile, he didn't know why, it wasn't

because he wasn't afraid, he was terrified. He looked for his cigarettes and lighter by the gear lever, still balanced there even through rundowns, crashes, off-road over the roundabout and driving down small country lanes like some sort of rally race. He tried to pick them up, but his arm just didn't move.

"Yes, you can help," he said. "Light me a cigarette."

The old man did as requested as Roland swung the car around bend after bend, sometimes only precariously in control, but it was certainly more welcome than being fired at again if the road straightened out. The old man placed a lit cigarette between Roland's lips and said, "You are very brave," before retreating to cover his grandson on the floor again.

A huge initial drag of smoke filled Roland's lungs and he felt good but within seconds the smoke was going up his nostrils and into his eyes and he couldn't take it out without taking his only working hand of the steering wheel. He grimaced and tried to roll the cigarette with his lips to the corner of his mouth but succeeded in dropping it onto his lap. He stared in frustration as it rolled between two folds of cloth and started to burn the trousers of his expensive navy-blue suit.

"Help me, help me. I've dropped the cigarette!" he shouted as the cigarette started to burn his thigh. The old man reached back in and picked it up and threw it on the passenger seat. Roland just did not care anymore that it would burn the beautiful leather. More importantly, he had to drive.

"Mr Johns, are you OK? Do you know where you are?"

The telephone car speaker came to life and his calm and efficient emergency lady was back on the line.

"I've been shot, so add an ambulance to the police; they are still chasing us about fifty to sixty yards behind, but I think in a few hundred yards I am coming up to a housing estate near the motorway entrance by Welford."

"Where have you been shot, Mr. Johns?" asked the calm voice.

"In the car," said Roland and then started to smile at his ridiculous answer. "I mean in the left arm – it's useless and dribbling blood all over the poor fucking car. Listen up, the housing estate is coming up. I am going to go through it across the Green, past the motorway entrance and straight to the police station at the next roundabout. Can you get some police here – we need help."

"Mr Johns, now we know where you are, police cars are being scrambled," an authoritative, calm male voice spoke. "Mr Johns, I'm Superintendent Geoff Wilson from Thames Police – we know what happened at Bedley Green roundabout, so don't lose it now, stick to your plan, you're doing great. We'll have armed police all around you in minutes."

Around the next bend was the turning into the housing estate full of young families and designed for commuters.

"God, let the roads be clear," said Roland as he braked hard and swung right into the estate. He needn't have worried, two short streets later and he mounted the pavement and headed across the Green towards the road on the opposite side, the car slaloming and skidding over the long, wet grass. When he was almost completely across, he saw the white van behind brake hard and stop.

"Yahoo, yahoo!" shouted Roland like some demented cowboy. The old man looked at him, puzzled. "They're not coming, they're not coming over the Green," said Roland and half turned and looked back with the old man.

"Oh fuck!" exclaimed Roland as the car shot suddenly over a particularly high pavement onto the road. By chance they hit no other traffic as Roland desperately pulled on the wheel as they slewed right up the road. Within a further 100 yards, two police cars with lights and sirens in full blast came racing towards him and drove past.

"I'm faster than you thought, you silly buggers," roared Roland and carried on to the roundabout where on one side was the local district police station. Standing outside the station in the front pedestrian court were about five men. Roland saw no guns but assumed they were armed and waiting for him. There was a small single road with a barrier that controlled car access to the station, but Roland was just suddenly too tired to comply and so instead he mounted the kerb yet again and let the car gently roll towards the station entrance. He stopped.

The door opened and a man said, "Mr Johns, we've been waiting for you; what have you been up to this morning?"

"I was on my way to work," said Roland.

Chapter 3

What Does This Mean?

That evening, after surgery, Roland woke in hospital to see a policeman by his bed. As his eyes became accustomed to the room, this fellow rushed out and returned within minutes with an obviously older, more senior man.

"How are you, Mr Johns?" asked the older policeman quietly. "I am from the national anti-terrorism squad. Can we talk? Are you up to it?"

Roland could not stop his eyebrows lifting.

"I always thought all you guys were like James Bond or something?" The older fellow (still no name) smiled as he sat down beside the bed. He leaned back and patted his portly stomach.

"We do not all have to engage in hand-to-hand fighting," he said. "Some of us are in the background trying to work on intelligence so we know what is likely to happen. We all serve, Mr Johns, and you did your bit today – can you tell me about it?"

"Your name?" asked Roland.

"Just call me Peter," he returned, no surname or title offered.

Together they chatted as Roland tried to explain what had happened and how it had happened while Peter just nodded and asked for clarity on a few occasions without it seeming like an interrogation at any time. As the conversation came to a close, Roland asked the one question he had been dreading.

"Peter, what happened to the man I ran down?"

Peter started to rise from the bedside armchair and said, "Good job there, Mr Johns. That is one less we have to track down. When a head is caught between a kerb stone and a Range Rover, I suppose the outcome is inevitable." He saw the horror and alarm on Roland's face and reached over to hold his right hand.

"Roland, you are a good, decent man who was caught up in a situation out of your control. It is not your fault and certainly not your problem – you will hear no more about that event, so just forget it. That might seem difficult right now but please believe me, I know what I am talking about. If you try you can and will forget about it." Then with a nod and a half smile Peter left.

Roland had no time to consider Peter's comments because as he left, in came a doctor.

"Ah, Mr Johns, awake and talking already I see. I must have done a fine job then. How are you feeling?"

"My left arm is bandaged from shoulder to wrist and perched up on some sort of bed-shelf. I cannot feel anything, but I know I was shot. What is the damage? Doctor er…?" said Roland as he struggled for yet another name.

"Dr Harold Chewson – your surgeon, Mr Johns. We met briefly before the anaesthetics but there was no reason then for social introductions. Yes, you were shot in the elbow or more accurately through the ulna as it meets the humerus. No bullet to dig out, just needed to clean it all up really. Bullet went straight through, unfortunately taking much of the pronator teres muscle with it, but I've stitched in some spare thigh muscle for the moment and now why don't we just let time and natural healing do the rest."

"Will I ever play the piano again?" said Roland with

weary sarcasm since he had not understood anything that the doctor had said.

The surgeon smiled. "Are you left-handed?" he asked, and as Roland shook his head he continued: "Well, that is good. The bone will sort itself out but there will be a need to support the joint for ten to twelve weeks during which time your good muscle will deteriorate while your damaged muscle will grow and develop. After twelve weeks your arm will be as stiff as a board and we shall put you on a course of extensive exercise therapy, hopefully organised by a very attractive young lady, and over the following three months you will regain about eighty per cent of your original function. However, you will never be able to throw or pull with your left arm without it telling you that it has been shot and as you grow older it will remind you on cold, wet winter days regardless of any throwing or pulling. Regarding your thigh's donation of some muscle, you have a slight cut and bruise that will ache for a few days and as long as you have no intention of doing the marathon later this week there will be no long-term impact whatsoever. Mr Johns, when a bullet comes in contact with a body it causes trauma – the body always comes off worse. You have been very lucky; in six months you will recover almost completely, many do not."

After that the surgeon briefly glanced at his medical charts and left.

Roland shook his head slowly; he wanted to say something and knew that there must be good words available, but at that moment all he could do was slowly shake his head. He had been in hospital now for three days and had been surprised at how tired he still felt.

Everything had moved quickly from the moment that he had stopped the car outside the police station. He vaguely remembered it all; it was just too surrealistic – more like a dream than real life but the throb in his left arm reminded him.

"How's the hero today?" asked his nurse as she came into the room. Roland didn't know her name but she had been his main nurse since he'd arrived at the hospital. She was about his age but although full of efficient hustle and bustle, she had a lovely smile and a nurturing, almost motherly way about her. Roland felt that he wanted her to just put her arms around him and to stroke his head as she said, "There, there, it's going to be all right, now go to sleep," just like his mother would have done had she been alive and of course, if he had been seven and back at home with a skinned knee or a splinter in a finger or if anything else in the world had upset him.

"I'm no hero, I was too scared to be a hero," said Roland.

"Oh yes you are," said the nurse. "Day three and still on the news and headlines of the newspapers, and all lined up outside to interview you whenever you want to see them."

"Please, please," said Roland. "I do not want to see anyone."

Roland had already had several visits and although all so very different, not one of them had been comfortable. Hayley's visit had been the most difficult. Early the second morning – before she started work – she arrived rushing in saying, "Roly. Oh, Roly, I was so worried, are you OK? It must have been awful. You have been so brave. Oh, Roly." It was all in a rush with no breaks for either a breath or a response from Roland and it all culminated in a full-blown hug with her burying her head in his neck and sobbing.

"Roly, I thought I had lost you and I realised that I cannot live without you. How did we ever get ourselves into this position? It must have been awful for you, terrifying. I did not know it was you until I got home yesterday... I mean Tony's place." Again, Roland recognised the same gush of words with no breaks for breath or input from him, but the mention of Tony brought them both up short and Hayley ended the hug and sank into the bedside armchair.

"Roly, sometimes it takes something like this to make you realise what we're missing – do you think we can try again? I know I have done and said some terrible things, but I will always love you."

Roland let out a sigh so big that it surprised them both. The meaning of the sigh was interpreted differently; for Roland it was despair but to Hayley it was a sign that they were back together again. She started to speak, but Roland recognised no words and held up his good arm.

"Hayley, I am so very tired. I cannot talk now, please let me be." She seemed to understand and jumped up, smoothed his blankets and kissed his cheek, and told him she would be back later that evening. With a flourish and almost a skip in her step she left the room, stopping briefly in the doorway to blow him a kiss.

She didn't come back that evening; Roland was relieved but curious all the same.

"Look, you are on the telly again," said the nurse as she put a thermometer thing in his ear and proceeded to update his charts and dole out his painkiller tablets. "You are the national hero of the moment and well deserved, I'm sure."

He glanced at the screen to see Frankie of all people standing outside the office building as the presenter said, "What makes a hero? Today, we have come to see Roland Johns' colleagues and friends at his work to find out, and here is Mr Francis Williams, a co-director with Mr Johns and someone who has worked closely with him for many years. So, Mr Williams, you know Roland Johns very well, what type of person is he?"

Dressed in his best suit, white shirt and silk tie normally kept for boardroom presentations stood a smiling almost bug-eyed Frankie staring into the camera.

"Oh yes, Roland and I are very close, we work together, we do everything together. I cannot tell you how shocked I was to hear the news..."

Roland tuned out as Frankie gushed and gushed but still managed to use the word 'I' more often than any other. It was ridiculous, but it was Frankie. It brought a smile to Roland's face.

"If you were able to say a few words to Roland now, Mr Williams, what would you say?" asked the presenter.

"Roland, with press like this, you are sure to get the promotion," spouted Frankie and with that Roland's smile burst into laughter. He laughed and laughed and only stopped when the nurse started to look at him in a slightly concerned manner. Even if everything else in his life was unclear, Roland knew from that moment he was never going back to work, to Frankie, to that life. It was not him and now all he had to do was work out what was him.

The television picture broke to the press outside the hospital and there was Hayley in the middle of a scrum of reporters. "Mrs Johns, Mrs Johns!" they shouted, and she quickly stopped to do her 'Frankie moment' for the cameras. She said that Roland was recovering, how his arm had been shot and how she was going to look after him, and how they were going to get away and take some sort of break, and she was going to do this or that… she this or that …I this … I that … smile for the camera and with an almost coquettish manner, she moved towards the hospital entrance and through the revolving doors. The camera panned from the doors back to the reporters and as it swung around, Roland saw something that hit him like a punch. There in the car park was Tony's yellow Mitsubishi sports car. No one in it but it was Tony's car – she had driven to the hospital to see her husband in Tony's car!

In the two or three minutes that it took Hayley to get to his room from the hospital reception, Roland had stared coldly at his bedclothes and ignored everything else in the room or on television.

"Hello, darling, how are you feeling?" she asked, without waiting for an answer. "You won't believe the number of reporters outside waiting for news about the hero," she said with a smile and excitement in her voice. Hayley paused for a brief moment realising that Roland had made no move, comment or recognition towards her since she had entered the room. She paused for a moment and then continued: "They just would not let me through without speaking to them. I was being filmed so it will probably be on television; we should try to find out what channel and watch it. I said that when you are fit enough and leave here, I am going to take you away for a vacation; we can go somewhere nice, perhaps something up market if you get a reward. That's what they are saying, the Saudis will give you a reward… have you heard anything yet? Probably not, too soon,

Roland, are you listening to me?" This now was a question and with a stupid smile on her face she leaned over Roland and looked into his face.

"I saw you," said Roland.

"When?"

"Just now on the television," he said, pointing to the small television up on the wall. "You came here in Tony's sports car."

"What do you mean?" she spluttered before realising what he meant. "Tony is out of town. I drove him to the airport yesterday and I'm just using his car until he gets back. I haven't told him about you and me getting back together, I'll do that when he returns at the end of the week. I'll return the car then, it's just so nice to drive. I didn't think it mattered. Does it matter?" She looked at Roland hard and even again answered her own question as she realised that it did matter. "Roland, I'll return it today, I'll never drive it again. Tony and I are over. He'll understand, it's just… it's just… it has been so crazy. We haven't had any time to talk."

Roland stared back at her, and she continued: "I mean, Tony and I haven't talked, you and I did yesterday, didn't we?"

"No, we didn't talk, Hayley, you did. You always do. You told me what you wanted to do, and you said it in such a way that by the end of it you were stating what we wanted to do… but I do not remember saying what I wanted." As Roland spoke, he had found his voice rising.

He calmed down and continued, while a stunned Hayley simply stood and listened.

"I know what I want. I want a divorce. This is lucky for you because now you don't have to tell Tony and you can continue to drive his little Fuck-mobile."

"No, Roland, you don't understand... it has come out all wrong. I love you and it's you I want to be with. I'm not going to divorce you... We can work this out," she whimpered. She asserted herself and stood up straight. "I am your wife. I am not going to divorce you."

Roland looked at her and smiled; he had always understood her, and now more than ever.

"Hayley, I want my clothes and my car and my divorce – nothing else. You can have the house, furniture, CDs everything. Let me tell you what I am going to do if you visit me one more time or if you give me any resistance in getting the fastest divorce possible in the western world. I am going down there to your reporter friends and tell them that you had left me forty-eight hours before this stupid hero thing happened, how you have been fucking your boss Tony because he lets you drive his yellow sports car, but how you haven't told Tony yet that you want to come back to me because you hope that you can stay in the centre of the cameras as we enjoy a reward from the rich Saudis. They will get to know you like I know you. You will be the most famous pond scum in the UK and by the way, I'm pretty sure that Tony will drop you like the poisonous self-centred little toad you are. Now, get out and only ever communicate to me via my solicitor when I get one. Until then, I want my clothes and car put in the garage and I do not want to see you again. You were right when we spoke last Saturday. We are not a couple. You deserve Tony and I deserve better. Now get out!"

Hayley was stunned, just stunned, and the pause, although probably only two or three seconds, seemed so much longer. She made an involuntary sound that was a mix between a sob, a yelp and a whimper before turning on her heels. She snatched up her coat, which she hugged to her lower face and stormed out of the room almost knocking the lovely nurse standing in the doorway with a large vase of flowers. The nurse looked down the corridor after Hayley and then anxiously came into the room. It was obvious that she had been in the doorway a while and had heard quite a bit.

"Nurse, what's your name?" said Roland in a now quiet, measured tone.

"Sally, Mr Johns," she replied.

"Sally, I am sorry about that. You must have heard quite a bit."

"Yes, I heard enough, but it has nothing to do with me."

"Sally, this terrorist thing, it has made me realise what is important. I have seen people killed, I ran a man down, and I ran over him as if he was a speed bump. He's dead, I'm shot in the elbow and a hero. Isn't it stupid?"

Nurse Sally had put down the vase and had approached the bed placing her arm on his shoulder.

"It must be very difficult to understand all that has happened to you, but it will in time, I promise. Now is not the time to make big decisions. Let yourself just relax and get better."

"Lovely Nurse Sally, you are so very wrong. Now is the very time to clearly look at your life and to decide exactly what you are going to do with it. And that is what I am going to do. I am going to sort out my stupid, silly little life and do what I want to do and what I value. I am not going to be a character in someone else's story. But you are right about one thing, I am going to take the next few days to relax and work out what I am going to do. Now, how about a cup of tea?" He smiled and with his good hand he reached up and squeezed Nurse Sally's hand to let her know how much he appreciated her and to confirm that he was not a raving lunatic or still in deep shock. His smile was rewarded with a bigger smile, and she left to get the tea.

When Nurse Sally returned with the cup of tea, she saw Roland reading the greeting card attached to the flowers. The card was written beautifully in blue ink and said, "Mr Johns, I send you healthy greetings from Abd al-Foud bin Nura."

Roland had a feeling who they were from.

Nurse Sally said, "Aren't they beautiful? They were hand-delivered by a young Arabian man and he asked about you and whether you could receive a guest this evening. I told him that you were receiving visitors; did I do wrong, Mr Johns?"

"Nurse Sally, the only wrong you could possibly do is if you keep calling me Mr Johns, that was my father's name, I am Roland. No, I lie, you could do wrong if you let that tea get cold."

"Roland," she said quietly and blushed a little as she handed him his cup of tea and then left the room with a smile.

Roland drank his tea, wriggled to get more comfortable and drifted into a gentle, untroubled sleep.

Sometime later, Nurse Sally woke him as she rolled up the sleeve on his good arm.

"Hello, she smiled. "Time for an injection."

"More pain," he muttered in a false grumpiness. "Do you take pleasure in injecting your patients, nurse?"

"Oh, what a hero you are," she replied. "You won't feel a thing and it will ensure that there is no infection in the bullet wound. I brought you the evening paper, there you are still on Page 1. Perhaps I will get a pay increase for nursing the national hero back to health."

"You could always sell your story and tell the world how I suffered in silence, a true man of grit and integrity. A man who willingly took on pain and laughed it away."

"I would probably get more if I told the truth about how you whimpered like a baby when you needed an injection, flinched when I took you temperature in your ear and complained bitterly if your tea was cold."

"My dear Sally, there must be a professional code of silence around the relationship between a patient and his nurse. The world will never know about the special things between you and me," Roland said with a smile and again Sally returned the smile and a slight blush as she left the room.

Simple, honest flirting and no more, but it did wonders for the spirit and Roland felt good for the first time in a long time – far before the last few days or events. He picked up the paper and there on the front page was his car. Driver's door open, blood all over the interior, the left side of the driver's seat in tatters with bits of stuffing hanging out, the back window shattered and the front and nearside of the car all scraped and dented.

"Oh, the car," said Roland. "What a mess. I'm sorry, Dad, I guess I didn't take good care of it." As he let the paper slip from his fingers onto the bed a young Arab man stepped into the room and then looked around before leaving; he returned soon after guiding an old Arab gentleman, his grandfather.

The old man smiled as Roland gestured to the bedside armchair.

"Mr Johns, how are you? Recovering well I hope?"

Roland reached again for the card that came with the flowers.

"Mr Abd al-Foud bin Nura?"

"Yes, that is my name. When we last met, we did not have any time for social introductions, did we?"

"How is the boy, your grandson?"

"He is back home surrounded by the love and security of his family, Mr Johns, and it is thanks to you. My family owes you a great debt; you are a brave man, Mr Johns, and we will always be in your debt."

"Mr Abd al-Foud bin Nura, sir – first am I pronouncing your name correctly? Is there a correct way but a little bit less formal way for me to address you?"

"Mr Johns, please call me whatever you want, we have been through too much to let such formalities bother us. I am an old man, in my country old people are treated with respect. When we were in the car you called me 'Old Man'. It can be said in a respectful manner. If you are comfortable, I would be honoured to offer this term to you to use when we talk." All this was said with a most benevolent, sincere, old-world gentlemanly style that Roland found almost overpowering.

"Old Man," said Roland feeling a little bit strange. "Thank you for that, now I am a middle-aged fool, but I would like you to call me Roland."

"Roland, that is good. Already we start to talk like friends," smiled the old man.

"Old Man, who were those people the other day? Why were they trying to kill you and your grandson? How can anybody be so indifferent to life, so indiscriminate in the use of violence?"

"Many questions, Roland, and I am sorry that there

are so few answers. They are people who are unhappy with what happens in my country, they do not accept the ruling family. They claim many inequalities and unfair issues and often they are right, but what they do not say is that they want to replace one ruling party that is trying to change slowly in a controlled way to the benefit of all our people to a far more radical approach that cares for no one but a small select group of fanatics. We cannot talk with them. It is sad but they will try to kill us, and we will try to kill them. Someone will win and I believe it will be us."

Roland looked at the old man and remembered how these terrorists were that day, how terrified he was when they first appeared and started to shoot at the limousine. He shuddered to think about them getting access to the old man and his grandson. He simply nodded as a sign of his understanding.

"So, Roland, tell me how can I repay you for your bravery and protection of my grandson?"

"Old Man, please, you owe me nothing. What happened was so crazy. I am not brave, I was terrified. I just happened to be there when it happened, and I just did what seemed to be right. Look at this newspaper headline," he said as he passed over the paper. "All they talk about is sensation, gossip, hero worship and rewards from the Saudi royal family for the brave hero. It is all false."

"So, Roland, you do not believe in all this," said the old man holding up the paper. "If not this, then what do you believe in? Let me understand, who is this man, this Roland Johns?"

"Old Man, I am a man with little spirit. I do not think I have ever been in control of my life. I have never done anything that I wanted to, I have just reacted to others. I think I am a good man, I have values, and I respect people. Last week I found out that my wife is having an affair and we are divorcing. I have a job that I really do not want to do and now all this. When I get out of here, I am going to start my life again. I am going to do what I want to do, what I value and love. I believe life can be good if you treat people with respect and if they do not treat me with respect then I will simply cut them out of my life and move on. I know all this does not make sense and I have to work out what it all means but I will or at least I am going to try." As Roland ended his little speech the younger Arab man stuck his head in the room and the old man looked up and nodded.

The old man slowly stood up from his chair,

"Roland, you are a good man and a brave man, and I hope now also my friend. I have to leave now but, in a few days, I will send someone to you, so please listen to what he has to say. I want to help you. I want to help you work out what it all means." He smiled, leaned over, and rested his hand on Roland's and quietly left the room.

"Work out what it means," Roland repeated the old man's words and pondered on the meaning.

Chapter 4

OK, so a New Start

Three days later, with an all clear from the doctor, Roland was getting dressed with help from Nurse Sally. The clothes he was putting on were the laundered clothes that he had entered the hospital wearing. They were clean but somewhat damaged in the left sleeve; he noticed it and tried to ignore the surge of old thoughts.

At that point, he became aware of someone standing in the doorway. The man looked English and in his late twenties, perhaps early thirties, and impeccably dressed. In fact, so well dressed that Roland almost subconsciously tried to hide the frayed bullet hole in his sleeve.

"Mr Roland Johns?" said the man and Roland nodded. "My name is Jeremy Gaul, I believe that Mr Abd al-Foud bin Nura, informed you that someone would visit you. I do hope that arriving unannounced like this is not proving inconvenient?"

There was a pause as everyone waited for Roland to respond. After a moment of silence Roland said, "Sure, no problem, please come in. How is the Old Man?" and as he said it, he realised it sounded disrespectful.

"Mr Johns, I do not personally know Mr Abd al-Foud bin Nura. I represent Coutts Bank and we offer business services for him and his family."

This bemused Roland.

"Then why are you here, Mr er…?"

"Mr Jeremy Gaul," he said smiling and offering his hand. Roland took it and as they shook hands he sat on the bed. Sally left the room and the visitor sat on the edge of a bedside chair and pulled a file of papers from his slim attaché case.

"Mr Johns, if you have a few moments, I have a remarkable situation to share with you. Mr Abd al-Foud bin Nura has instructed the bank to set up an account for you."

"Ah, the reward, is it?" Roland sighed. "Mr Gaul, I am no hero. I am no paid bodyguard. I am just an ordinary man caught up in an extraordinary… thing," as he struggled to find the words. "I want no reward, I do not want to be paid for my deeds, I want to be just left alone to get on with my boring humdrum little life that has no place in it for shoot-outs, car crashes and newspaper headlines."

The visitor heard all this but did not react, and after another short pause he continued: "Mr Johns, please hear me out. There is no reward as such, it is altogether a different situation. I have a letter here that I am to ensure that you and only you get to read it. The letter is from Mr Abd al-Foud bin Nura." He handed over a small envelope and Roland took it, and after a moment's hesitation, he opened it and began to read:

Dear Roland

I am now back in my homeland, and it may be some time before we can meet again in person, although I do hope that we will meet again.

I have spent some time thinking about our last conversation as well as remembering how you decided, when you could have looked the other way as a bystander, to help my grandson and me.

You talked about wanting to start again with your life, to do something different with your life. You said that you did not know what it would be but that you wanted to live a good life, be surrounded by good people who share the same values as you.

Roland, I want to help you achieve all this. I cannot give you happiness, self satisfaction, contentment, indeed all these things that you seek. What I can give you is the freedom through resources to follow this goal.

The Coutts Bank, instructed by me, will provide you with the financial backing to allow you to be independent and do or go wherever you wish as you establish this new life you seek. Roland, you are a good man and good men deserve to achieve their goal. I cannot look the other way and act as a bystander when a good man needs help.

We will always be able to stay in touch via Coutts and so until we next meet, I wish you well.

From an Old Man

Roland rocked on the bed, as Mr Gaul leaned forward.

"Mr Johns, I have taken the liberty to set up an account for you in your name and to provide you with a debit card on this account that you may choose to use either to access cash or make payments. We offer full banking facilities and if you ever have any questions, you have my card and you can always contact me personally at this number day or night. I will get your message and can then contact you. All I need from you to set it all in motion is your signature on this form here and on the card," he said and pulled an expensive pen from his inside pocket and proffered it to Roland.

Roland took the pen, signed and before he handed back the pen he pondered. "How much money is in this account?"

"Mr Johns, there is no money in this account, there is

a secured credit authority backed by Mr Abd al-Foud bin Nura."

"A credit authority?"

"Yes, it means that Mr Abd al-Foud bin Nura will personally cover your debts up to a certain amount."

"So, there is a credit limit – so what is the limit?"

"Mr Johns, the credit limit is one hundred million dollars," said Jeremy Gaul with a slight smile on his face. "Please take my card and contact me anytime you wish." Roland handed him his pen back and Mr Gaul stood up ready to leave.

***

Sometime later, but exactly how long he could not be sure, Roland became aware of Nurse Sally standing by his side.

"Are you alright?" she asked. "You look ashen, if you are not feeling well, you do not have to leave this morning. You can stay here longer if you need to".

Roland, stood up and putting his good arm around her shoulders said, "No, Sally, I am fine. It is time to get on with my life." Then switching to a flirting voice he continued: "Although it will break my heart – to match my broken arm – Sally, to leave you, I must go," and with that he hugged her and kissed her on the cheek and strode out of the hospital room holding his Coutts bank details in his hand, leaving a blushing nurse behind.

As he exited the hospital reception, he realised he had no idea where he was going. "Home, I suppose, at least to start," he said to himself and then walked across to a taxi as someone dismounted, and giving his address jumped in and sat back.

The trip home took a few minutes, and he asked the taxi driver to wait as he walked up to the door. Roland's key did not fit the shiny new lock in the door, and he immediately understood why. He entered the side door into the garage and saw her note which was written on a bank statement of their joint account – balance zero!

Take your clothes and go!

His clothes – suits, ties, shirts, socks, shoes and underwear were in an unreal pile on the floor of the garage and thrown on top of them were two empty cans of lawnmower oil, which had been liberally sprinkled over all his clothes.

Roland looked at it and shrugged: Nasty things are done by nasty people, he thought.

He walked back to the cab and said, "Take me to a cash machine and then how about a trip to the city?" As the taxi pulled away, Roland wondered what he would do if the Coutts card did not work. Of course it did not work, and Roly huddled by the cash machine and called Jeremy Gaul, more in hope than confidence with an ever more anxious taxi driver straining to hear. The phone rang and was answered at the second ring. Jeremy took control and although he did give the humblest of apologies for not emphasising the point that the card needed to be authorised before use, he did manage to point out, "But it does have a sticker on the card." He then asked to speak with the driver. "Take Mr Johns to this address and call me as you arrive. I will pay you twice what is on the taxi meter."

When they arrived, Jeremy was waiting outside; he paid the driver and ushered Roly into a side room off the reception area.

"You are booked into The Westbury Hotel; I will take you there personally. Perhaps, you would like to have some pre-theatre drinks with me and my wife this evening, as it is our wedding anniversary."

"I am sorry, but I have no clothes – none, only what I am wearing with bullet holes in the sleeves as well." He told Jeremy about his wife's actions.

With raised eyebrows Jeremy said, "Well, that can be sorted, let me make a phone call." He picked up his mobile and was soon into a conversation. Roly simply looked out of the window as the hustle and bustle of London rolled by. "Done," said Jeremy and started to usher Roly towards the door.

"This is most impressive, Jeremy; I never got this service from my High Street Bank."

"Mr Johns, it is amazing what we will do for clients who have a healthy credit authority limit," he responded with a smile. "Right, we are off to the hotel and Jamie will be waiting for us," and it was once more outside and the hailing of another cab. Roland sat back and let someone else take control and although bemused, felt in the company of a nice person.

At the hotel, they met Jamie.

"Mr Johns, Jamie and Jamie, Mr Johns," announced Jeremy without breaking step.

Jamie was a true gay stereotype – he minced, with limp wrists and a falsetto voice with a giggle and a smile that was just infectious. In full efficiency mode, Jeremy had a suite booked, and they exited the elevator to enter into a luxurious other world for Roly.

As he stood and stared, Jamie and Jeremy chatted. Jeremy announced he would be back in a few hours and Roly was left still standing bemused, with Jamie moving into full-on work mode. First, he took all Roly's measurements and then announced, "Smart casual and off the shelf," before promising to be back within the hour. One minute after leaving, he popped his head back in and with a delightful giggle said, "Sorry, shoe size?"

When finally left alone, Roly sat down on the sofa and sighed. He was tired, he felt confused, and he was worried – no, he almost said to himself, not worried just confused that any sense of normality in his life up to that point had vanished. He agreed with himself – he had no worries but then realised that perhaps Jamie's concept of smart casual would be very different from his.

He must have dozed because the next thing he was aware of was the inevitable "Yoohoo" from Jamie as he entered the room with a full set of parcels and baggage, which he simply dropped on the floor in the centre of the room.

"I am shattered," he announced. "I cannot go on for a moment longer without a cup of tea."

"Jamie, please allow me. Sit down and I'll put the kettle on," responded Roly and Jamie promptly kicked off his shoes and sat in the middle of the room and started to unwrap everything announcing as he tidily built a pile of new clothes in front of him.

"Underwear boxers set of three; Socks, selection of colours pack of five; three shirts plain colours button down blue, white and cream; trousers, navy and khaki; and blazer, navy, but without those horrid metal buttons, instead we have these brown buttons. Oh, I do hope they are not made from the horns of some poor animal." Jamie's look of despondency lasted for the few seconds it took him to realise that Roly was holding up a cup of tea in front of him with a small packet of chocolate bourbon biscuits.

"Ooh, just what is needed," he sighed. "Finally, we have a pair of Church's Oxford Brogues in burgundy so they can be worn with either khaki or navy trousers. What do you think?"

Now it was Roland's turn to smile, "Thank you, this is so good of you, far better than I expected."

"So, what did you expect?"

"Oh, I don't know – perhaps something not quite so conservative, this is just right."

With seriousness in his voice, Jamie replied. "I know what you needed. I would not be seen dead in this stuff but for you it is right," and then burst into a giggling fit while munching on a biscuit.

"Now do not forget your wash bag, razor, shaving cream, hairbrush, after shave and deodorant. I think it is time for you to smarten up – go shower and get dressed, I want to see the real you." And with that he pounced onto the sofa and turned on the television, allowing Roland to pick up everything and disappear into the bedroom.

Roland washed and dressed and was admiring himself in the bathroom mirror when the telephone rang, and he heard Jamie answer. Shortly afterwards Jamie knocked on the door.

"Quick, quick, Mr Johns, Jeremy and Lucy are waiting," and as Roly left the bathroom Jamie looked him up and down and smiled. "There you are, didn't I do good? I have turned you into a most elegant gentleman, Mr Johns."

"Jamie, I am very grateful and please, you cannot buy my clothes and call me Mr Johns – my name is Roland, my friends call me Roly. I would be pleased for you to call me Roly."

Jamie giggled yet again.

"Thank you, Roly," and then he linked arms with Roly and ushered him out of the room towards the elevator and down to meet Jeremy and his wife Lucy.

By the time they met, Roly had managed to disentangle their linked arms and after the initial introductions they sat and chatted like four friends. Roly, being the only new person, saw that it was clear Jamie, Jeremy and Lucy went way back.

Conversation was not awkward as Roly had anticipated. After introductions, Lucy simply smiled and said, "Mr Johns, this must be a difficult time for you." In that statement she seemed to recognise and acknowledge everything, and then turned to Jamie and got into giggles over gossip and names that had no meaning to Roly.

Jeremy spoke to Roland about his young family and twin toddlers, and about being at public school with Jamie, but within the hour, Jeremy and his wife were making their excuses and Jamie and Roly were left behind. More drinks were ordered, and they slipped into a semi-formal conversation with Jamie enquiring about Roly's ideas on his style of clothes, and giggling when he announced that Roly did not have any fashion sense.

"Jamie, you have been so kind buying me all these clothes, I do not know how to repay you for your kindness. I assume Jeremy has sorted out any expenses and stuff," said Roly, as he grappled with what to actually say.

"Don't you worry about money and stuff," teased Jamie as he fed Roly's uncomfortable words back to him. "This is a perfectly legitimate business and after we have sorted everything out, I will fully invoice Jeremy. Now, onto more important things, are you going to buy me dinner?"

"Of course." Roly smiled and they walked towards the restaurant only to be faced with quite a queue, all trying to get the attention of the Maître d'.

Roly looked at Jamie and shrugged, whereupon Jamie giggled and said, "I know, let's order room service," linking arms with Roly again, who simply smiled as he was led back to the elevators.

Two hours later, after smoked salmon, steak and crème brûlée and well into the second bottle of Rioja, Roly and Jamie were stuffed and content and chatting freely on the sofa.

"Jamie, how did you get to know Jeremy? I got the impression you were old friends."

"Jeremy and I were at the same school; he has been looking after me for years. School was a horrid place all rugby, cricket and Latin. A cruel place where anyone who was a free spirit could be cruelly bullied."

Roly simply nodded and Jamie continued: "Jeremy was not like the others, he was never a bully and he looked after me. He still does. Everyone eventually went on to university or the military, I went to fashion college. Many ended up in the city, like Jeremy, and through Jeremy I have started my own small business as a sort of concierge service providing confidential and reliable services to people working too long and hard to have a life themselves. It works for me, I have my life and I help sort out others, but let's talk about you! Jeremy has told me a little bit; I know from the papers that you are the terrorist hero who got shot saving some Middle Eastern royalty. Now you must tell me more about that!"

Roly sighed and tried to explain, starting with his standard "I'm no hero" comments. He was tired but comfortable and Jamie was a terrific listener and as they finished the wine, Roly went on to explain about his failed marriage and how he was at the crossroads of his life and trying to work out what he could, should and would do next.

"Roly, we are all struggling to get through life as best we can," said Jamie. "Take your time, you deserve it. I will help you any way I can as a friend, not a service provider. Tomorrow, we will get your clothes all sorted out and, in a few weeks, you will be able to face the world dressed most elegantly."

"Wait a minute, you just bought all my clothes," said a startled Roly.

With hoots of laughter Jamie squealed, "That was just to stop you walking around in torn, bullet-holed rags. We haven't started yet! You have many things to work out, let me do this for you." Jamie collapsed back on the sofa in hysterics at poor bemused Roly.

The wine was now catching up with both of them and they decided to call it a day and when Jamie staggered to rise, Roly invited him to stay over and sleep on the sofa with a blanket and pillow from the wardrobe.

In the morning Jamie was gone and had left a note that said he would return later in the day and that was the start of a growing friendship. Over the next five weeks, they shopped during the day, went to the cinema to see old films, ate together, drank far too much together and swapped opinions on what was important in life and slowly allowed Roly to decide on his next steps. They had agreed that at the end of the week it was time for Roly to move on.

On Thursday evening, they were sitting in a corner of a small bistro restaurant that they favoured far more than the elegant, over-priced show restaurants that they had soon got tired of and were both trying to not talk about Roly checking out of London the following morning.

"Everything all done then," said Jamie quietly. "Did the car get delivered?"

Roly's eyes lit up and he smiled, "Yes, delivered this morning. It is an exact copy of Dad's car apart from being brand new. I feel kind of guilty buying a completely new one. Do you think I am taking advantage of my benefactors?"

"Ridiculous, you save their grandchild and the grandfather, they have more money than they know what to do with and you want to save them a few thousand by repairing your dad's car which was only damaged because you saved them, ridiculous, ridiculous!" All the time this ever-louder tirade came his way Roly was trying to calm Jamie down but as per normal it had no effect.

"So where exactly are you going? What are you going to be doing?"

Again, a sigh and Roly responded, "I've told you, somewhere down on the coast but a little bit further from London where people cannot commute to London. I know what I want, a small place with a slow pace. I want a boat and I want to learn how to take it out on my own. Not a Gin Palace, a proper boat with character."

"So, you are still running away then, I mean small place, fewer people, slower pace and if that gets too hectic for you… you go to sea on your own. That's no way to live," said Jamie, taunting Roly now.

"No, not running away, not anymore, but I am going to run my life on my terms and my rules and if people don't fit in, then that's their problem," said Roly a little bit more forcibly than he intended.

Now Jamie looked hurt. "Do I fit in?"

43

"My God, Jamie!" exclaimed Roly. "You more than anyone has helped me get my perspective back on life. There will always be a place in my life for dear friends. But I am not going to visit you in those dodgy Fulham nightclubs that you dance in. When I'm settled you can visit me – simply any time you want to."

Jamie responded with a giggle and a smile and said, "Good, so what are these rules?"

"Well, I haven't written them down. I mean, they are not laws, and I am not questioning the Ten Commandments, but they are my twist on things."

Jamie smiled and grabbing a paper napkin from the table and fishing a pen out of his bag he wrote "Roly's Rules" and under that wrote 1…

Jamie smiled and responded, "Declare an asshole free environment!" They both laughed and by the end of the evening, there on the napkin, stained with a little red wine and a fingerprint of bolognese sauce were the six principles:

1. *Surround yourself with people who share the same values but be open to new things.*
2. *Never knowingly hurt a person and if you do apologise at the earliest.*
3. *If you can help people then do so willingly, but do not be taken for a mug.*
4. *Be polite and have good manners and try to face each day with a smile on your face.*
5. *Find something to be passionate about and when you find it explore it with energy.*
6. *Find someone new to share your life with and do not let the first mistake scare you off intimacy.*

With a teasing smile, Roly leaned across the table and grabbed Jamie's hand, "I will never forget that you helped me create Roly's Rules and apart from Rule 6, you fit in pretty damn well!" and with a squeeze on his hand they both knew the evening was over. Roly carefully folded the napkin and placed it in his wallet.

"OK, so a new start," said Roly to himself as they left the restaurant.

Chapter 5

Julian has Found his Power

Jules came down the stairs ready for school. His mother, as usual, stood in the hallway, looking old and careworn and with a weary smile to send him on his way. All it did for Jules was to remind him how different things had been before his dad left home over two years ago now. His mother had been a very smart, classy woman and to see her now poor, well a lot poorer than they had been before, and having to work to provide Jules and her with this two-bedroom Victorian flat was all it took to cause anger and bile to swell up in his stomach.

"No, I do not want any breakfast. I don't do parental kisses and if it rains, I will get wet because I am not wearing an overcoat," he announced as he side-stepped his mother and headed for the door.

"You can't always be in a bad mood, Julian," his mother wailed, and she sat on the stairs in bewilderment as he slammed the door and left. She knew something was up but not what and she struggled to understand.

Jules was not in a bad mood, this was Jules. He savoured his own identity, and as he swaggered down the street, he recognised that people treated him differently, with respect or more accurately most people avoided him at every opportunity. What Jules regarded as respect was seen by many as either fear or disgust. Jules was known by many in town, with the complete exception of his mother, as a teenage vandal cum gang leader cum general tearaway. All this had come to pass in just a few short months but for Jules, he now felt 'a someone' for the first time.

Julian Fox was sixteen years old and lived with his mother. Two years earlier, his parents had divorced. His father had had an affair and left them both for a younger female. If he had just left, then perhaps things would have not changed so much. After all, Julian and his mother were used to him always being away on business but no, it was not that simple. First, there was the anguished weeks of his occasional visit. His father said it was to check that they were OK but every time he came, he seemed to have a list of things he needed and slowly but surely all the stuff he wanted was picked up. Also, each of these visits was an opportunity for his mother to cry and wail and bleat and beg his father to come back but to no avail. As time passed, the raw emotion in his mother turned from tears to anger. Visits came to be screaming matches where she called him, and he called her, and Julian retreated to his bedroom and tried not to hear all the hurtful things said.

The turning point came just a few months later. His father arrived, as usual unannounced. As usual, they tried to start a conversation in a sensible but strained manner until he mentioned a divorce. Worse was to come – the tart (his mother's favourite phrase) was pregnant. His father wanted the family home sold and as he tried to explain to his shell-shocked wife, that he would buy them something smaller but still nice. The house was too big just for her and Julian but it would be a nice place and they would be happy. His mother launched herself at his father screaming like a banshee, slapping and pulling and completely out of control. His father tried to fend her off but after a short while he, too, lost his temper and simply lashed out with a slap that hit his mother to the side of the face. Her knees buckled and she slumped to a semi-kneeling position on the carpet and then his father hit her again and would have hit her a third time if Julian had not run into the room himself screaming and leaped at his father.

At fourteen, he was not a man and could not fight like a man and all he did was react by screaming, "Leave her alone, you fucker!" as he scratched his fingers across his father's face. "Leave us alone, we don't want you here!" His father shrugged him off and looked desolate, more so when he felt the blood run on his face. It is surprising how effective fingernails can be in making their mark. His father looked into the mirror in the hallway. Three blood-red scratches were starting to swell on his face diagonally from across his temple over his nose and through his cheek, leaving weals that looked like he had been attacked by a tiger. Socially, for a successful businessman with a young trophy girlfriend going through a difficult divorce it sent a different message – no tigers here!

His father turned and looked at his wife and son still kneeling together now on the carpet.

"Fuck you, fuck you both. You are not staying in this house, I am selling it and I will fight you for every penny. You have held me back like a weight around my feet for years. Well, no more! From now on, everything is through solicitors."

He stormed out and that was the last time Julian had seen him. And he was true to his word, the house was sold, the money that went to his mother was just sufficient for the flat they now lived in and the maintenance for Julian was not enough to keep him in the private school he attended.

This was where Julian's agony really started; he had to attend the local comprehensive and to the mindless thugs there he was the ideal target for merciless bullying.

For over a year, Julian was bullied because he was posh and spoke differently. He was bullied by several but one bully in particular made Julian his pet project – Dan Holvey. Several times a day at every school corridor meeting or inter-lesson break, Julian had his nipples tweaked, or his legs dead-legged or his ears pulled with such ferocity that the pain made him squeal and then cry. The more he squealed and cried the more fun everybody seemed to have, and the more Dan Holvey seemed to revel in his role of tormentor.

With his mother depressed and no one to talk to, for Julian suicide seemed to be an option worth considering and then something changed. Either puberty started to kick in or perhaps the unfairness of it all just started to build. He had done nothing wrong, why had all this come about and changed his life? It was not fair, it was not right, and he decided to fight back. He knew he could not match Holvey physically, but he became determined that he would inflict some sort of pain in return. It was strange because at first it seemed when he tried to fight back that all he had managed to do was to trade "Nipple Crushers" and "Dead-legs" for split lips and bloody noses, but if he managed to get in one or two licks from his side he noticed that Holvey seemed to prefer to change the torments from several times a day to several times a week. As good as that was, the thing that was better and truly surprised Julian was that it did not hurt so much when you fought back and sometimes when he saw it coming, he almost relished the moment of conflict.

It all changed just a few weeks ago. It was Saturday morning and Jules was walking back from the corner shop with milk and bread when as he turned the corner Holvey, and his band of thugs appeared.

"Hey, snot rag, you've brought me breakfast," said Holvey and grabbed the bread. "Breakfast anyone?" he shouted to his goons as he proceeded to deal out the bread slices as if they were cards. Jules stood just for a short while and then in one smooth motion flipped off the top of the milk bottle and twirled it over his head, spraying milk over everyone except himself. "I'll kill you this time," dripped Holvey and launched himself with flailing fists.

Fights don't last a long time, they are often over in seconds, at worse minutes, but strangely time can seem to pass very slowly indeed. Even so, they had not really got started when Holvey's sister appeared. For sure, Julian was losing but still every time he got knocked down, he got back up. Now girls usually get agitated when boys fight, but Holvey's sister was no doubt well used to it. Anyway, she was far more disturbed about something else.

"Dan, Dan!" she shouted. "Mam said you have to come home, a chicken is dying."

Holvey's attention was grabbed mid-swing of another punch and you could almost see his brain processing this urgent message – and then he was gone! He was running home holding his little sister's hand as if a family member was dying, not a chicken.

"What is happening?" asked Julian aloud and to no one in particular. Yet, a Holvey thug giggled and decided to answer.

"A chicken is dying, and he must get home to kill it before it dies or they can't eat it." Everyone laughed and for a brief moment Jules was almost one of them. The other boys explained to Jules about Holvey's home life – Dad a drunk and gambler; his mother a saint trying to feed him and his two younger sisters. Home was a wreck with a tin-sheeting rusty shed in the garden where the chickens were kept. Apparently, Dan Holvey had a soft spot. He might be a Neanderthal thug and bully to the outside world, but he would do anything for his mother and sisters. Immediately it became clear to Jules that Holvey did not have a soft spot, he had a weakness. Jules decided on revenge, he was going to attack mercilessly what Dan loved. That evening was to be the start.

The Holvey house was a semi-detached property that had certainly seen better days. This was made even clearer by the comparison to the homes around it. They had crisp paintwork, polished brass door handles, flowers in a smart front garden and a gate. The Holvey house had gone decades without any attention, the front garden had mud and abandoned toys and household rubbish and no gate. The back gardens of the street ended with a back lane and the comparison was even greater. Where some houses had greenhouses, vegetable patches, lawns and patios, the Holveys had an even greater area of mud, abandoned toys and household rubbish and a rusty tin-sheeted shed that had a roof that hung over the back wall to allow rain to drip into the back lane.

Jules crept up and sniffed at the shed. The unmistakeable smell of chickens made him wrinkle his nose in disgust. He lifted the spout of the petrol can he had taken from his own garage and prodded it through

51

the gap from the shed wall and roof. One or two chickens clucked but did not seem to object. Anxious though he was, Jules quietly continued until the petrol can was almost empty and he could not pour anymore without lifting the can so high that it threatened to break the roofing sheet. Satisfied that he had poured enough, he put the cap back on and pulled from his pocket the book of matches he had taken from a kitchen drawer. He hesitated, not because he doubted what he was about to do but more how he was going to do it. He decided not to drop a match into the shed and that is probably the only reason why he ended up keeping his hair and eyebrows. Instead, he put the lit match to a small piece of wood baton that some petrol had dripped on. It flared up a little but disappointingly soon returned to a steady flame.

In frustration, Jules prised it from the wall and it fell into the shed. No sooner had it dropped out of sight than there was an almighty whoomp sound and, as the roof lifted about six inches, flames shot up in all directions. Jules, protected by the wall, saw flames shoot above his head and he managed to maintain enough presence of mind to run down the lane, stopping as he reached a side road and looking back as he proceeded to walk home. He had left the petrol can behind but the garden looked like one almighty bonfire so there was no going back for it now.

The next day in school there was no Holvey. The whole school seemed to be giggling and laughing and making jokes about roast chickens! Everyone except Jules claimed they had seen or at least heard the fire engines in the night. That evening, the local newspaper, The Cranport Citizen, warned its readers of the presence of an arsonist in the town – but no clues as to who.

Days passed, and it was soon forgotten, Jules felt it was time for more action in his attack on Holvey's soft spot. If the removal of chickens did not provide a period of personal torment for Dan Holvey, then the stakes had to be higher.

It took a few days to identify it but as Jules realised what he would do, a satisfied smile crept over his face. In the middle of Holvey's street was an alleyway of steps that led upwards quite steeply to the next street where there were several shops. It was to these shops that Holvey's mother went to buy the family's groceries. Laden down with multiple plastic bags, she slowly and carefully negotiated the steps back home. At least that is what she normally did.

One Monday morning, Jules was skipping off school and checking out Holvey's street. Sure to form, Mrs Holvey came out and headed to the shops. Excitedly, Jules followed the long way around to arrive at the shops as a weary Mrs Holvey appeared. She was a gentle, careworn lady – old before her time and struggling to keep a family home together. For most people, this would have elicited sympathy and a desire to help in some way but not for Jules. He never even recognised her as an individual, a person with feelings, someone who had done him no wrong – to him she was only another part of the soft spot of his enemy, Dan.

Jules waited and surprised himself with his patience. Timing was to be everything. Mrs Holvey came out of the mini-supermarket laden with six or more plastic bags and slowly walked back towards the top of the steps. As she approached them, running from behind her came Jules, and just as she made to make her first step down,

Jules shoulder barged her ferociously taking her off her feet and sending both her and the groceries headfirst down the steep stairway. Her scream echoed in the alleyway but faded to Jules as he kept running and within thirty more yards, he had turned a corner and slowed down to a normal walk as if nothing had happened.

Back at school days later, Jules again had the good fortune to find out what had happened. Holvey had been off school and on his first day back he was with his gang talking loudly in the rain room during morning break.

"Fuck, she is a mess!" he exclaimed, "She has a broken arm, a black eye, a cut over the eye that needed stitches and she is black and blue all over."

The gang listened attentively, as did Jules, as one of them asked, "How did it happen?"

"She doesn't know," said Holvey. "She thought she had been pushed, but now she feels she must have tripped over her bags – what a mess she's in," he repeated.

Jules felt excited and knew what the next step had to be. It needed to be a face-to-face conversation with Dan Holvey at the end of the day.

As school finished, Jules left at speed and headed off towards the road he knew Holvey would take on the way home. Several minutes later, in the distance he saw Holvey wave farewell to some boys and head alone towards home. Jules stood quietly almost completely hidden in a building's back doorway as Holvey advanced. When he was no more than three steps away, Jules stepped out in front of Holvey causing a surprised step back.

"Hi, Holvey, what's for tea, roast chicken?"

"What the fuck? What did you say?" growled Holvey.

"And how is your dear mother? What a terrible time you and your family are having," continued Jules as a total look of bemusement crept over Holvey's face.

"You know they say that bad things come in threes, I wonder what will happen next. Do you think it might be one of your little sisters?"

At this, Holvey suddenly realised what was being said and a strained, guttural scream erupted from his mouth as he leapt forward and grabbed Jules very tightly by the neck with his fingers dug around his Adam's apple.

"I don't believe it you evil little shit, now I am going to fucking kill you."

Outwardly appearing cold and calm, while inwardly worrying if he had gauged things right, Jules tried to speak: "Holvey, you had better kill me because if you don't, you know I am going to hurt the things you love."

Holvey, physically strong, seemed to struggle with what he should do next, so Jules helped him.

"It seems to me, that you have three options," croaked Jules.

"One, you can kill me, and your Mum and sisters will be left alone when they send you away for a very long time; or two, you can let me go after a beating and spend the rest of your life frightened to go anywhere and leave your sisters unprotected for my next evil deed; or three, we can be friends and you and your gang can join me – your choice, Holvey, and you need to make it now."

The grip on the throat loosened as Holvey struggled to process the three clear options that Jules had presented to him. Eventually he said, "You want to join my gang?"

but this was more of a statement to himself than a question to Jules and he shrank back with shoulders hunching as he realised that Jules had a frightening coldness about him, something he had never realised before. Holvey started to realise that it was he who was now the frightened one. In a pantomime macho swagger, Holvey let go of Jules' throat and shrugged his shoulders to get some more height into his body and stepped back saying, "OK, I guess you can join, if the others will let you in. Meet us tonight in the Brickworks at about seven," and with an exaggerated nonchalance, Holvey stepped back, turned and walked towards home but not without showing his insecurity by looking anxiously over his shoulder.

Jules looked on with disgust at how weakly Holvey had crumbled. "Join his gang, if the others will let me in," Jules sneered to himself. "I think it is my gang and no one is keeping me out."

That evening, a good twenty minutes after 7 p.m. Jules headed to the old, ruined brickworks. Sliding a fence sheet sideways, he entered and listened. He heard laughter and voices coming from a two-storey old office block twenty yards away and he moved towards it. Inside, stepping over a rubbish-strewn floor, Jules tentatively headed up the stairs where the sounds were coming from and soon stood in the doorway. Several of the local thugs were there and a few girls and the moment they realised Jules was there everything stopped and became quiet.

"What the fuck is he doing here?" said one of them.

Holvey looked over and said, "Listen up, he is my friend. I invited him, come on in, Jules."

Holvey led Jules into the centre of the room and

everyone crowded around, but it was clear that the gang were not impressed so Jules decided to impress them.

"Not your friend yet, which hand used to pinch me?"

A bemused Holvey tried to laugh it off and said, "This one," holding out his right hand.

Jules picked up a piece of brick and told Dan to put it on the bench – now he had everyone's attention.

Holvey, still nervously laughing said, "Are you nuts?"

Jules' reply hung in the air for longer than anyone except Jules felt comfortable with.

"Yes I am, how about you?" He stared at Dan.

Dan understood and said, "OK."

The gang were mesmerised. Jules smashed the brick on Dan's hand and Dan screamed in pain. Jules smiled and left. Dan went home and then to hospital – he had broken two fingers, a knuckle and his thumb.

Now the gang were impressed but they were never told why Dan let Jules do it, but it became the start of the Jules "psycho" legend.

As Jules walked that day down the road from his house towards school it was hard to believe that all that had happened just a couple of months ago. He had gone from #1 Snotrag to Psycho Gang Leader and Dan had become his number 2.

One of the first things Jules got the gang to do was to work and organise the old brickworks into their headquarters and started a campaign of thieving for their needs. They kept the ground floor waste-strewn in order not to attract attention but the first floor was now cleaned up with old chairs, cushions and carpeting from the recycling centre and cupboards with drinks and biscuits and cigarettes and booze – all the result of shoplifting expeditions. The gang felt good, they had their place, and it was all down to the organisation of their new leader.

There were three girls who hung around with the gang – they had their uses. They cleaned the place and made up drinks and fended off most of the boys who wanted to see their underwear or touch them. Most of the boys, but not all of the boys. Jules was awakening to the fact that with his new power he had become an attraction to the girls. With a snap of his fingers, they would come to his side on a big cushion that he had deemed to be his throne.

Everyone seemed happy, even surprisingly Dan, who seemed to be relieved at the removal of his gang leader decision-making responsibility and relished the freedom of being just a thug or even Jules' thug.

Everyone that is except Jules, who felt that something was missing and there were things that they should be doing rather than playing in their private rather rugged and wild youth club – because that is what it felt like, a fucking youth club for wayward kids under the rule of the wayward kids. Tonight, he was going to tell them all that it was time for doing different things, time to make them a group that was feared by the folk in Cranport.

As Jules turned the corner into the high street, from the other side of the road Tina waved and ran across to join him.

"Hi, Jules, going to school?" She smiled and linked arms with him to demonstrate to all the other students as they approached the school that she was his. Jules looked at her and smiled back; gang leaders had their privileges and Tina was one of them. She was tall and thin with the start of budding breasts all packaged up in a mini-skirt, boots and school blouse opened just one button more than it should be and an attitude that showed she knew she was attractive to the boys. She was an alpha girl deserving of an alpha guy.

All through the school day Jules gave minimal attention and went through the motions of sitting in class and walking quietly from lesson to lesson when the rooms changed but deep in thought. The indifference to lessons was obvious to all. Fellow students didn't want to interrupt him for fear of a backlash of some kind and the various teachers were inwardly pleased that for once they didn't have to rival him for the students' attention, always aware of his powers of disruption. For the teachers it was an easier day and they welcomed it.

After school, and after dodging any conversations with his mother, Jules wandered listlessly towards the brickworks. As usual his gang were there messing around like big kids, some throwing stones trying to break one or two distant windows that had somehow managed to remain intact. Inside, some of the boys were arguing about football team games coming up that weekend, a few girls were huddled in the corner trying to have their conversations while two boys tried to engage their attention by trying to lift skirts or brush their hands across breasts which resulted in screams and slaps.

Jules was stood by the door and took it all in. Just a few weeks ago he had wanted to join this group. Just a few weeks ago he had felt so damned good when they all rolled over and took him as their leader and now, he saw them for what they were; weak, childish and completely lacking discipline. Anyone could lead this group because they were not going anywhere, leading this was not something to be proud of and he wasn't.

"Listen up," he shouted, and they did.

"Gather round, everyone, we need to talk."

Most but not all responded immediately. The two prats who had been tormenting the girls were still childishly trying to grab a bit of girl and it was just one thing too much for Jules.

"You two, fuck off and if you come back ever again you will regret it – you're out of this gang!"

"Ah, Jules, don't be like that, we're sorry aren't we, Dan," said the youngest looking.

Jules turned to Holvey in a cold, quiet manner but allowing everyone to hear and understand that this was not a point of discussion.

"Dan, take them out and if one of them opens their mouth and says another word give them both a good fucking kicking to send them on their way."

Holvey, his eyes widening just a little, shrugged and grabbed one of the boys and pushed him to the door and followed them down the steps.

Everyone now gave Jules their full attention and there was silence for the long two minutes it took for Holvey to return. When he did, Jules stood up and started to speak again.

"Look at us. What are we doing?" he started. He could tell, as they looked around at each other that they had no idea what point he was making. He walked around the room, kicking and grabbing everything he saw laying around.

"What have we got? A shitty little den, a few bottles of coke, a box of crisps, a plastic bag full of cheap biros. All from corner shops if they are stupid enough to leave them within reach of the front door. Oh yes, we still have some vodka and whisky and a few packets of cigs left from Joe's uncle, who is still convinced he left his duty-free bag on the bus – well done, Joe." Everyone sniggered and Joe got a slap on the back from the boy next to him. "I nearly forgot," continued Jules, "we still have sixteen packets of condoms of various colours donated by the machine in the bog of the Trafalgar Arms. God knows what we are going to do with them," and now the sniggering broke into loud laughter while the girls blushed.

"We can't just carry on like this, we've got to decide what we want to do. We need money then we can do whatever we want, and no one can stop us." Jules paused and surveyed the group. Some of the more mature gang members were now catching on and were nodding slowly. "I don't give a fuck about anyone or anything except my mates. Do you feel the same way?" They nodded. "I want to do what I want to do whenever I want to do it. Fuck parents, fuck teachers, fuck the police – fuck them all."

"Yeah," said a few as now they all nodded.

"We've got to get focussed, we've got to get money, we've got to stay tight together. It's us against the world out there. Fuck 'em all!"

"Yes!" and, "Yeah!" shouted the group.

"I'm going to do it, whatever it takes. Kiddy stuff is over. Think hard now, if you're with me, great, but if you want something different then fuck off with those other two clowns. If you stay now there is no turning back, we are going to be gangsters not a gang of kids. You choose, I am going outside with some of uncle's vodka. Tell me when I come back – think hard."

Jules took a few swigs from the bottle and waited. Now he knew what he intended to do, and he was confident that the others wanted him to lead them. After a few minutes he headed back and as they heard him coming up the stairs the others ended their conversations and looked up.

"OK, it's fucking simple. Who's in and who's out?"

One girl whimpered and said in a mouselike voice, "I don't want to get into trouble, I just want some fun."

"Play with kids then," said Jules harshly. She started to cry and ran out.

Tina stood and moved across to Jules and linking her arm with his for the second time that day she said with a sexy little grin on her face, "I think this might be fun, I'm in."

Holvey and Joe were next. "Yeah," they said and stood up.

The others followed, "Yeah," and everyone stood up.

Laughter was breaking out when Jules raised his arms and quietened them down. "From now, we only steal things for money, or we steal money. And when we've got it, we are going to buy what we want and go where we want. We are going to be organised. Better than the police, we are going to steal scrap metal, steal from cars and get into empty houses. Joe, when your brother got done for handling stolen goods, find out who he sold things to, we are going to get rich but not flash it around. Nothing must cause too much attention. When we want to rave, we go out of town and have a blast. And you, girl," he said pointing at Tina, "you're my girl and I am going to buy you a leather jacket, a shorter skirt and a bigger bra if those tits keep growing." At this, they all laughed, and Tina snuggled up.

"Stand in a circle and link arms," Jules announced. "We are family, we rely on no one but us. There is no going back now. Is everyone happy?"

"Yeah!" they shouted.

Only Joe hesitated, "We don't have enough girls," he said. "We need more than three... another three and we all have one each."

Tina smiled, "Leave that to me."

"Right," shouted Jules. "Let's have some more of my uncle's vodka." He passed the bottle to someone and as they all reached for it turn, Jules realised he had the power.

Chapter 6

A Need to do Some Thinking

Four months after leaving the hotel in London and Roly was still a lost person. He now lived in Cranport on the Dorset coast and one morning he looked out over the sea from a bench in the private communal gardens in front of his newly refurbished apartment, watching the sun start to shine through a few broken clouds, and in a thoughtful mood he asked himself, "Am I happy?" Well, he wasn't unhappy but that was not the answer he wanted.

He had been busy and had allowed himself to get immersed in key projects. First priority had been to find a place to live and that had been successful. Cranport was a mid-sized coastal town with probably a far more successful trading history than a predicted future. Yet it had been able to decline gracefully and to maintain a charm that seemed to signify that it chose not to compete with an ever-accelerating modern world and it managed to stay young with the County Teacher Training College supplying enough, but not too many, enthusiastic and energetic students during term times. In the west of town, he had found a Victorian terrace of very large houses and bought himself a ground floor, two-bedroom apartment. There were private communal gardens in the front that overlooked the bay and at the back he had a small courtyard and double doors that allowed him to park his car and still have space for a little patio and the enjoyment of the evening sun. The neighbours were friendly but kept a distance and that suited Roly. They were kind enough to share details about tradesmen, who was good, who was bad, who charged a fair price etc., but no one asked him who he was or offered to share their life details with him.

For the first few days, he literally slept on the floor. In the living room, where the previous owners had left just one rug but over the next few weeks, he had had each room decorated and filled with furniture and now it was complete. For the first time in his life, he had exactly what he wanted and needed – his home. Although he had worried about how much he was spending he allowed himself to argue in his favour. No gold taps or marble bathrooms but good quality stuff and just the basics, no unnecessary things.

On reflection, it looked like the hotel room that he had left, nice but not personal. Sure, he had some dirty linen in the laundry room and dishes in the sink in the kitchen but no photographs, no history.

Second project was the boat and again Roly had chosen well. Not for him those big, plastic and chrome gin palaces that had more electronics on it than the first rocket to the moon. Instead, it was an old classic wooden boat, a forty-foot motor cruiser in the old trawler style. "Oh, wood is just too much maintenance," said all the boat brokers but that was just what Roly enjoyed and although the boat had been well looked after and sound when he'd bought it, he was forever rubbing down this bit and painting that bit, but it was not a chore. Now the mechanics was something different. Roly found for the first time in his life that he just did not get diesel engines! His boat had two and even after a three-day Marine Mechanics course, he still found it all too bewildering beyond the simplest of tasks. He had found a sanctuary at the local marina. They had been more than willing to look after him and answer his questions.

And now after morning coffee in the gardens he was off to the marina to see if a certain spare part he needed had been delivered so they could make a final fitting of an impellor that would allow his engines to cool with sea water and not set off all sorts of alarms and red lights which had happened last time he'd tried to take the boat out the previous week. Roly smiled to himself, he enjoyed talking to the mechanics, and he knew they treated him as a complete incompetent, but he also knew that they recognised his love of the boat and his efforts to improve.

So, after depositing the coffee mug into the kitchen sink, with last night's dishes still to be washed, he set off. He crossed the road and started on the coastal walk around the headland that would take him into the next bay and the marina on the edge of the main harbour and centre of town. A twenty-minute walk at best and time for some more pondering. But the mood had passed, and he soon got engrossed in watching the soaring of the seagulls as they made small wing adjustments as the coastal breeze bounced off the seashore cliffs, and he saw dogs chasing balls thrown by their owners and returning with tails wagging and ever hopeful that it would be thrown yet again.

As the walk dropped down into the next bay, the marina was the first place you reached. It was out of season now and mid-week, so the big car park was almost empty. It was about a hundred yards wide and sloped down quite steeply for about a hundred yards to the public launch slip, boat docks and the marina buildings of office, chandlery, maintenance yard, cafeteria, and bar.

Roly ambled along as he approached the launch slip and was suddenly woken into the real world. "Stevie! Brake, Stevie! Pull the brakes, Stevie!" screamed a young woman near the top of the car park as a young child wobbled in panic with his feet already off the pedals as his little bicycle accelerated down the car park.

The child cried out "Mum!" in abject fear as the bike unerringly headed towards the slip that ended in the water.

Without thinking, Roly took a few steps forward and grabbed the child off the bike as it passed in front of him. The child's momentum was such that they were swung around and collapsed into a heap on the ground, but Roly had managed to protect the child fully with his body and the child was crying and sitting on his chest unhurt when, just a few seconds later, the mother appeared and snatched him into her arms also crying and shouting, "Stevie. Oh, Stevie. Are you hurt, Stevie?"

For a brief moment it was almost as if Roly did not exist, and he started to rise from the floor. As the mother realised what he had done she clutched at him with the child still in her arms and said, "Thank you, thank you, oh my God thank you!"

Roly simply smiled as his head raced to find words but failed. "The bike," said Roly and he stepped into fifteen inches of water and reached further to pull out a wet but undamaged bicycle. It was as he stooped down to wipe away the water that they both realised that his trousers were torn across the knee and he was bleeding from a bruised cut.

"Oh, you are hurt, please let me help you," the young woman said and knelt down, put Stevie to the side and pulled a tissue from her bag and proceeded to examine Roly's knee. "And your trousers are ruined, I must buy you a new pair. I am so sorry."

"The trousers are old work jeans and the knee is nothing but a scratch. How is the boy?"

"Stevie is fine," she said as the child cowered by her side. "Stevie can sometimes not listen when I tell him to do things and perhaps this has been a shock to teach him a lesson." She looked crossly at the child and as he started to cry, her face broke into a wide grin, and she wrapped her arms around the child and hugged him for all her worth. "Thank you, thank you," she started to repeat, "and I am so sorry for your knee and trousers."

Roly politely backed away repeating that it was nothing and then turned to continue his walk to the maintenance yard. His knee hurt like hell but as he looked over his shoulder, he could see the woman and child looking at him, so he tried hard not to limp.

Forty-five minutes later, after a friendly discussion with the maintenance foreman who had assured him that Cariad I, his boat, would be repaired and ready by the end of the week, and Roly was in the bar sitting in the corner reading a newspaper and finishing a pint of beer. As his right hand moved down to rub his throbbing knee through the torn jeans another pint was put in front of him. He looked up questioningly.

"It's from Chrissie," said the barman pointing to the child's mother who waved from the other end of the bar. "She said thank you."

Roly looked across, waved, and said, "Thanks," and sipped his free beer. For the first time he saw her as a woman, she was probably late twenties, slim, and attractive but with a smile that could light up any room.

Her smile simply made others smile, and Roly smiled back.

That afternoon, after a hobbled walk back and two beers at lunchtime, Roly welcomed a siesta on the sofa.

Two days later, with a swollen, bruised knee and a definite limp, Roly hobbled to the car to drive to the marina and settle up the bill for the boat repairs.

"As you get older it takes longer for your body to repair itself," said Roly to no one in particular as he awkwardly got into the driver's seat.

At the marina, he noticed that Cariad 1 was in her slip and bobbing slowly up and down in the light breeze. He wandered over but, because of his knee, hesitated to climb the three feet over the side into the boat. Instead, he leaned against the hull and allowed his hand to stroke the heavily varnished and smooth gunwales.

"Yes, she is a beauty. You have a fine boat there, Mr Johns." Roly turned to see Trev Wright the maintenance foreman walking towards him wiping his oily hands on an almost oilier rag. "So, where to now, because she is ready to go, and this type of boat was never designed to just pootle around the bay; this boat was meant to go places."

"So was I, Mr Wright, so was I," replied Roly. They shook hands and after more small talk walked back to the maintenance bay for Roly to pay the bill.

"Mr Johns, you go out single-handed, don't you?" Roly nodded. "She is a safe boat, safer than many but the sea can be a wild place at times. It can be risky for someone on their own."

"Oh, I am careful. I'm no danger merchant. If the weather is bad, I don't go and if I am already out, I can always go in the other direction to the weather. It is never that important to be anywhere if you have to take risks."

Trev didn't look convinced but still nodded and smiled. "Well, that's me done for the day; half-day today because I have to be here Sunday morning for the Marina Welcome Day. There'll be members and no doubt visitors, and the boss is quite keen to demonstrate the marina has full facilities and to try to get a few more to join. We are not as full as we have been in earlier years. There'll also be a barbeque and it's a great chance to meet people. Will you be coming?"

"I don't know, I hadn't thought of it," said Roly honestly. "But I tell you what, I would be happy to buy you a beer now as thanks for fixing the boat."

"You don't have to thank me, you've paid me, that's enough."

"I know I don't have to, I would like to," smiled Roly.

"Well, that would be grand," said Trev. "So, let's not talk about it, let's get the beer."

He laughed, slapped Roly on the shoulder and walked past him to the stairs up to the bar above the cafeteria.

Trev was quicker than Roly up the stairs, and Roly was hurrying to buy his guest the beer. As he entered the bar he heard, "Hi, Dad, I thought you were going shopping with Mum this afternoon."

"All in good time, my girl. I am being bought a beer by a satisfied customer," said Trev as he held his arm wide towards Roly entering.

"That's him, Dad. He saved Stevie," said the barmaid. Roly looked over and there behind the bar was Chrissie. Embarrassed, he stood and smiled.

"Of course," said Trev. "I should have known what

with that crippled knee and all. Now after saving my grandson, I think it should be me that buys the beer. Set them up, Chrissie."

That afternoon was the start of Roly making new friends and the breaking down of the barrier that he had erected around himself. He and Trev chatted freely with Chrissie joining in the conversation in between serving a few regulars. An hour into the discussions and there was no let-up in the topics. As the three of them got to know each other, Margie, Trev's wife, joined to find out why the delay, with little Stevie in tow. Shopping was forgotten, little Stevie chased the marina cat around the bar and the four of them chatted freely and openly while Trev and Roly bought each other beers in turn.

Roly learned that the family was Cranport born and bred. Margie and Trev had been teenage sweethearts and were still sweethearts. Trev was an apprenticed marine engineer who had never wanted anything more than to work at the local marina with the exception of five years in the Merchant Navy where he had learned his trade. He had travelled throughout those five years; Singapore, Hong Kong, Africa, Scandinavia and East Coast USA and constantly made references to them in almost every comment he made: "In Oslo they…" he would start or, "Waiting outside of port in Hong Kong was like…" "It was a most magnificent site Table Mountain as we entered port in Africa…" but all these references were said in a non-boasting manner using them as almost adjective phrases to emphasis some point or other in a charming somewhat eccentric manner that always raised a smile or at worse a slight benevolent roll of the eyes from Margie and Chrissie, who had of course heard them for decades. Chrissie, he was told, was separated from her husband (the father of Stevie), who had not been seen or heard from for over fifteen months. The talk almost stuttered and the atmosphere cooled as this subject was raised and it was not helped by Trev announcing that "Chrissie picked a 'bad 'un'", only to be shushed angrily by Margie as she looked over her shoulder to see if Stevie was aware of the topic. Stevie wasn't – he was flicking beer mats at the cat.

"So, what brought you to Cranport?" asked Margie. It was the one question that everyone had tiptoed around. Roly paused briefly and then, deciding that he was in the company of nice people, he chose to tell them. He told them all; his old job, his divorce, the terrorist attack, his recuperation, his desire to find a new way and purpose in his life – leaving out nothing with the exception of his new found benefactors and unlimited wealth.

"Trev," said Margie in an almost quiet whisper, "we are in the company of a hero."

"I know that woman, he saved our grandson as well. I think that calls for another beer," roared Trev.

Everyone laughed and as Chrissie poured the beer, Roly thought he saw a little smile on her face sent in his direction. This was to be the last beer of the afternoon and soon, after agreeing to meet up again on the Sunday Marina Open Day, everyone made their excuses, and the session broke up. Leaving Chrissie behind to finish her bar work, Margie gathered up Stevie and informed all that Trev was in no fit state to go shopping but he could still manage the walk home and Roly left them in the car park. He was certainly in no fit state to drive, so he pulled a bag out of the back, locked it up and ambled home wondering along the way if this was a turning point of some sort.

This question and that possible slight smile from Chrissie were all that preoccupied Roly, not only that day but for the rest of the week as Sunday morning slowly approached. He had not been back to the marina, he was too anxious to see anyone again until he had sorted out things in his mind. He had picked up his car very early the following morning, far too early for the bar and café to be open, and he felt guilty as he drove away looking all around to make sure that he was not seen by anyone.

Sunday morning arrived. Roly was slow to get going and over a small breakfast he pondered. He found himself arguing in his mind that perhaps he shouldn't go, he could always make an excuse later that he had had something else to do. He had almost convinced himself when he suddenly realised that he was being cowardly. It was just a marina barbeque with some new friends – why was he building it up into something more? In the past few months, he had made very little progress with his new life, he was no further forward in identifying a purpose, he was doing what Jamie had predicted – he was still running away.

Now angry with himself, he flung on a jacket and headed out the door. As he stood by the car, he realised that he would likely be drinking beer and so he should walk to the marina and checking his watch he set off at a fast pace now concerned that he was going to be late. After fifty yards of 'Olympic Walk' pace, he already out of breath and had broken into a sweat. He then proceeded at a more leisurely pace, and he laughed out loud at himself, which startled an old couple who were walking past.

The Marina Open Day was in full swing when he

arrived. People were milling around – many it appeared were regulars that Roly had seen about but didn't know and Trev waved over from a small group that he and the marina manager were chatting to. Always uncomfortable in groups, Roly's tendency would be to stand like a wallflower on the fringes and observe but as he lowered his hand after waving back to Trev, he found Chrissie's arm linking under his.

"Glad you could make it, Roly," she said with a big smile. "Now, who do you not know and let me introduce you." She squeezed his arm and walked him into the group, introducing him to almost everyone there. Each conversation was kept short as she manoeuvred him around, never letting him go and eventually saying, "Well that's enough for the moment. Time for a drink, don't you think?" They sat down on stools at the end of the bar, Roly's back to all the other people.

As they received their free beers, Chrissie moved in a little closer and said, "I thought you might not come. I am so glad you did."

Pleased as Roly was to hear that, he asked awkwardly, "Why?"

After an uncomfortable pause, Trev broke the silence. "Roly, glad to see you, young man. Is Chrissie looking after you? Just been talking to some people who have been admiring your boat; I told them it was owned by an intrepid explorer who was going to sail it around the world."

And with that he slapped Roly on the shoulder and broke into laughter that not only caused Chrissie and Roly to laugh but removed every bit of awkwardness between them. They were not left alone again but Chrissie never left his side.

After the sausages and burgers on the barbecue, and just a few more beers, Roly announced that he was going to see his boat.

"Can I come?" asked Chrissie and he nodded with a smile.

"Dad tells me that you love your boat," she said as they walked across the marina pontoons.

"Yes, I suppose I do," said Roly as they arrived next to Cariad1 and he lovingly stroked her hull. "She is what I always wanted and when I am out on her I am as happy as anyone deserves to be".

"What does Cariad mean? It is not a word I know," said Chrissie as she copied Roly's body language and stroked the boat's name on the side of the hull.

Roly looked at her blushed a little and smiled, "It is a Welsh word. My father was Welsh, and it is what he called my mother – it is Welsh for darling."

"Roly, what a romantic you are," teased Chrissie.

They climbed on board and stood together on the upper helm. It was a perfect, calm, late spring/ early summer's day. A few high white clouds and sun rays were shining through the cloud gaps.

"Can you take the boat out now, Roly? I mean, just you and me for a few hours?"

Roly, feeling in control for the first time in a very long time put his arm around Chrissie's shoulder and said, "Yes, we can."

It was the first time he had ever used a sentence with 'we' in it for such a long time and it hit home. Chrissie sensed the change and putting her hands around his waist, she looked up at him. As she opened her mouth to say something, they heard Trev leading a group of people around the marina shouting:.

"There they are, on probably the best boat in the marina. Can we come aboard, Captain?" and before Roly could answer or even acknowledge them Trev was leading three strangers onto the boat.

Chrissie and Roly dropped their arms from each other and stepped back a little.

"What's the draught on this lady, Roly?" asked Trev and Roly stepped into the group to talk about his favourite possession, Cariad 1. The intruding group roamed over the deck and Trev and Roly engaged them on general topics of the boat, the marina, the river down to the sea and all the other aimless and harmless topics strangers engage in to pretend they are not strangers. Only in a brief moment of respite as Trev took on the conversation was Roly able to glance over his shoulder towards Chrissie and he saw her climbing back down to the pontoon and heading back to the marina.

Twenty minutes later, when he too was able to amble back with the group, Chrissie had gone. He stood there looking around him and didn't see Margie approach.

"She's left, Roly. I think she needs to do some thinking. Perhaps, you do as well." She kissed her fingers and pressed them to Roly's cheek and moved on.

"A need to do some thinking," said Roly to himself as he quietly turned and left.

Chapter 7

Only This Was Their Business

Over the last few weeks, Jules and the gang had been busy. No longer did the old brickworks appear like a delinquent kids' youth club. Now it was a mixture of their place of work and their home.

They had done their research, they knew who they could pass stolen products to and what were the expected prices they would be paid for car radios, laptops, printers, Nintendo or X box games, DVDs or lead or copper piping. It was good to know but it wasn't much.

As they sat around the room, they discussed the situation.

"Not much for the risk, is it?" said Joe. "What we make from this won't keep Liz in knickers." He laughed as he grabbed his newly acquired girlfriend.

"She don't wear any," laughed Dan and the others.

And this was followed by, "Oh yes I do," from Liz as she pirouetted in front of them raising her skirt as she spun around for them all to see. Everyone laughed but it became serious again as Jules spoke.

"It is simple arithmetic, if someone wants to buy something stolen from a stall in the market, a car boot sale or the pub then he wants a bargain. So, if he can buy it new with all the packaging and a manufacturer's guarantee for fifty pounds, he's not going to buy it stolen for more than twenty-five. The guy selling it wants to make a tenner so he buys it from the warehouse for fifteen pounds. The warehouse wants to make a tenner so he buys it from the street urchins for a fiver. The street urchin is taking most of the risk for the least amount of money. Do we want to be another bunch of fucking street urchins?"

"No fucking way," said somebody but apart from shaking heads no one else spoke, as they sensed that Jules was not finished.

"So there seems to me to be just two solutions to this problem – we become a warehouse or we steal money." Still not clear of the implications, they all nodded and waited.

"Now, if we lift a car radio, or a laptop in a briefcase from a back seat, cops don't care and give out a crime reference number to the loser who makes an insurance claim, and everyone is happy. Now, if we tunnel into Barclays and blow up the safe, we become national villains and every copper in the country is out looking for us for ever and when they find us, and they must, they get a promotion, and we get thirty years like those poor sods in the Great Train Robbery." Everyone laughed but got the point.

Jules continued, "But lifting things from cars, or shoplifting, or breaking into poor people's houses, isn't going to get us the money we need,, is it? So, we become a warehouse for other street urchins. But we need to get our contacts set. Dan, you walk the streets and let those who need to know that they bring things to us from now on. Joe, I think you and I need to go and visit Lawrence."

"Why Lawrence, Jules?"

"Who do we take our stuff to? Lawrence, right, who does he take his stuff to? We don't know, do we? So, we need to find out."

"Look, sorry to be thick, but why would Lawrence

tell us anything? He is more likely to set some goons on us if he thinks we are taking business away from him."

"Joe, my thick friend, we are going to visit Lawrence to assure him that we are in partnership and not competition with him." Jules smiled. "We need to anyway. He has to give us the money to pay off the kids on the street."

Lawrence was an old man in his early sixties but looked older. He ran an old car servicing and filling station on the outskirts of town. He always had a couple of guys around repairing cars, and a large-chested woman taking the money for self-service petrol but the whole place seemed to be in a run-down fifties time warp. It appeared as if they barely made enough money to get by and that is exactly how Lawrence wanted it to look. Lawrence himself did not look much better during the day, stained clothes and unshaven, but he was a dresser in the evenings when he visited the clubs and he certainly always had someone twenty or thirty years younger on his arm. It was in the evenings that Lawrence spent the money he made from the warehousing he did at the back of his building.

"Tomorrow," said Jules, "we start by visiting Lawrence. For now, why don't we check if all the girls are wearing knickers." Everyone laughed and paired off as the boys groped the girls and the girls hoping for some privacy guided the boys to various corners or old sofas and bean bags. This was not a problem for Jules and Tina, they had already claimed a small side room as his office, and they entered confident of not being disturbed. The room had a small desk and some wobbly chairs and a two-seater sofa that rolled out into a sort of futon mattress. Tina rolled it out and perched on it with her knees and legs tucked under her.

"You are going to do it, aren't you?" smiled Tina.

"Do what or do who?"

"You are going to become a gangster".

"Tina, I don't know what to call it, but I am never going to let anybody control me again. Whatever it takes, I can, and I will," scowled Jules.

"Anybody? What about this body?" smiled Tina, immediately lightening the mood as she straightened up and pushed out her developing chest. Jules reached out and grabbed her breast but gently as he lowered himself to her side on the mattress. Tina straightened out beside him, and they entwined their bodies as they kissed. They had not made love yet for all their coarse talk when they were in the gang and although it was never mentioned they were both virgins. Together they were nervous, careful and loving and each time they seemed to move closer and closer to the point where they would. Tina was falling in love with Jules, and he was already in love with her. They were two different characters when alone together – she was not the brash, knowing tart and he was not the glowering, frightening psycho. They both knew this and valued the fact that it was special just to them, but they didn't ever talk about it. Words might make it evaporate.

Surfacing from a heavy kiss, Jules leaned back and let his eyes cast down over Tina as she lay beside him. Her chest rose as she breathed and as she raised her knee and turned towards him, her short skirt failed to cover her bum and he reached down and cupped her cheek in his hand. As good as it felt he knew it could feel better and moved his fingers around and pushed under the thin material of her underwear to cup the skin. As he squeezed Tina groaned and he slowly pushed her back onto her back.

"I want to kiss you all over," he said.

She giggled. "Who's stopping you?" He sat up and straddled her waist and with a smile he unbuttoned her blouse and pulled it aside to reveal her small pink bra. He reached behind her and fumbled like a child with the clasp, as his frustration grew so did her giggles so he calmly reached across to the desk and picked up a knife. Tina's eyes opened wide as he hesitated for a moment and then reached forward and cut the bra between the cups. As the bra parted her breasts almost bounced up for attention. They were small and pert with dark areolae and nipples at full attention. Jules leaned forward and cupping one breast in his hand his mouth covered the other one. "Ah, my God, you are beautiful, these are beautiful," he said as he transferred hands and mouth from one breast to the other. It took another while before he raised his head again and with a smile and a giggle on his part he said, "Let's see what else I can kiss." Slowly and deliberately, he started to undo the small belt of her skirt and then the side zip, but when he tried to pull down the skirt, Tina froze and didn't lift her bum to help.

"No, Jules, not here, not with everyone just out there." She gestured to the growing giggles and groans outside. "I want you and only you, but it must be special because we have something special."

Jules, feeling half-relieved but incredibly frustrated, jumped up and sat on a chair.

"OK, Tina, but it has to be soon, look what you are doing to me," he said pointing at the tent in his jeans.

"Perhaps I should be kissing you," smiled Tina and kneeling in front of him started to unbuckle his belt.

"Oh Jesus, Tina, that would be fantastic," said a surprised Jules. Up to now she had been hesitant to do anything more than give him a hand job making sure that it never pointed her way when he came. This was now another step. He moved forward on the chair and leaned back, allowing Tina to undo the belt and unbutton the jeans. His white boxers had just one fly button that seemed under considerable strain. Tina, giggling, reached forward and fumbled with the button a few times with each touch being a torment for Jules who, with eyes wide open and groans of pleasure, desperately wanted her to succeed. With theatrical calmness and slow purpose, Tina reached behind her and picked up the knife from the floor. Holding his underwear in one hand she cut off the button, which shot out over her shoulder and Jules' dick sprang to attention inches from her face. There was a shriek and a giggle from both Tina and Jules but then they calmed down and both aware that they were breaking new ground, paid attention and with a desperate deliberation they both prayed it would go well.

"Tell me if I do anything wrong," said Tina as she reached forward and grabbed him.

"Just don't bite it," said Jules almost seriously. She kissed the tip and around the end and then opened her mouth and took in as much as she could, which was not all of it. Slowly but surely, she moved her mouth over and back. When she had taken as much as she could, she backed off to just the head of his dick, her tongue free to roam around him, causing Jules to squirm in delight on the edge of his seat. "Oh God, I'm going to come," he said, and no sooner was this said than his first ejaculation exploded in Tina's mouth. With a shriek of surprise, she moved back only for a much bigger second ejaculation to explode into her face as she retreated and for the third ejaculation to arch out over the increasing distance and splash over her blouse and skirt.

Jules looked relieved and Tina sat back and looked surprised and then she sneezed.

"Oh, it went up my nose," she said, grabbing a tissue and they both burst into laughter.

"God, Tina, I do love you."

They took the next few minutes to dress and tidy themselves up and Tina threw the cut pink bra into the corner of the room grumbling, "Shit, I hope Mum doesn't notice or I'm in deep shit." As they stood up, they heard more groans and giggles from the main room and looking at each other with a grin they burst into the main room shouting, "Tarrah!"

"Everybody up!" shouted Jules as various bodies scrambled in the dim light to cover themselves.

"I'm already up, way up," drawled a satisfied Joe as Liz, who was straddling his waist, flattened herself on his chest and put her hands on her bum to try to cover her nudity.

To roars of laughter and continued scurrying Jules announced, "Early to bed, children, school tomorrow and another day of fun." And with that he and Tina left the building and headed home.

The next day after school, they all met up briefly and started to put the plan into action. Jules and Joe were to try and get a meeting with Lawrence while Dan was left with the others to walk the streets and various cafes and clubs and get the word out that they were ready to receive products for a good price.

To get to Lawrence you simply visited the service station and asked the cashier woman. The service station was not like some modern Esso or Shell filling station where the payment area was filled out like a small supermarket and people could buy their general provisions along with the petrol. This was a concrete flat-roofed hut with a large, glass front and door. Inside the door and within six feet was a stained, wooden partition with a door in the middle that split in two like a stable door. Around the walls on nails and shelves were fan belts, light bulbs, cans of oil, air fresheners, and all other associated auto stuff. Hanging over the half door was the large-chested lady with the till. Behind her and almost out of sight was Lawrence and many other things that drove his prime business interests – the warehouse. Down the side of this back room, which appeared bigger than perhaps it was, was a side door into the service bays building. There were three bays, almost always two of them occupied by various old piles of junk but the main value was that vans could drive in when invited and unseen, and empty dubious contents through the side doors into the warehouse.

For a few weeks now, Jules and the guys had been bringing the odd thing to Lawrence and had walked away knowingly ripped off but with some money in their pockets. So, they were known, not strangers but not regarded as anything but street kids.

"Excuse me, Miss, we are here to see Lawrence."

"Are you now?" she said to Jules. "But does Mr Lawrence want to see you?"

"Tell him we have a business proposal for him," smiled Jules.

Lawrence, who had heard all this, reached up and squeezed the backside of the cashier and grunted, "Let them in, Edie."

Edie got down from the high stool with a grumble and moved it aside to open the door for the boys.

They entered and stood awkwardly in front of Lawrence's old armchair. Edie shut the door and as she pulled across the stool and stepped up to sit down again, Lawrence reached across and grabbed her backside again. She jumped and slapped at his hand, but both shared a smile of understanding before Lawrence moved his attention to the boys.

"Now, why would I be interested in a business proposal from two school kids?" he asked. There was a pause as Joe looked to Jules and Jules just stood there smiling. To fill the silence Lawrence continued, "So, what do you have for me? More car radios, any home electronics, anything you might have picked up in your travels back-and-forth to school?"

"Mr Lawrence, as you know we have been bringing things to you now for several weeks."

"Yes, and out of the kindness of my heart, I have given you pocket money in return."

"Exactly," said Jules, "we have come to realise that this won't do. It is not a way to get rich."

"Get rich," laughed Lawrence, "look around, no one is rich in this shitty little place."

"Now, Mr Lawrence, I might be young, you may think I am foolish but we both know I am not stupid. I know that you are too big a man to spend your life in some derelict armchair in a broken-down business unless it had an extremely valuable sideline that allowed you the lifestyle that a man like yourself must demand."

Lawrence, recognising the challenge from this young pup, changed the atmosphere by growling, "What do you want, for fuck's sake spit it out."

"All I want, Mr Lawrence," said Jules in the same calm voice with a smile on his face, "is for you to listen." Lawrence waved him to continue.

"I see it this way, you're getting older." At this Lawrence almost started to rise from the armchair as Jules protested and continued: "No, wait, I said older, not old or too old. Rather, I am simply recognising that as you get older you want to protect and enjoy the rewards of your hard work but that's it, it needs to be a time when the work is not so hard. Look, at this time in your life, what is the worst thing that could happen? You give a kid a fiver for a pinched radio, and he blabs or gets caught and bring the police down on you."

Without taking his eyes off Jules, Lawrence reached over to his side table and pulled out an old revolver.

"Listen. you little fuck! Is this a shakedown, do you seriously believe you kids can come in here and threaten me?"

At this Joe was as white as a sheet and probably ready to wet himself. Edie had gotten off her stool on the other side and now held the stool in front of her almost like a shield.

Jules had simply paused and now continued: "Listen, Mr Lawrence, you are not listening. You recognise this threat, we all recognise this threat. I am suggesting how you can protect yourself from this threat. You pay peanuts for two reasons. First, it is the lowest amount the kids and junkies will accept, and they are all idiots. Second, you need to pay that low figure to compensate yourself for risks you have to take before you are dealing with the professionals you sell to. I am offering you a chance to reduce that risk by dealing with professionals when you buy. It is quite reasonable for you to accept a little bit less for a dramatically reduced risk, don't you think?"

"Who are these professionals?" mocked Lawrence, knowing what the answer was going to be.

"Why, Mr Lawrence, two of them stand before you and there are twenty more in the town who listen only to me, and I do not need one of these." At this, Jules stepped forward and grabbed the pistol off Lawrence. Six eyes stared in horror and Joe probably more than Lawrence and Edie. "And you will not need one of these to work with me, Mr Lawrence," said Jules, handing back the gun.

Lawrence looked at this special kid in front of him in a new light. "Let me think on it, kid. How about coming back in say two days and we talk more?"

"What time?"

"Any time that is convenient for you. We don't need to predict specific times, do we? Let the boys out, Edie, we'll talk again in a few days."

Edie moved the stool, opened the door and visibly sighed when Jules and Joe walked out. With the door shut and back on her stool she swung her legs around towards Lawrence.

"What was all that about?"

Lawrence smiled and said, "Just a business proposal, that's all. Must give it some thought," and he reached his hand up and put it straight up Edie's skirt until he hit the target. Edie didn't slap away his hand but squirmed on the seat as Lawrence looked away in thought.

Across town, Jules and Joe were heading into the brickworks. They knew their world was changing but they had not spoken.

Holvey was there with some of the guys and looked

up as they entered. "How did it go?" he asked.

Jules smiled as he started to sit down before answering and Joe jumped into the speech gap.

"Jules was fucking awesome; Lawrence pulled a gun on us! Jules took it off him and then gave it back! Oh my God, I think I not only pissed myself but I also shat myself!"

"Guns? What the hell happened?" asked Holvey.

"Calm down, everyone, let me give you a clearer description of what happened and what is going to happen," smiled Jules, who knew that Joe had now added to his growing legend of Teenage Psycho Gang Lead.

Jules sat them down and then explained in detail what he intended to do for Lawrence and how it would work. They discussed money and how much they could make, they discussed volumes around how much business they could bring in and Holvey told Jules how everyone on the street preferred to do business with them rather than traipse up to Lawrence. It was their first serious business meeting and all they had to do was call it Sales for Money, Margin for their cut, Revenue Growth for how big this could be and Sales Force coverage about how they would get out to the street urchins and druggies, and they would be discussing exactly the same points their parents did in offices throughout the town. Only this was their business, and they knew it.

Chapter 8

The Start of a New Relationship

Roly gave Monday a miss but was back in the marina bar on Tuesday. He tried to casually read his paper and drink his pint but chided himself each time he found himself looking around, scanning everywhere for Chrissie. She did not appear to be there but then he heard her voice and she passed briefly from the kitchen to the bar and looking across she saw Roly. They both smiled and it was awkward and then with a wave and "Hi" she ducked back into the kitchen like a rabbit diving into its burrow.

As despondent as Roly was when he thought she wasn't in, now he had seen her and received an awkward smile, followed by a "Hi" and then a dash back into the kitchen – now, Roly was concerned. "Another beer?" asked the barman, and Roly shook his head, drained his glass and headed out.

The walk back along the coast was normally such a delightful setting, the waves, the hills, the birds – so much to just observe and make you smile but not that day for Roly. Head down, eyes tracing his feet as each pace took place and his mind whirling.

He asked himself questions: Did I misread the situation? Did it mean far more to me than Chrissie? Of course, it did, why would she be interested in me? What made me think I could be something to her? My God, how could I be so foolish? I have made her feel awkward, how did this happen to me so quickly? Why am I acting like some moonstruck teenager? What do I do now? How do I save face? I am so embarrassed, what do I do next?

As he reached the entrance to the community garden he sat down on the bench and with a big sigh said out loud, "Get a grip, you fool. She is at best a friend, don't spoil things, calm down."

He nodded to himself sadly and decided there and then that he would re-establish the distance in his relationship with Chrissie if he could and get on with his life.

He entered the building and picked up his mail, the normal selection of bills and advertisements but his spirits rose to see a card with his address written on it in a recognisable scrawl. It was a letter from Jamie.

With the weather changing and the sun appearing I thought, who do I know that lives by the seaside who I could visit. No one else would have me so I am coming – see you Friday afternoon, love Jamie. X

Roly smiled, some time with Jamie was just what he needed to take his mind off Chrissie and feeling energised, he looked at his flat and started to clean up and prepare.

All that week he avoided the marina, even when sitting on the garden bench on Thursday afternoon and admiring the boats out in the bay. His time would come.

***

Friday afternoon, and Roly was standing at the station awaiting Jamie's train. The flat had been cleaned top to bottom and the second bedroom had been made up with fresh towels and bed linen. Roly stood there excited and as the train stopped, he peered on tiptoes through the arriving passengers, anxiously looking. His smile lifted and he broke into a loud laugh as everyone turned to stare as Jamie shouted out so very loudly, "Yoohoo, Roly. I'm here!" and there almost running towards him was Jamie in neon bright clothes and flipflops with dark sunglasses looking like some fifties B-movie starlet.

Next came the big hug and Roly took Jamie's bag and directed them towards the car park.

"Well, the sun is shining, Roly, and I feel we are going to have a wonderful weekend. What have you got planned?"

"Well, I thought we could go out one night, the restaurants are not up to our usual standards but there is a bistro that you'll like, all check tablecloths, candles in bottles and young waiters with strange Italian accents."

"Ooh," squealed Jamie

"Also, I have my own patio and barbecue so I thought we could stay in one night and I'll cook for you, and on Sunday lunchtime before you go back there is a traditional pub in town and they do a marvellous roast beef Sunday lunch."

"And in between meals, I want some time on the beach, I want some time on your boat, and I want to casually flaunt myself as we stroll along the promenade. You do have a promenade, I hope."

"Well, we have the front, and I am sure it will do. But now the big question, tonight – bistro or barbecue?"

"We can't barbecue if it rains or is cold, why don't we barbecue and tomorrow come rain or shine we bistro?"

"So be it, we just need to stop off at the supermarket and buy some meat and there are no reservations at the bistro to worry about."

Five minutes later they were parking in the supermarket. Roly and Jamie strolled towards the door. As they approached, a little girl no more than three or four came skipping out in her summer frock with ribbons in her hair and flipflops on her feet. Catching the toe of one of her flipflops on the floor she sprawled forward and fell on her hands and knees just in front of Roly. Other than a scuffed knee and red palms, she was not badly hurt, but it was enough to frighten the little one and as she broke into tears Roly was quick to run up to her. Kneeling down in front of her, Roly tried to comfort her with a hug and using his hands he proceeded to rub away small pieces of dirt and grit from her hands and knees.

"There, there, princess. Are you OK? Where's your mother?"

Still frightened and crying the child stepped back and stared at Roly open-eyed. The child's mother came out obviously searching and seeing Roly kneeling down, with his hands on her daughter's legs and her child crying she screamed out "What are you doing with my daughter! Take your hands off her, leave her alone!"

People looked and stared as the mother ran over and snatched the child out of Roly's hands. Roly looked at this woman full of horror, it was just so incongruous. "What do you think I was doing, you stupid woman!" he shouted back at her, understanding for the first time the implications of her original comment. "She fell over and I picked her up."

At this the mother started to cry and hugged the child, who also continued to cry, and more people stood around and stared.

"What the hell is going on here?" asked a young man, obviously a partner to the woman.

"He had hold of her and was stroking her legs," said the mother not looking up.

"She fell over, I picked her up," said Roly as simply as he could, expecting reason and logic to reconnect with the world any time soon.

"You dirty old bastard," said the man as he moved towards Roly.

Jamie stepped and in his high falsetto voice said, "Don't be stupid, why would he want your snotty little kid?"

Frankly, that did not help but rather it inflamed the man who simply exploded saying, "So, you're in it as well. A couple of fags is it?" and started to throw a punch at Jamie. Roly just reacted and grabbed the arm at the wrist and twisted it. There was an audible click, and the man sank to his knees with a gasp saying, "Fuck, he's broken my arm!"

By now the watching audience had grown and started to mutter amongst themselves as the latecomers asked those present what was going on. Roly turned to Jamie and said, "Let's get out of here."

As they walked back to the car, they heard someone shout, "Yeah, get out of here, we don't want your type here!"

Almost in a trance and without words, they drove home. They carried Jamie's luggage into the flat and sat down in the living room.

"What a crazy thing," said Jamie. "How in hell did that happen?"

Roly shrugged and said, "It's nonsense, let's not allow it to spoil the weekend."

But it had. There was an almost funeral pall over the flat and just no way to allow it to pass.

Things got worse. About forty minutes later there was a knock at the door and there were two policemen. Over the next hour, they explained as clearly as they could that the girl had fallen over and had been picked up, the mother had got the wrong impression, the guy had got overexcited and tried to punch Jamie and Roly had simply grabbed his arm to stop it. On the other side, the policemen explained they had been called to the supermarket because of a disturbance; the woman accused Roly of groping her daughter, the man accused Roly of assaulting him and dislocating his elbow, people in the crowd had said that Roly and Jamie had run off and someone had given them Roly's car registration, so they were able to track him down.

"What a screw-up," said one of the policemen. "For what it's worth, I believe you, but I'm afraid it is not me who has to sort that out. Tomorrow, you will have to come to the police station and be charged with common assault and possibly a child offence, although I would hope that that goes away."

It was an enormous relief for Roly to have someone in addition to Jamie who simply saw this as an incredible misunderstanding and the burden seemed to lift from his shoulders as he showed the police out.

"Come on," said Jamie, "forget the barbecue, let's get shit faced. The weekend can start after the police station tomorrow. Where do you keep your booze?" And that is what they did.

In the morning, feeling hungover and with a light breakfast they headed to town and parked in the town's multi-storey car park. As they entered the small shopping precinct and headed out the other side towards the police station, Roly stopped and pointed in horror. There on the local newspaper The Cranport Citizen was the headline for the day: "Hero and Gay partner accused as paedophiles".

Jamie bought a paper and together they read: "Roland Johns, who recently moved to Cranport after being injured in a terrorist attack on the Saudi royal family, was yesterday accused of common assault and having sexual contact with a little girl at an incident outside the Sainsbury's supermarket in Deadworth. Police were called when they ran away from the scene, and we are informed that Mr Johns and his unidentified gay partner will appear in the magistrate's court next week." It went on and on with various non-specific comments from people, or witnesses, as the paper described them and then ended with, "Mr Johns was not available to comment."

"My God, not available to comment. No one asked me to comment," said Roly as he visibly slumped. "This reads so wrong, it was not like that."

The fact that it was not like that was soon recognised at the police station. The constables had found two shoppers who had seen the little girl fall over, the girl's father had admitted throwing a punch and as quickly as it had blown up all charges were dropped. Life started to seem normal. So, Jamie and Roly drove back to the flat determined to enjoy their weekend.

Back at the flat, they started to get ready for Jamie to have his stroll on the promenade and Roly was in his bedroom when he heard Jamie shout, "Roland, you're on the telly now!"

As Roly rushed into the living room, he saw the local

lunchtime news programme was on and standing in the marina was one of the local presenters. As the camera panned around the marina bar the presenter was heard saying, "So, as we heard, Roland Johns and his partner will not be prosecuted for molesting a female child; the police say there is insufficient evidence, but we ask, who is this man that some call a hero who has chosen to relocate from London to Cranport? Today, in the marina bar we will be asking those that know him."

As the reporter turned towards the bar, several of the regulars looked over but no one made a move to speak when the reporter asked, "Who here knows Roland Johns? Who is he? What does he do? What type of guy is he?"

The ensuing silence was like a collective holding of breath. As the reporter started to approach the nearest person, Chrissie came from behind the bar, angrily pushed away the reluctant reporter and at the same time pushed back the TV presenter.

Chrissie jumped in: "I'll tell you what sort of guy he is – he is a really nice caring person. He saved my son from a serious accident just a few weeks ago when he fell off his little bike in the car park. You TV people don't want the truth, you are just trying to get a sensational story – there isn't one. What's this nonsense of insufficient evidence – there was no evidence at all. What are all these implications around his partner? He doesn't have a partner, it is his friend! This was just a stupid misunderstanding and if you want to be regarded as serious journalists then stop making up stories and just honestly report them!"

As the presenter's blushes became apparent and as he mumbled and bumbled while slowly but surely closing down his exclusive and backing out of the bar you could hear general cheering and laughter in the background and at least one, "That told the buggers, Chrissie, my girl!"

Roly did not realise that he was standing there staring with his mouth open but Jamie made him aware of it. As he reached up to close Roly's mouth he smiled and said, "Mmmm, it seems you have made another friend down here."

Roly hesitated and then smiled and said, "I must call her and explain or at least say thanks."

The telephone in the bar rang and the barman simply shouted, "Chrissie, for you!"

There was no advance warning as she picked it up to hear Roly say, "I've just been watching you on the television."

"I've just been reading about you in the local rag."

"You do know it is all nonsense, don't you?"

"Of course, I do, Roly. Why don't you come back down the marina? I feel you have been avoiding us."

"I thought you were avoiding me; last time I was there you didn't seem to want to speak to me."

"Yeah, I know, and I am truly sorry for that. I just had a wobble, my feelings were racing ahead too fast, I got a little bit scared because I didn't think that I would feel that way about someone again – at least so soon."

"Feel what way?"

"You know, we seemed to get on very well at the marina Open Day and when you have a failed marriage on both sides and a young child it cannot be like a teenage love affair. It has to be different, don't you think?"

"It is different and that is what surprised me, but if we are going to struggle to work out what it all means, can't we do that together?"

"Yes, I think we can. I get off at three, why don't you come down the marina and we can talk more."

"OK, but can I bring my gay partner with me?"

Chrissie laughed and said, "Of course," which made Jamie laugh out loud after having hung on to every word.

That weekend, originally planned for two, now became for three. For Roly it was the start of a new relationship with Chrissie, an extension of his friendship with Jamie and for Chrissie and Jamie the start of a special friendship focussed on their love and respect for Roly.

Chapter 9

There was no Going Back

Over the next few weeks Jules and Lawrence set up the new ways of working together. Jules' gang was funded by Lawrence, and they had a book to track every transaction. Business was good and the gang found they had more money than before, but Jules recognised that there was only so much crime that could go on without there being a substantial crackdown by the authorities. Cranport was never going to be big enough for Jules. He was anxious to know who Lawrence passed things onto and was introduced to the concept of criminal warehousing. Lawrence was supported by – and a part of – a gangster group in London and they passed things into and out of central warehousing in an efficient manner to ensure that they were not constrained by the localities that tied down Jules. It was like a small corner shop going to a 'Cash & Carry'. You not only had the chance to buy into whatever specials were on offer (perhaps a shipment of microwave ovens somehow 'lost' during a major launch to department stores or cases of wine that never made it out of the docks), but also the chance for you to move on your local 'stocks'.

Jules proved to be an avid student and spent time and attention on Lawrence. Slowly the older guy started to lower his guard and to enjoy the apparent open admiration from his young admirer.

A few months into the relationship and Lawrence mentioned he was planning a visit to London. As Jules raised his eyebrows, Lawrence smiled and said, "Come along, you cannot attend the actual meeting but come for the visit." Lawrence had already built up these quarterly meetings as something along the lines of a Mafia family meeting of the Dons as per Hollywood, implying that he 'represented' the south coast. While Jules had his doubts about this, he was still anxious to know more.

"Bring a partner," said Lawrence.

"Will you be bringing Edie?"

"Hell no, she's my daytime blow job at best; she was good, but her good times are behind her, all in that big arse of hers."

***

On the day, Jules took Tina, and Lawrence was with someone almost as young with big breasts and no brain but a big smile and happy and excited by the trip. The drive up was in Lawrence's big Mercedes with Jules and Tina raising eyebrows to each other as they tried to watch the countryside and ignore the dirty talk between Lawrence and Sal as he told them what he intended to do to her that night and how much she would enjoy it while his hand reached over to grab whatever body parts came into reach.

Lawrence had arranged a big suite in a mediocre hotel with two bedrooms and a living room. That afternoon, he left for his meeting with promises of a big-time dinner and show that evening in the city and so the girls prepared to shop, and Jules decided to just wander around.

During the shopping, the girls got on well. Tina and Sal had been given a wad of notes from Lawrence and told to make sure they looked good that evening. It was like a schoolgirl's dream but surprisingly just three hours later they were being dropped by taxi back at the hotel with arms full of purchases but tired of the thrills of Selfridges in Oxford Street. As they entered the suite, dropping packages as they walked, Tina headed for the kettle and the thought of tea and biscuits while Sal took one particular package into the bedroom.

"It's not right," she wailed as she returned a few minutes later with a figure- hugging sheath of a mini dress. It was a beautiful, clinging, dove-grey dress but just one or two sizes too small for Sal. "I knew I should have got the bigger size. What do you think? These tits look as if they are going to break free and it even shows the crack in my arse."

Tina looked across as she poured the tea and she had to smile, Sal looked like she had been bandaged. "I guess you're right, but it is a beautiful dress."

"You try it on, Tina, you have a slimmer frame than me. It would look terrific."

"I'm not that sophisticated really, my style is more casual," said Tina.

Sal pulled the dress over her head and then standing there in just a black thong she said, "Just try it on, girl."

Tina stood there for a moment and then shrugged. In turn, taking off her flat walking moccasins, waistcoat and blouse, jeans and then pausing just briefly she removed her bra. Now giggling along with Sal, she reached out for the dress and started to pull it over her head. It did indeed fit her like a glove. Tina looked into the full-length mirror by the door and Sal looked over her shoulder and they both said "Wow" together.

"You keep it, girl. That dress was meant for you," said Sal as she walked back into the room, still content to get her cup of tea before dressing.

Tina took another look in the mirror and then started back into the room saying, "Thanks, Sal, it is nice. I have never had anything so expensive before. Do you think I should wear it tonight?" As she walked and talked, she started to pull the dress back over her head. This time as the skirt part of the dress came over her head, but with her the arms and shoulders still in the dress, her hair slide and dress got caught. Tina pulled and twisted but it was caught fast. As busy as she was, she did not hear the door open, and Lawrence walk in.

"Help me, Sal, help me. It's caught and I don't want to damage it."

Sal looked at Lawrence and as she was about to speak she saw him signal with a finger on his lips. Tina continued to fumble forward until she came up against the sofa back. "Sal? Sal?" she called just as Lawrence made his grab.

Taken by surprise, he bent her over the sofa while his left arm circled her body, grabbing a breast and his free right hand went straight under her flimsy knickers from the back and reaching up round the front to her pussy.

As Tina screamed in surprise, Lawrence roared with laughter and said, "Just like I like 'em, all trussed up like a turkey for Christmas."

Lawrence had been drinking and continued to grope Tina as she ripped off the dress and, in a fury, slapped Lawrence's face.

"Damn you, girl, you always seem to think you are better than everyone else but you're just a pretty pussy like all the rest, now calm down." And as he said this, he backhanded her to the mouth, and she was knocked down on her backside with a mouth full of blood.

Suddenly, the large table lamp from the side of the sofa crashed against his head, and Lawrence staggered forward.

"You dirty old bastard," said Jules. "Why can't you keep control of your dick?"

Jules took a step forward and hugged Tina. "Are you alright?" he asked.

Sal's scream took his attention again and looking over to Lawrence he saw the old man, with the back of his head now streaming blood, crawl towards his briefcase and struggle to pull out his old pistol. As the pistol came out of the bag, Jules took two steps and almost casually stepped on Lawrence's arm, pinning it to the floor. He calmly reached down and took the gun from Lawrence's grasp. He knew there was no going forward now, and he put the barrel to the forehead of an astonished Lawrence and pulled the trigger. The loud bang shook them all and Lawrence's head exploded over the armchair. There was a huge pregnant pause as Jules, Tina and Sal stared at the scene.

Sal was horrified and close to screaming. "I won't tell anyone, please don't hurt me." Jules knew she would and picking a cushion to muffle the next shot he walked towards Sal and pulled the trigger.

"Tina, are you OK with this?"

"That bastard deserved it, she didn't but that's what you get if you fuck scum!"

They hugged again for a moment and then Jules started to think out aloud. "We're leaving now. Take everything we brought, everything you bought." As Tina started to pick up various bags and ran into the bedroom for their stuff, Jules walked over and reached down into Lawrence's briefcase. Within ten minutes, after checking and double-checking, they left with their stuff plus Lawrence's gun, wallet and keys. They casually left the hotel and after walking two streets hailed a passing taxi and within the hour, they were back on a train heading for Cranport. They would have to change in Bournemouth for the local train and travelling down to Bournemouth with all the commuters meant they couldn't talk. They both knew that now things had changed, murder was not a misdemeanour. Jules had said he was going to be a gangster and now he acted like one. They hugged as they remained locked deep in their own thoughts, which would serve them well before the next conversation. Things had happened so fast.

On the local train to Cranport they were able to sit at the end of an almost deserted carriage and talk.

"Oh my God, I don't think I can do this. I never thought we would kill someone. What do we do now?" whispered Tina.

"We do nothing," responded Jules. "When we get back, just go home. Your parents thought you were going to London with Liz and her parents for a show. Tell them that her dad had to come back for work, so it was just a shopping trip. By this evening or at the latest tomorrow, the police will be on it. Hell, they might even be trying to work it out now. Either way, they will be in and around Cranport by tomorrow. The gang just know that you and I were going somewhere. We didn't tell them anything. Did you?"

"No, you said not to, so I didn't".

"Good, so we're OK on that front. The police will get to know that I have been working with Lawrence but that's all. Nobody saw us check in at the hotel. I think we will be OK but listen, this is important. I want you to stay away from me and the gang for a few days."

"No," interrupted Tina. "We are in this together."

"Yes, we are, but if things go wrong there is no way I am going to let anything happen to you."

"I just want to be together," repeated Tina, still whispering.

"OK, we are always together but listen to me, if the police are talking to me and others in Cranport over the next few days, let's not let them see us as a couple. They will be looking for a couple. Let's not make it easy for them. Stay away until I tell you. I'll tell the gang you have a bad cold or something. In a few days, I'll call. I promise, and then we will be together for ever."

Tina had a tear in her eye when she whispered, "OK, but just for a few days."

When the train pulled into the station, they kissed and Tina walked the short distance to her home looking over her shoulder every few steps until Jules was out of sight. As she walked up the front garden to her home, Jules' last words echoed in her head: "Just act normal. Be normal. Don't let anyone feel like asking what's wrong." She opened the front door and as she walked in she shouted, "Hi, Mum. I'm back."

Jules was not heading home, he had things to do. He headed to Lawrence's place.

It was fifteen minutes before the garage closed at eight p.m. and only Edie was there.

"Hi, Edie"

"What are you doing here? I thought you were going to London with Lawrence."

"Nah, the bastard let me down. I'm standing on the street corner waiting for him as planned and he drives up, winds down the window and says, 'Change in plans, kid, can't take you this time. I got people to meet. We'll do it again sometime,' and then he just drives off. What a bastard."

"Was he with a woman?" asked Edie and Jules could tell that she hated the fact that he wanted younger women now.

"Yeah, young with big tits and no brain. You know what he's like. He can take her but not me."

"He's a pig, I know what he's like," spat Edie.

"Why do you stay working for him, Edie?"

"What else am I going to do? To be honest, when we are together during the day we chat and things and he's nice. It's just when he goes out with the boys. He wants to impress them all with some young thing and I guess that's not me anymore."

"Edie, you deserve better," said Jules and he gave her a little hug.

The hug was so out of character that it made Edie realise that she had spoken perhaps too openly to Jules. She backed off a little and said, "So anyway, what do you want? I'm closing up in a minute."

"Can I have one of those DVD players that Lawrence just got in? It's my mum's birthday and I want to get her something."

"Sure, you can, but I will have to make a note of it. Lawrence will want to charge you, you know that."

"Ah, Edie, couldn't this be our little secret? He owes me for what he did today."

"Yeah, you're right. Just take one. Serves the bugger right," giggled Edie, "but be quick. I want to get home tonight."

Jules entered the warehouse and picked up a small boxed DVD and as he returned, he blew Edie a kiss and with a big smile he said, "Thanks, Edie, you're a star. I'm off home." But he wasn't.

Jules hung around out of sight and watched Edie lock up and eventually drive away in her old car. He gave it five more minutes and then returned. Without turning on any lights he used Lawrence's own keys to enter the premises. Again, with a separate key on the key ring, Jules sat in the old, battered armchair and opened up the safe. Inside were several documents that after a short examination were left behind but Jules did take a small notebook and a wad of banknotes that when counted in his room later came to £2,300. His final act was to wipe down everything, in particular the old pistol, which he left in Lawrence's drawer.

The following morning, just as Jules had predicted, the murder of Lawrence seemed to dominate all news. Jules had surprised his mother by sitting in the kitchen and having breakfast and, while he shared a stilted conversation with his delighted mother, he paid particular attention to the small television on the sideboard broadcasting breakfast news like it did every day in his house. National News talked about the 'Hotel Gangster Murder' with all the implications that it was OK if the lowlife kept it amongst themselves. At the break for local news, there was more detail with a reporter standing outside the petrol station talking about how a trip to the capital had turned to tragedy for a local small-time criminal. Behind the reporter, Jules was interested to see several parked police cars and police in and around the store entrance. He would not be there today or indeed soon. There was no going back.

Chapter 10

Roly's Purpose

That Sunday was a most perfect day for Roly. He had wanted to make the weekend visit special, not only for Jamie but also for himself after his disappointment with Chrissie. The surreal activity of the supermarket episode and the resulting local press had driven him to distraction, but it was that craziness that had brought Chrissie back to him. Sunday, with high energy from all, everyone was determined to ensure that each minute was packed with enjoyment. In the morning, Jamie got his stroll along the promenade and this time Chrissie was in between him and Roly – all three holding hands and chatting and laughing together. In minutes, Chrissie and Jamie were like old friends. There must have been three times the conversation and laughs between them than between Roly and either of them. Roly smiled to himself, these two were special to him and he appreciated it. The new game was to make Roly the subject of all conversation and the butt of all jokes and comments. Chrissie and Jamie teased him and at times almost collapsed with high giggles. Roly took it in the good humour it was intended, and at worse rolled his eyes under higher eyebrows and pretended to get cross with an angry glower, which of course just created more squeals and giggles from the other two.

At two in the afternoon, they met up with Trev and Margie with little Stevie for a beach picnic. If there was any hesitation on Trev and Margie's side in welcoming Jamie into the family fold, it was almost instantly banished when they saw him playing in the sand with Stevie. They built sandcastles, ran to the sea for buckets of water, and Stevie helped Jamie find the water which seemed to get lost when they poured it into a castle moat they had made. "Where's it gone? The water's disappeared. Quick, Stevie, let's get some more." And they ran back to the sea again for more.

"A nice young man there," said Trev. "He cares and that's all that counts, I think."

"He has helped me more than anyone else beyond my parents. I cannot imagine him not being around."

"Neither can I," said Chrissie grabbing Roly's arm and causing Trev and Margie to look at each other and smile.

As the afternoon ended, they packed up and walked to the car park, and made arrangements for Chrissie, Jamie and Roly to meet up for dinner.

At the agreed time, all washed and freshened up and with no sand particles left to irritate parts of the body, Roly and Jamie arrived at the restaurant. As they were entering, they heard a horn beep and turned to see that it was Trev. As Chrissie stepped out of the car, Trev rolled down the window and said, "Jamie, is it tomorrow morning you are heading back to London?"

When Jamie nodded, Trev continued, "Well, lad, you look after yourself, it was special meeting you and make sure you come back again soon. Now, you three have a wonderful dinner and, Chrissie, do you want me to pick you up?"

"No, Dad, I'll make the arrangements this end. Have a quiet night in with Mum and make sure Stevie gets to bed early."

With waves from all, the three entered the restaurant

and were shown to their table.

The half-full little restaurant was an Italian bistro, as promised by Roly to Jamie, and they were given a small table for four in the corner. Jamie and Chrissie sat on one side and Roly faced them. Immediately, the conversations started and again it was Chrissie and Jamie speaking about Roly and talking about him in the third person as if he was not there.

"Chrissie, I am so pleased that Roly has met you. He has been down here now for months just drifting about."

"I know, I was surprised when he told me he didn't have a job, God knows how he spends all his time."

"Now wait a minute, you two" said Roly, "stop talking about me as if I wasn't here. If you want to know what I do then ask me, and I am not drifting, I am planning. I have my boat, I have my flat, and I am taking things one step at a time."

"Nonsense, Chrissie, he is drifting and when we wrote Roly's Rules I told him he would. It is his tendency to drift. I should have insisted on a seventh rule – Do not drift but get a purpose in your life."

"What's Roly's Rules?" asked Chrissie.

Jamie for once stayed quiet and simply looked to Roly, and with a sigh of exasperation, Roly continued: "Chrissie, I told you about my background. My marriage and divorce, the crazy terrorist attack, how I got shot and how in hospital I decided that life was so precious that you had to live it the way you as an individual wanted to. Not to do so meant that all you ever did was build up an ever-increasing list of regrets. Well, Jamie also got this speech from me several months ago and in a restaurant not that different from here, where we made up a list of things and called them 'Roly's Rules'."

"And what have you done with them?" said Jamie. "Are they still relevant? Do you even have them anymore?"

"What, I don't believe that you said that. It is the most important document in my life," shouted Roly, "and here they are." With that, he pulled his wallet out and very carefully removed the original napkin from it. Chrissie held out her hand and with great care and respect took the napkin from him and read them:

1. *Surround yourself with people who share the same values but be open to new things.*
2. *Never knowingly hurt a person and if you do apologise at the earliest.*
3. *If you can help people then do so willingly, but do not be taken for a mug.*
4. *Be polite and have good manners and try to face each day with a smile on your face.*
5. *Find something to be passionate about and when you find it explore it with energy.*
6. *Find someone new to share your life with and do not let the first mistake scare you off intimacy.*

"OK, one is done, he has us. Two?"

"That's OK as well. When we were in the flat, he stepped on my foot and said sorry," giggled Jamie.

"Great, and three – well, he helped Dad carry the picnic basket back to the car this afternoon. Well, Roly, you are on a roll, only three left."

At this, Roly started to get a little irritated and disappointed that they were teasing him about something that he held so dear.

"Four, be polite – well he did say thank you to the waiter when he gave us the menus."

"Enough now," said Roly a little loudly. "This is not a thing we should joke about. It means so much to me. It is not a checklist or a game. It may not seem like much to you guys, but it is almost everything to me. It describes who I am."

"Oh, Roly, I am sorry," said Chrissie. "I didn't mean to ridicule the list."

"No, we didn't, Roly. You know we love you, but we are trying to make you realise that the list outlines a philosophy of life, a way of life but it doesn't have a life unless you apply it to a purpose," Jamie added, while reaching across the table to hold Roly's hand.

"What's your purpose, Roly?" asked Chrissie.

Roly thought hard and then, as his shoulders sagged, he said, "I don't know."

Jamie lifted the despondency by saying, "No matter, we will help you find it." With laughter they sat back and sipped their drinks as Jamie unfolded another paper napkin and wrote 'Roly's Purpose' on it.

"What do you want to do?" said Chrissie.

"Don't know."

"OK then, what do you not want to do?"

"What I was doing."

"You're not helping," warned Chrissie. "So, what do you like doing?"

"Spending time with you two," smiled Roly.

"That's not good enough. Let's get serious," she said, showing her frustration.

"OK, I love the water and boating. I love helping people. I care for people who through no fault of their own have fallen on hard times. I like openness and honesty. I want to be surrounded by people I respect, and I refuse to have to compromise. Yes, I am a megalomaniac, but hopefully a nice one."

"Do you dream, Roly?" interjected Jamie.

"Not of anything specific but yes. I sometimes have a feeling that I could do something good."

"Why did you come here?"

"I love the seaside, the harbour and boats, the old Victorian buildings. For example, I love that old warehouse on the edge of the harbour. Used to be storage for goods coming into the country and things being exported but when the trade died so did the harbour and building. It is such a beautiful building; it should be preserved."

"So, fix it up, Roly, why are you waiting for someone else to do things?"

"I suppose I could, with help, I could turn it into a hotel. A harbour in the front with a small but good restaurant, the beach can be accessed at the back, and I could even moor my boat out front and take guests out for day trips. But who would come? Everyone flies away now for the sun."

"Not those who through no fault of their own have fallen on hard times," said Chrissie.

These words were almost like a switch going off in Roly's brain. "Yes of course. I could make it a holiday home for those that really need it. But I need help."

"And you need money," said Chrissie.

There was a big pregnant pause and Chrissie looked from Roly to Jamie and back again. "What haven't you told me?" she quietly asked.

For the next half-hour Roly explained as clearly and straightforwardly as he could, stopping only when the waiter appeared to either bring food, pick up dishes or pour wine. Chrissie understood the words but struggled with the meaning.

"So, you have no money of your own, but you can spend what you like as long as it doesn't go over a hundred million dollars?"

"Well, yes, I suppose, but it's not like winning the lottery. I mean I only spend as little as I need."

"And when he does, he always feels guilty don't you, Roly?" said Jamie.

"I cannot waste it. It was not given to me as a toy. The Old Man wanted me to do something meaningful with it," said Roly.

"Like opening up a seaside hotel for those that most need but cannot get a holiday break, some respite in their tired worn-out unfair lives?" asked Chrissie.

"Yes, I guess that would fit the bill," agreed Roly. "OK, let's do it but it is only viable if you two join me in doing it."

"Yes, I'm in," said Chrissie excitedly.

Jamie looked on and pondered before smiling broadly and nodding. "Yes, count me in,' he said. "It might take a few months to sort it out and to sell up, but that promenade was meant for me. So Cranport, look out, Jamie is on his way."

"Hooray, Hooray for me!" shouted Roly. "I cannot tell you how happy this makes me. But let's get down and seriously do some planning. We will call it The Water's Edge. We will seek out those most needy and deserving from all the charities and offer them a simple quality holiday or at least a break away from their problems. We could solicit funding from companies who want to show their corporate good heart."

"I could do that," said Jamie. "I know so many corporate executives."

"You must tell Mum and Dad," said Chrissie. "I am sure that they would want to help. I know I will, we can make this happen, Roly."

"Yes, we can. Let's do something nice, let's do good. It sounds silly but there is no reason why it cannot work. We will use my provided money to get it up and running but then we will ensure that it pays for itself and start up another and another. Why not – all we have to do is commit ourselves to doing what's right. Tomorrow, I'll start by finding out how to buy that building."

That night they started the planning and discussions that would change their lives – all of them. As the evening ended, the bill paid, Jamie slid the napkin across the table to Roly with Roly's Purpose written on it as a headline and underneath it simply The Water's Edge. Roly smiled and took it and gave Jamie a hug and turned to Chrissie and gave her a kiss. It had been a most memorable evening.

Chapter 11

What Would a Gangster Do?

That first day after the murder of Lawrence, there was frenzied police activity throughout the small town of Cranport. Police were everywhere asking questions but the intensity soon diminished as no obvious leads were found. Some of the gang were stopped in the street and asked but clearly they knew nothing. Jules waited to be contacted but again, nothing. After three or four days, it all calmed down and reverted back to normal. It was clear to the police that this was a big city gang crime and locals were not involved. For the local police, the removal of Lawrence and his black-market trading was a positive step. The crime was not on their patch and so frankly, who cared.

Jules and the gang cared. Not emotionally for Lawrence but without him and access to the warehouse, their business was finished. Things became quiet and boring, and they all started to drift a little. That evening at the brickworks the gang had started to kick around a small cushion and as the game got more excited, they whooped and hollered like the gang of teenagers they were. Perched on some old furniture at the side of the main room, Jules looked on with Tina. She saw the distaste in his eyes and nudged him.

"What's wrong? You seem upset."

"Fucking Youth Club."

"They are just having fun, you worry too much. I'm glad that the Lawrence thing is over. To have it calm and carefree for a while seems like a great idea to me."

"Fun because they still have a few pounds in their pockets but soon, when that's gone, they will just be bored kids again."

"Perhaps that's what they are," mused Tina who looked at Jules sadly as he vigorously nodded in agreement.

"That might be them but it's not me. Tina, you have to decide if it is you," he said coldly and quietly. Tina looked at him and felt frightened. She thought she might be a little bit more like them, but she couldn't and she wouldn't say that. She was relieved to realise that Jules had not picked up on her lack of a response. As she looked at him, he came back from wherever his thoughts had sent him and said, "Cranport is just too small for a life of crime. How could I have been so stupid? If ever we did anything of any size or value, the whole town would be down on us in a minute. We have to leave this place and get back to London."

Now it was Tina's face that looked on with confusion.

"London? Where are you going to go in London?"

"I'm going to meet up with Lawrence's contacts," replied Jules.

"You don't know them."

"I've never met them, but I know where they hang out."

"How do you know that, did Lawrence tell you?"

"Tina," said Jules now looking straight into her eyes, "Didn't you ever wonder how I just happened to come back at just the right time while that lecherous old bastard was grabbing you? When he left in the morning and you girls went shopping, I followed him. I followed him to the pub he went to. I saw him enter and through the window go into a back room. That's where they are. I can find them again."

"How? You don't even know who they are."

"I do not know them by name, but I know where they are – I will manage."

Tina could no longer hide her fear and she turned away.

"Tina, I'm going tomorrow. Don't tell anyone. The last thing we all need is for this Lawrence thing to start up again, but if I don't do this then in a few weeks' time, when we leave school, you and I will be signing on with the rest of these clowns. You can be a shop assistant and if it is a clothes shop in the high street, you can get ten per cent off as an employee," he said with a sneer, "and I can sign on with the council and avoid work at every opportunity and finish up each day going to the pub with the rest of the lazy wasters. Don't you realise, our lives would be over. I can't live like that, I won't live like that."

Tina was scared but wanted to be supportive. She moved across and hugged him but realised he was off again in his thoughts.

After a brief pause he continued, "Tomorrow, I'll go. You stay here. Tell the gang I have some family thing I got to do and wait for me. I'll call when I'm back. It might be a day trip, or it might be a few days but don't call me, if I'm delayed, I'll call you."

"OK, Jules. But be careful."

Jules simply shrugged. Tina sensed that he had already made some key decisions and was already in action mode.

"I'm off, I got a few things to arrange. Do you want me to walk you home or will you head back with some of the others?"

"I'll walk back with them; you go if you need to. Just be careful, please."

Jules did not acknowledge that he'd heard her and simply turned and walked out. Tina loved him but was surprised that she was glad he had left.

Jules spent that evening in deep thought. He told his mother he was going to London to explore a job opportunity that he had heard from at school, and he was bemused by how gullible she was in believing him. She did not even query him in detail about the job and seemed satisfied when he had simply said it was an Events Coordinator. That evening she ironed shirts and put out a suit for him and even polished his old black school shoes. In disgust, he ignored them the following morning putting on his normal 'street' clothes before leaving and heading to the station. Just after the morning rush he bought an open-ended return and settled down in a carriage half-full of middle-aged female shoppers and stared out of the window as the train headed across the country. Again, changing at Bournemouth, he spent the last hour of the journey trying to get his thoughts together. He was simply going to introduce himself as Lawrence's partner and try to re-establish the business link. Once this was established, he intended to get closer to them, like he had done with Lawrence, and eventually end up moving to join them in London. That was the plan.

Arriving in Waterloo, he felt he deserved a taxi and happily paid the cost of the trip asking to be dropped outside the hotel that Lawrence had booked for them just a few weeks before. It felt strange being back there and he paused briefly on the opposite side of the road

119

looking across and noting that all was back to normal. He shrugged and turned to follow the streets that Lawrence had walked to get to the pub where his meeting had taken place. His mind raced even though to an outside observer he was just a young fellow somewhat aimlessly wandering along the street.

Suddenly, a question occurred to him: how was he going to introduce himself as Lawrence's partner when he didn't even know Lawrence's surname? Lawrence of Cranport, that is how he would refer to him. Not exactly Lawrence of Arabia, he chuckled to himself, but it would have to do. He paused briefly outside the front door of the pub and then walked in. It was almost empty, after no doubt the normal lunchtime visitors, and so Jules felt a little exposed as the few people there all turned to look at him. No matter, he simply looked squarely ahead and started to walk towards the corridor that headed to the meeting room.

"Hey kid, the gents are that way," said the barman, pointing to the opposite side of the room.

Jules hesitated, then continued. The barman ran around the end of the bar and grabbed Jules' arm as he entered the corridor.

"Hey, you little prick didn't you hear me?"

"I'm sorry," said Jules smiling, "I should have said that I'm here to meet someone."

"Who?"

"Just a man," smiled Jules.

The atmosphere changed and there seemed like a chill in the room. The barman started to squeeze Jules' arm and said, "Listen to me, smart arse. Unless you tell me who you want to meet, you are going to find yourself outside standing on your head with a broken arm."

Jules believed him, this was not going to plan. He tried to smile but it came out like a grimace. As he prepared to say something, a guy no older than about early twenties stuck his head out of a room into the corridor and spoke, "Hey, George. What's up?"

"Nothing I can't handle, Ronnie. This prick says he wants to meet someone but won't say who, will ya?" he said to Jules, adding even more pressure to his arm.

"Get off me, you clown," shouted Jules who had already recognised George as not being a decision maker.

"Now, now gentlemen," said Ronnie with even more false politeness. "Let me see if I can help. Let him go, George, and bring us both a drink over in the corner there. What do you want, kid? A coke?"

Jules nodded and Ronnie asked George for two cokes.

They walked over to the corner table and Ronnie bowed to two people sitting at the next table and said, "Gentlemen, I am sure you will want to give me and my guest some privacy. Why don't you move a couple of tables over?"

All said with a quiet voice and a big smile, but the two older men got the message loud and clear and almost scuttled several tables away with obvious haste.

Jules and Ronnie sat. Ronnie said absolutely nothing at first but examined Jules with his eyes and it was only after a protracted pause he started.

"What's your name, kid?"

"Jules."

"Well, Jules, where you from?"

"Cranport on the south coast."

"Hey, a long way from home. Are you lost or looking

for something?"

"I guess I'm looking for something. If you could help, I would be very grateful." At the thought of Jules' gratitude, Ronnie laughed, and Jules joined in.

"Can I call you Ronnie?" asked Jules, trying to make an even closer connection.

"Sure, Jules, but listen, just tell me straight what you are looking for. I'm a busy man, Jules. If I can help I will, but I don't have all day, y'know."

"OK, Ronnie, as I said I am from Cranport. In Cranport I worked with a guy called Lawrence. Lawrence came up here a few weeks back and somehow, he ended up shot in his hotel room. Now that was bad for him, but it was also bad for me and my gang. We used Lawrence to fence stuff that we acquired. He took his cut, but he also provided us with cash flow to allow us to do some trading from the street. Now he's gone and everything has stopped."

"Interesting story, Jules, but what are you looking for in this pub?"

"Lawrence told me that he had contacts in London and if he's gone, I thought perhaps I could keep the Cranport side going."

"So, who are his contacts, Jules?" shrugged Ronnie.

"I don't know, he never said," said a resigned Jules. "I just know they were here."

There was an even longer pause, while Ronnie pretended to wrestle with this problem.

"I tell you what, Jules, I'll ask around. No promises but if you come back here tomorrow at say 10:30 in the morning, then perhaps I'll have some more for you. Will you do that?" Jules nodded, Ronnie stood up and continued: "Finish your coke, kid, but I got to get back to work."

Jules tried patiently to sip his coke but was constantly aware of the glowers coming from George and so he waited as long as he could without appearing rushed and then gulped down the last of the drink before standing and walking out. He was pretty sure that he had made contact, but he couldn't be one hundred per cent certain. He had been willing to stay overnight but did not expect that he would have to arrange his own sleeping arrangements.

While Jules had been finishing his drink, Ronnie had already been busy. As he left Jules, he signalled to an old pub regular to join him in the corridor.

"Jack, I want the kid followed. No contact do you hear, he must never know anyone is there. Tomorrow when he comes back. I want you to tell me where he has been, who he saw, who he talked to – everything."

The old man nodded vigorously as Ronnie spoke and eagerly took the bank notes offered to him.

"Do this right, mind, get others in if you need to but be back here tomorrow at 10:30." And with that Ronnie left the corridor and re-entered the room he had been in some twenty minutes before.

As Ronnie entered the smoky room, three older guys in a corner hunched over a table looked up.

"What's up, Ronnie, trouble?" said the oldest of the three.

"Not sure, Mr Hopkins. It's a kid from the south coast looking for someone."

"Why the fuck do we care; but that's not what's got you looking worried, so spit it out, Ronnie."

"Remember that guy, Lawrence Simmons, the greasy, lecherous bastard from down Bournemouth way who got shot just the last two weeks – well, the kid says he worked with him and wants to re-establish a trading link to us."

"Who shot him, Ronnie? It wasn't us and have we heard anything?"

"Shot him and his slut, but no one is saying a word. I haven't pushed it because the filth were all over it but I have a young guy who has a mother who cleans rooms at the hotel. According to this kid, the police believe that that there were more than two people in the room, another couple, but who?"

"How did the kid know to come to this pub?"

"I don't know, but he just said that this Simmons guy had contacts in London but never said who."

"So how the fuck did he end up on our doorstep? Where is he now?"

"I offered to ask around and try to help him, so I told him to come back tomorrow at 10:30."

"So where is he?" repeated the older guy now just a little bit irritated.

"No worries, Mr Hopkins. I have Jack following him. If anything funny happens he'll let us know."

"OK, Ronnie, if it's clean then we can chat with this kid tomorrow, but if it's not clean and this kid is playing on the other side then this is a problem for you to sort out – understood?"

"Understood," replied Ronnie, now a little concerned that suddenly this had now become his problem.

***

Jules wandered a little outside not knowing where he should go and how he should spend the next twenty hours. He was so perplexed that he never noticed the old man following him. He had money so he decided to head towards the West End He would treat himself to a hotel room and a night out on the town. Smiling to himself, he looked forward to just being free from all constraints. What would the next few hours bring, he wondered and allowed an almost childish excitement to grow. The excitement did not take long to fade; none of the hotels he walked into would let him book a room without a credit card, even though he flashed a wad of cash. One hotel even suggested that a minor should only book in with an adult. In frustrated disgust, he wandered for over two long hours before he found a small bed and breakfast house that was like his grandparents' home. The old lady was willing to let him a room for the night when he told her he was waiting for his father to arrive the following day by train. She took the money upfront, and she wanted to mother him and asked if he wanted dinner and was surprised when he said a little too forcibly, "No, I thought I would eat out tonight."

Jules wandered around Leicester Square and Piccadilly Circus; no one looked at him, no one spoke to him. He was surrounded by people who were all going somewhere or doing something, and he had never felt lonelier. It was as if he was not part of life, just an observer. He hated it, he hated them, so he headed back to the bed and breakfast with a burger and chips and a can of coke. His little room had no television but some old books on a shelf. He hated the room and after a short while and still early in the evening he crawled into bed and curled up facing the wall and fell into a fitful sleep.

As disappointing as the evening had been, Jules woke up as the morning light broke through the undrawn curtains and felt well rested. The old lady was pleased when he presented himself for breakfast and he let her fuss over him as he enjoyed a surprisingly good full meal. He left shortly after and even waved to her as she watched him walk down the street and at the first corner his stride turned into a more determined step as he headed back towards the pub and the meeting.

As he arrived on the street, he took no notice of the old guy who was walking in front of him and who also turned into the pub. As Jules entered his first sight was George the barman.

"Morning, George," said Jules with a smile.

"Wait at the corner table," scowled George, no smile returned.

While he sat and patiently waited, a different conversation was taking place in the back.

"Where did the kid go, Jack?" asked Ronnie.

"He was like a fucking tourist, walked around the streets of Leicester Square and Piccadilly, spent the night in a cheap Bed & Breakfast, saw no one and spoke to no one," reported Jack.

"Did he telephone anyone, did he use his mobile?"

"That I don't know," said Jack.

"OK, thanks, and here get yourself and your friends a few drinks on me," replied Ronnie, handing over a few notes.

Ronnie pondered a short while before heading out to meet Jules.

"Hi, Jules, how's things?" asked Ronnie with a smile as he slid in beside Jules.

"Hi, Ronnie," Jules replied and waited for Ronnie to drive the conversation.

"Jules, I want you to meet someone. He might be able

to help but be careful what you say as this is an important man around here and his patience is short, especially with kids. You got a choice, either walk away now or have this chat. Your choice, what is it to be?"

Jules understood the message, loud and clear, but there was no way that he was going to give up on this contact.

"Ronnie, this is great thanks. Let's go meet the guy."

"For fuck's sake, kid," said an exasperated Ronnie. "He's not a guy. He is a very important man. Show him respect."

With that Ronnie grabbed Jules by the arm and led him down the corridor into the back rooms of the pub. They stopped at one room and Ronnie knocked lightly before entering. Two older men were sitting around a table and they both stopped talking and looked over as Ronnie ushered Jules in.

"What you got here, Ronnie, a play pal?" sneered one of the men and Jules found himself becoming irritable. He had expected the same respect that Ronnie had shown him.

Mr Hopkins had not spoken but had certainly registered Jules' reaction. Now he spoke quietly and everyone, including Jules, strained slightly to hear him.

"Ronnie, is this the fellow from yesterday that you told me about?"

Ronnie nodded and he started to speak, but Mr Hopkins held up his hand to stop him.

"Young man, what are you doing around here asking about a man that was shot in a hotel? No one here knows anything about that. If you're not careful, people might think you know something about this or worse, that people

127

around here know something about it. That wouldn't be good now, would it?"

Jules made his first critical mistake when he chuckled before he spoke, and Ronnie's eyes rolled as he knew how much this was going to upset Mr Hopkins. He was wondering if this upset was coming his way for making the introduction as Jules started to speak.

"Look," said Jules, "I am not here to cause you trouble, I'm here to put some business your way. As I see it, with Lawrence gone, you have lost some good south coast contacts. Seems to me, it is in our mutual interests to re-establish the link and to work together."

With this, Jules had made his second big mistake and the last for the day. His ego had made him try to establish himself as an equal or at least a respected player. He had also greatly overestimated two things; first was how important Lawrence was, he had been regarded as an inconsequential foot soldier at best and second, how equally inconsequential was the south coast business, as they hadn't and wouldn't miss it. Jules waited for a response, his anxiety rising as he realised, he could not read the man.

After a slight pause, Mr Hopkins ignored Jules and looking at Ronnie he said in the same quiet voice without emotion, "Hit him."

There was no pause from Ronnie as he jumped up and threw a full swinging punch into Jules' face, knocking him off his chair, splitting his nose and leaving him on his hands and knees on the carpeted floor.

"Ronnie, you should know better," spoke Mr Hopkins. "Now, take this piece of junk out of my office before his blood stains the carpet. You have a choice to make; either kill him and come back and tell me it's done or give him the beating of his life and come back and tell me how he is going to be your respectful and most humble foot soldier. I swear to God, if I hear his voice ever again, I will take it as a personal insult from you."

"Yes, Mr Hopkins," said Ronnie as he grabbed Jules and simply picked him up and walked out of the room.

Jules was semi-conscious and struggling to work out what had happened. He was dragged down the corridor and into storeroom where there were three more guys who looked up in surprise. Ronnie threw Jules like a rag doll into a corner.

"God fuck it, kid, I told you to show respect," shouted Ronnie.

"Ronnie," bleated Jules through his broken face, but before he could say another word Ronnie had taken two quick steps and kicked him hard in his side.

"Shut the fuck up. That voice of yours got you into this," shouted Ronnie, "and me," realising that this was now his problem. "Not another word from you. Grab him," instructed Ronnie to the others. "Take him to the flat and give him a hell of a beating. Now listen, no broken bones or damaged innards but a hell of a good beating."

Ronnie glowered at Jules as the other three got up to follow orders. "If he speaks, hit him again. I'll be along in the evening, I gotta think this through." And with that Ronnie walked back out of the room.

Ronnie paced up and down the corridor for a few minutes and finally, he realised what was his best course of action. He walked down to the room and again knocked gently on the door before entering. The two men were still there, and Ronnie simply sat down with them and joined in the conversation as if nothing had happened.

Sometime later, they decided to go into the pub for a drink and something to eat. It was at this time that Ronnie decided to ask the question he wanted to ask.

"Mr Hopkins, I would appreciate some advice."

"Sure," smiled the older man. "How can I help?"

"What would you do, Mr Hopkins? Should I simply get rid of the kid or knock some sense into him and set him to work?"

"Ronnie, the kid thinks he is too important to be a foot soldier, but he knows nothing. If you can't knock that out of him then he is dangerous so, get rid of him before he causes you problems."

Ronnie noted that the possible problems would be coming his way not to anyone else.

"However, he is not unintelligent and with the right coaching might develop into something. It is not so easy to find intelligence in the ranks these days, so when you find it, you need to nurture it. Like I did to you, Ronnie," continued the old man and he reached over and ruffled Ronnie's hair. "Ronnie, he has got to be your kid and no one else's. That's not for you to understand but for him to understand. Got it?"

"Yes, sir," smiled Ronnie.

"You've got him, and I've got you," said Mr Hopkins as they approached the bar.

Now Ronnie knew what to do.

Chapter 12

Getting Started

The very next morning after waving Jamie off on the train back to London, with a list of things to do and follow through on, Roly started in earnest to outline his planning for The Water's Edge.

The harbour warehouse had been derelict for many a decade and was actually owned by the local authority, who had made a compulsory acquisition when the last owners had failed to take any actions to secure the crumbling building and surrounding land. Roly needed a solicitor and of course knew none apart from the solicitor who had helped him purchase his flat. Roly disregarded him; he had been a nice enough fellow but an older far more traditional type of solicitor. He sensed that a good solicitor would be an almost permanent member of the planning team as they tried to transfer his poorly expressed ideas into practice. His solicitor would have to share that vision.

That first afternoon Roly met up with Chrissie and her parents and they talked long and hard.

"So, you are independently wealthy with this Saudi reward then Roly?" asked a bemused Trev.

"It's not really a reward but I suppose it is since they allow me access to money. You see, it's best to think of it as an allowed overdraft."

"You mean you have to pay it back at some time?"

"No, overdraft is wrong. Look, it is very simple. After it was all over, I met the grandfather and talked. They wanted to give me a reward but I would not accept one, it didn't seem right. The grandfather asked me what I was going to do when I came out of hospital and I told him honestly that I did not know. We chatted and I explained that my marriage was over and that I did not want to go back to my old job. I told him I wanted to do something different; have an impact, live by a different set of rules, help people, help me to become someone different, at least to try to be different and to make a difference. The old man, because that's what he asked me to call him, said that he would make the money available to me so that I could have the independence to seek out what I wanted to do with my life. And I am eternally grateful to him. That allowed me to come to Cranport and to meet Chrissie and both of you."

"We don't really understand, Roly; our life has been much simpler but if you're asking will we help you then yes, my love, we will. Of course we will," interjected Margie as Trev nodded. "I don't work, although I do look after Stevie, but I would be willing to help right now. Trev retires next year and when that's done he can also join us," she said as her husband continued to nod in agreement.

Now that her parents were on board, Chrissie picked up the conversation.

"So how can we help, what's first to be done?"

"Well, not too much really. The first few steps are all around getting the building bought and going through all the rigmarole that I suppose is inevitable in setting up a hotel. We need to work out if it is a charity or a business and again there are rules. What I really need is to find a solicitor to help us through all this legal wrangle. I want to find someone who can understand what we are trying to do. I need someone who can become almost a member of the team."

Margie, who had only been half listening, looked up and said, "How about Cousin Kate?"

Roly simply raised his eyebrows and held his arms out and looked around in bemusement.

"Yes, Kate of course, Mum's brother's daughter and a fully-fledged solicitor currently coming to the end of her maternity leave. I wonder if she would want to help."

"Please wait," said a concerned Roly. "I'm sorry but it just cannot be any old solicitor who happens to be in the family. It must be the right person, someone who can understand our vision, someone who I can be confident with… this is not an automatic thing. I need to meet her and feel comfortable. I'm sorry, but this is too important a role to involve the wrong person."

"Of course, Roly. You have to meet her and then you decide. Don't let us hijack your project. Now come on, Trev, if we go now, we can get some shopping done before we pick up little Stevie. Chrissie, you and Roly work out a plan and simply tell us how and when we can help." With that Margie gathered up Trev and with kisses despatched to Chrissie and Roly, she left them on their own.

Roly smiled and sat quietly with Chrissie, both of them happy but not knowing what to say or do next. Roly broke the uncomfortable silence first.

"Chrissie, I don't know how to start but I do know I want to start. Does that make sense?"

"Yes, I don't know either and I am frightened of getting too involved."

This statement caused Roly to raise his eyebrows.

"Chrissie, you are involved. I want you involved in

everything. I want you involved in my life," he said with concern in his voice.

"Oh, Roly, I know that and it is the same for me. I didn't mean it as it sounded. What are we doing? We are tiptoeing around each other frightened in case we spoil something special – because I think you and I are going to be very special. This is your dream and I want you to achieve it and I don't want me or my family getting involved and possibly spoiling it for you. Why don't you just tell me and Mum and Dad when you want us to do something and until then we can just support you in the background?"

"No!" said Roly quite forcefully, which surprised not only Chrissie and everyone else in the café but also himself. He paused and continued, "OK, these are the rules. There is an inner trio of you, Jamie and me. We share the same vision and values and there will be no tiptoeing around amongst us. We simply say what we feel – right?"

"Right," responded Chrissie, as her heart leapt to be in the trio because she wanted that more than anything else.

"OK then – first task is we need to buy the property no matter what and we need a solicitor for that so let's go and see Cousin Kate."

"We can do that," said Chrissie. "Let me ring her now."

Ten minutes later and it was all done. The phone call to Kate had taken two minutes to arrange a meeting the following day and eight minutes of girly conversations around the subject of Roly. Who was he? Were he and Chrissie a couple? Was he special? Roly only heard half the conversation and noticed that on certain queries

Chrissie actually went red and almost whispered into the phone looking away from him. He did hear the occasional whoop and giggle from the other side and a clear "You go for it, girl" comment as the conversation ended.

Now the conversation dried up again and they looked over the table at each other.

"So, Roly, what do you want to do now because Mum has Stevie, so I'm free until after tea."

"You want to know what I really want to do?" he asked.

"Yeah," Chrissie responded quizzically to a small grin on Roly's face.

"I want to spend the afternoon with you in bed at my flat. I'm glad we have several hours because I think we are going to need it."

Jumping up with a squeal of delight Chrissie responded with laughter.

"So come on then, I do not want to waste a minute!"

That afternoon sealed a closeness in their relationship that neither of them had ever experienced with anyone else in their lives. It had started with squeals, giggles and grabbing as they tore off each other's clothes from the moment the flat door had been closed behind them. They were both semi-naked by the time they reached the bedroom and as they fell together onto the bed the mood changed from an almost teenage slap and tickle into a deep passion. Their lovemaking was physical, strong and deep, consuming all their energies but resulting in a tenderness that almost bonded their sweaty bodies together as one. Both spent, they lay in each other's arms not wishing the moment to ever change.

"We must do this again sometime," smiled Roly as he

held Chrissie.

"I agree," she smiled looking up into his face.

"I tell you what. Let's doze here for a little while and see if we can do better later."

"What a great plan," Chrissie smiled, snuggled in even deeper and closed her eyes.

The next day, Roly picked up Chrissie and they drove into the town. Kate, the solicitor, worked in a legal firm of several solicitors that covered all types of law. The offices were on two floors of an old, well-preserved building in the predominantly business quarter. The ground floor was the reception and conference rooms, and the first floor was for various individual lawyer offices with an administrative team in an open plan area. They waited for a few minutes while the receptionist rang for Kate.

"Well, hi there, Chrissie," announced Kate as she arrived, "and this must be Roly. The whole family are talking about you."

All this with a big smile and hugs and Roly found himself smiling at a woman about his age with a clear, familial similarity to Chrissie.

"How's the baby?" asked Chrissie.

"Come upstairs and I'll tell you over coffee, and then we can discuss some business for Roly."

Kate and Chrissie chatted briefly but when the secretary brought the coffee, Kate seamlessly turned the conversation to Roly and business.

"Roly, Chrissie tells me that you want to buy a property. Is that how I can help?"

"Well for starters, yes," said Roly and immediately regretted how it had sounded. "I mean, we have great plans, but it starts with this specific property."

"Tell me about this property and what you want to use it for – the other things can be dealt with later."

Roly spoke about the old harbour warehouse and how he wanted to turn it into a hotel or rather a holiday home for people, children mainly, who had fallen on hard times. He wanted it to be free to those who could not pay but he wanted it to have an income if he could secure sponsorships from corporations to allow it to become self-financing. If it did, he wanted to be able to open others eventually.

Kate listened without comment or reaction. Only when Roly had finished did she speak. "That building is owned by the town and has been regarded as derelict for about twenty years. However, before you buy it or try to buy it two things must happen. First, the town's planning committee must agree that the town has no use for the building or land and second, they must approve your intended use of the building. Only then can you negotiate a price and then, frankly, because all this is done in an open public manner, you may well find that you have others who may wish to buy."

"But it has been derelict for twenty years. No one wants it."

"You have an exciting plan for the building, and such a plan may well excite others. That's all I'm saying."

"Sounds like a long, tedious business."

"Not necessarily, at least a couple of months for sure to get to step one. Afterwards, perhaps only a few more weeks if there is only a sole buyer – longer if it becomes a competition."

"Well, we have to start – so let's start – how do we start?"

"First, I need to explain to you, my costs. We have a

standard rate card and …"

"If it is a standard rate then that's all I need to know… next step?" interrupted Roly.

"OK," said Kate, a bit surprised. "I believe there is a Planning Committee meeting next week, let me see if I can get some agenda time."

"Great," said Roly as he perked up with the sound of action.

"In preparation for that meeting," said Kate, now interrupting Roly like he had her, "I need you to type up on A4 sheets of paper in no more than three pages everything about your plan. Describe your vision, your plans – just like you spoke to me earlier. I need it by the end of this week. I will work on it to prepare a briefing document for the committee and modify it as required."

At the words modify as required were spoken Roly could not help but react. His eyes opened and he sat up straight, but before he could speak Kate continued: "If I make any changes, you get full and final approval. The document that gets distributed is yours."

Roly smiled and stood up, he held out his hand first to shake Kate's but then thought better and rather clumsily held out both arms wide and enveloped both Kate and Chrissie into a big bear hug. He laughed out loud, "We're making progress, we're taking action, wait till we tell Jamie – I am so happy!"

"I wish all my clients were so easily pleased," said Kate with a wry smile. "But it is a start."

They left the building and walked towards the car.

"What next, Captain?" asked Chrissie.

"Do you have any plans for today?"

"Well, I start my shift at one."

"It's quarter past eleven, do we have time for the

flat?"

Chrissie beamed a big smile and said, "Oh yes, race you to the car," and sprinted up the street. Roly was so happy at that moment and could not think of a time in his life when he had been happier. He didn't run but he did walk rather fast after her.

Chapter 13

Five Weeks of Freedom

That evening, Ronnie arrived at a small nondescript flat on the ground floor of a large three-storied terraced house. The house, the street and the area had all once had refined times but now were simply rundown. Elegant people had moved on and poorer more desperate people had moved in, all too busy chasing their own agendas, or protecting what they had, to bother about what was happening to a neighbour. To that end, the place was perfect as the 'home' for Ronnie's direct gang. Ronnie's day had picked up since that crazy session with the boy and Mr Hopkins. In fact, Ronnie had only just started to think about the kid on his short drive to the flat.

On entering the flat, Ronnie heard his lads chatting in the main room while some sports programme blared out of the television.

"Hey!" he shouted and immediately got their attention. "Where the fuck is the kid?"

One of the guys pointed half-heartedly towards an understairs cupboard along the side wall and Ronnie took a few paces across and clicked open the simple latch.

"Jesus, kid, look what your mouth brought you."

Jules was huddled in the corner in his underpants; from the look in his eyes he seemed in total shock and from his body you could understand why.

"Come on, kid, out of there," spoke Ronnie with almost care and consideration in his voice. When there was no response, Ronnie turned angrily and stared at his two henchmen who were totally absorbed in the television. There was an old mug on a side table, Ronnie reached over and picked it up. Then with a roar of rage he flung it at the television screen.

"Whoa," said one as he almost jumped out of his armchair.

"What the fuck," echoed the second as he stepped sideways off his chair. "What you want to do that for, Ronnie?"

"Because you aimless bastards, I want your attention. Now, help the kid out and gently put him on the sofa."

They moved forward and, as requested but perhaps without the description of gently, carried Jules across to the sofa and then stepped back for Ronnie. Still with a look of disgust in his eyes, Ronnie took a couple of twenty pound notes from his wallet and holding it out to one of his guys said, "Here, get some stuff in. We need bread, milk, tea and coffee and something for a sandwich and for breakfast... yes, get some eggs and bacon. You guys are staying here tonight so make your calls and be back with the food in an hour, an hour from now not fucking two!"

They were gone in seconds and the quiet in the flat now seemed to close in on Ronnie as he sat down besides Jules on the sofa.

"What did they do to you, kid?" he asked but it was not a question, he knew what they had done, they had done what he had told them to do.

Jules' nose was certainly broken, his lips swollen and one eye fully shut with the other partially shut. Dried blood was on his face and also from one ear lobe where it appeared to have been pulled away from the side of his face. The kid had bruises starting to come out on almost all parts of his body, shins, thighs, sides and shoulders. All, no doubt, the result of a sustained kicking. One instep was particularly bruised and swollen with blackening toenails and a strangely twisted big toe.

"Kid, never ever forget this and perhaps it will never happen again. If you do forget it, then for sure the next time will be worse and probably fatal."

Ronnie got up and walked into the kitchen and finding no clean towel or rag took out his handkerchief and wet it with warm water and returned. Slowly and gently, he wiped the dried blood from Jules' face as he talked.

"Kid, you thought you were the man! You were the smart one, you knew what you wanted and you were going to get it. Kid, listen to me. I know, I was there myself. Kid, what am I, eight years older? Not much really and I remember. Kid, you were a big fish in a small pond and now you are in the big pond and the big fish just don't give a fuck – about you, me or anything other than what they want. You want to be tough? Fine, but not against these guys, not until you know the rules. In all walks of life, you have to do your apprenticeship. With a trade, playing football, boxing, as a doctor or accountant – all start with nothing more than promise and then learn their specific trade. Now you have to decide if this is your trade because if it is then you are my apprentice. Do you understand? I said, do you understand?"

All through this little speech from Ronnie, spoken in a soft, older-brotherly way while he gently cleaned the kid's face was too much for Jules. The mixture of softness, kindness and gentleness of his words overwhelmed him, and he broke down and started to sob.

Great big heaves of sobs that lasted for several minutes. Ronnie waited for a short while and then moved away back into the kitchen. He waited for a few minutes more until the sobs seemed to die down. He had more to say and wanted the kid to pay attention, this was harder than he had thought. In the past he had often given people beatings, but this was not just a smack in the face, or a club to the head and move on. He had to turn this kid into one of his soldiers and if he didn't then the kid had to go. It all depended on the next conversation.

When he walked back into the room, Jules was still huddled up on the sofa curled up into a foetal position. He was no longer crying, his eyes were on Ronnie. Jules had never been more frightened in his life, but he knew he had to pay attention.

"Sit up, kid, I need to talk to you."

Jules slowly moved around to a hunched sitting position. He winced at every little move as pain shot out of all parts of his body.

"Kid, do you have any idea of the position you are in?"

Ronnie paused for a response and let the silence hang there so that Jules knew he had to say something.

"I'm sorry, I didn't mean to cause so much trouble."

"What the fuck did you expect?"

"I don't know, but it wasn't this. I wanted to join up with you guys not threaten you."

"Kid, you don't know the rules," repeated Ronnie as he shook his head.

"Tell me what you had in mind and I'll explain the situation to you. Now listen clearly, if you tell me anything that is untrue, I will personally kill you. If you cause me any more problems, I will kill you.

Understand, no one will miss you except perhaps your mother. Now, I will ask the questions and you talk."

Jules nodded and the critical conversation started.

"Tell me again, who knows you are here?"

"My girlfriend, she knows that I am coming to London to meet up with Lawrence's London partners, but she doesn't know who they are or where they are."

"Shit, that old fuck. He wasn't a partner, he was no more than a foot soldier. So, who killed him, do you know?"

"I did, and his girl, with his own gun."

"Now, why the fuck did you do that?"

"He was a dirty bastard and he tried to touch up my girl."

"So, you shot him?"

"Well, I hit him over the head at first with a table lamp and bust his head open but then he tried to go to his bag for this old gun he had, and I realised that I couldn't work with him again so I took it off him and shot him. The girl was hysterical and screaming so I shot her to quiet her down."

"Jesus, kid, you don't take prisoners, do you?" laughed Ronnie at the thought of this young kid just blasting people away. "So, you and your girl went back home to the coast. OK, but why come back?"

"In Cranport, Lawrence used to fund my gang when we handled all the stuff that people stole. Without Lawrence, we had no money to keep things going. But also, it wasn't much money really and it never was going to be because the town is too small. I thought that if I could make a contact then I could get involved in bigger stuff. Not the gang really, they are just kids who do as they are told by me, but I wanted a free life for me and my girl and I wanted it in London with the big guys."

"Well, you met them. The question is, though, do they want to work with you? Listen, kid, to them and me you are just a..." Ronnie struggled for the right words, "an inconsequential little turd with no redeeming qualities. Someone they don't need who can only cause them problems, especially if they think they are a big guy. Sure, every so often an up-and-coming kid catches their eye, and they invite the kid in and give him something to do, something small to see how it goes. If it goes well the kid gets some more, if not the kid goes away knowing almost nothing. If he knows too much and it doesn't go well then, he goes away permanently, understand?"

Jules was listening and paying attention. He did understand and he certainly did not want to upset anyone again. So, he nodded.

"Kid, this is it. Tonight, you sleep here. In the morning, you have to explain to me why I need an inconsequential turd. What have you got to offer? If I am not convinced that you bring any benefit, then…"

Ronnie didn't finish but Jules understood and nodded.

"Now get yourself into the bathroom, wash up and get dressed. The goons will be back soon, and you can have some food before sleep."

Jules, with head hung low and knowing his place, hobbled off the sofa to a corner of the room and picked up his clothes and retreated to the bathroom. Ronnie watched him go and wondered. Had he broken the kid's spirit? If not, the kid had to go. If yes, the kid had to get some back or he had no value and had to go. If the kid could recover and be willing to learn, then he was smart enough to be of use.

Jules quietly locked the bathroom door and sat on the throne. His spirit had been broken, he felt lost. He had thought he could outsmart anyone and everyone, but these guys were animals. What he had found so difficult to get was that these people just didn't care about him or anything other than what was important to them. Ronnie had said "an inconsequential turd" and it was an accurate description. He had also said that everyone had to learn their trade. Jules wondered what trade he wanted.

There was a big bang on the door and Jules jumped.

"Don't hang about in there," growled Ronnie.

"OK," shouted Jules and started to wash and get dressed, still wincing as he moved. A few minutes later, after combing his wet hair with his fingers, Jules tentatively left the bathroom.

Ronnie was standing by a window on his telephone and glanced over. He ended his call and pointed at the sofa for Jules to sit down.

"Kid, you still look like shit," he said but with less of a growl in his voice than earlier. "Now, let me tell you what you're going to do. When my guys come back there will be something to eat and then I want you to go into a bedroom and sleep. Nothing else, just sleep. I will be back in the morning, and we will have another chat. Think about all I've said, tomorrow's conversation is the most important one of your life. You understand that don't you?"

Jules just looked at him and nodded and almost as if it had been timed, the door opened and in came Ronnie's guys.

"What you got?" asked Ronnie.

"Just stuff like you asked," responded one of them,

opening up the plastic bag and offering Ronnie to look inside.

Ronnie ignored it and said, "OK, whatever it is you lot have to eat it, I don't care. Do you have something for the kid?"

The guy looked surprised.

"Jesus, you are one stupid bastard," roared Ronnie as he grabbed the bag and searched inside. He came upon a pork pie and a plastic litre of milk. The rest he tumbled out on the table. "Kid, have a pie and drink some milk then go to bed. Guys, no more beatings. Don't let me come back tomorrow and see any more marks on him. You got my number if you need me, but I'll be back about eight." And with a quick glance around to ensure everyone was in agreement, Ronnie strode out of the flat.

With Ronnie gone the atmosphere changed again. One of the guys walked over and said, "Don't you drink much of that milk, it's for our teas and coffees as well and that pie was for me, so I hope you choke." Harsh, unfriendly words but no physical contact, Jules recognised that these two knew the rules and would never disobey a Ronnie command. One put the kettle on as the other settled back into the only armchair and started to read some sports magazine, passing comments to his partner as he moved from topic to topic.

Jules decided that bed was best for him, he wanted and needed to be in a separate room. He stood up and as they looked at him, he said, "Ronnie said I had to sleep in the bedroom tonight. I'm not that hungry, thanks for the pie but I cannot eat all of it and I've had enough milk." He tried to smile as he spoke but was not sure if one came out, it certainly did not get any reaction from them. Jules wandered towards a bedroom and entered the first one he came upon. As he made his way towards the dirty, unkempt bed with rags for blankets the door was wrenched open.

"No shutting doors here, kid. We want to hear you snoring." The guy half closed the door and went back to whatever he was doing. Jules curled up on the bed facing the wall and tried to shut out the world while he thought through the situation he was in. He was scared – no, he was terrified. He couldn't take another beating, and he was not sure if he wanted to live in a world where these things could happen. He wasn't sure that he wanted the big time anymore. He wasn't sure if Ronnie was ever going to let him go. He wasn't sure, he wasn't sure, he wasn't sure – everything just seemed to bubble up inside him as his head whirled with thoughts that sometimes were just not connected. He wasn't going to cry, he was sure of that. As he lay there, he suddenly gave an almighty sigh and so much tension seemed to drain out of him. Slowly, he relaxed and without even realising it he slipped into a welcoming sleep.

"Get up you lazy bastard," were the words that woke him in the morning. Which of the guys had shouted it from the other room didn't seem to matter to Jules. He stretched on the bed and winced as he felt all the bruises and bumps on his body. Slowly, he walked into the other room, which reminded him of the brickworks' old office before he had the gang clean it up. The air was stale from smoke and people smells, rubbish was strewn over tabletops and around the floor of the chairs and the two guys lolled on the armchair and sofa.

"Put the kettle on, kid, and make some tea," said one with a half-smile. From the smell of whisky and the sight of lager cans lying around, the guys had obviously spent a significant amount of time drinking from the previous night.

Jules pitied them and smiled. "Sure, no problem, tea is coming up or would you prefer coffee? If you like I could make some bacon sandwiches?"

"My God, we've kidnapped a butler. Go for it, kid, tea for me and a bacon sandwich would be just great."

Jules went at it with gusto and saw how easy it was to get these two goons on his side. Within ten minutes he had mugs of tea and bacon sandwiches piled up and he was encouraging them to join him around the table.

"No fucking ketchup but still, this is good, kid."

Slightly more hesitant at first but even the other guy hauled himself out of the armchair to join them at the table and that is how it was when Ronnie walked in.

"What's this? Happy families?"

The atmosphere changed again as the two guys tried to reassert themselves as tough guys to Jules in front of Ronnie.

"Just having breakfast, Ronnie. The kid's good at cooking."

"Well, finish up, you two, and wait for me in the car outside."

There was a serious look between the two guys, but they immediately started to grab a few things, making sure they each grabbed a last sandwich in a free hand as they headed towards the door and left.

Ronnie sat at the table, making sure that his elegant suit did not touch any of the stained table surfaces by moving his chair back out of reach. He looked at Jules but let the silence hang out there for long enough for Jules to feel and understand it.

"Kid, time for our chat. Have you been thinking

about what I said yesterday?"

"Sure, Ronnie, apart from frying up bacon and making tea, it is all I have been thinking of."

"And so?" snapped Ronnie. "What value can you be to me?"

Now purposely Jules let his silence hang out there and only when Ronnie looked like saying something did he start.

"What are you looking for, Ronnie? What do you need because I can do many things, but I'm not like those goons and you know that don't you?"

Ronnie smiled, "What makes you different from them, then?"

"God, Ronnie, my mother's dog is smarter than them."

Ronnie almost laughed out loud and had to put his hand to his mouth to try to hold it back.

"Are you smarter than me, Jules, is that what you think?"

"I might be, Ronnie, but I do not know what the rules of this new game are and I'm hoping you will teach me. In return, I will be your right-hand man, someone you can unquestionably rely on to do things that you would hesitate to send others to do."

"And when I've taught you all you need to know about the rules, kid, what then?"

"Hell, Ronnie, by then you would have become the top man and if you haven't you can always work for me. I will look after a good teacher."

Ronnie could no longer stifle his amusement and leaned back and simply chuckled before getting desperately serious. He leaned forward and grabbed Jules by the neck.

"Kid, this can only work if you seriously understand that I can and I will kill you if you ever fuck up. This is a game but a very serious one that demands a hundred per cent loyalty. If you think I'm wrong you can question it once, openly and only to me. After that, hesitation, taking no action, talking to others, or doing what you think is right are all offences in my book. You might have heard of the principle of three strikes and you're out. Well, in this game it's one strike. You don't work for the big man, you sure as hell don't work for yourself, you work for me – I own you, kid. Look me in the eyes, kid, and tell me you understand."

"I understand, Ronnie, I really do," said Jules quietly. And he did.

"What now then, kid, are you expected back home?"

"Ronnie, I still have five weeks in school but after that I want to come up here and work with you. Could I bring my girl with me?"

"School! Jesus, what the fuck am I doing? Do you want to bring your mother as well and perhaps your gang of boy scouts – should I hire you some hotel rooms and set up a welcome party?"

"Ronnie, it's just me. I will look after my girl. Give me a few weeks to sort out things back home and then I promise you that you are going to look back on this as the smartest thing you ever did."

"OK, kid, I am going to remind you of that. So go home, tell them you were mugged or something. Get yourself better and lose all that black and blue shit. "Here, take this." Ronnie threw him a cheap disposable mobile phone.

"The number is on the back, you ring me if anything strange happens on this number." Ronnie scribbled a number from the back of another mobile phone onto a strip of newspaper. "I want a text each day telling me that all is OK. You know that if I don't get this, I'm coming looking for you, don't you?"

"Ronnie, you don't have to say that. I'm on board, you are my boss from this moment on."

"Yeah, you are. So do this; go back, get healthy, finish school for fuck's sake. Get out of the boys' gang business. Do you need money?"

"No, I have some," said Jules as he stuck his hands into his trouser pockets and then frantically into his jacket pockets. "Those thieving bastards have pinched my wallet, I had almost three hundred pounds."

"Anything else of importance in the wallet?"

"No, nothing else except some condoms."

Ronnie smiled again, "Well, leave your wallet to me to sort out, get some new condoms and take this." Ronnie peeled off quite a hefty wad of twenty pound notes and threw them on the table. Jules picked them up without counting but at a glance he quickly estimated that he had made a profit on his loss.

"Kid, you've got five weeks of freedom and then you start your apprenticeship with me."

"Thanks, Ronnie, I won't let you down."

Ronnie got out and started to head for the door.

"Ronnie? Is that it? What do I do now?"

"Questions, oh so many questions. Kid, you said you were smart so work it out. Go home and keep in touch. Now, I've got work to do and those clowns in the car owe me some money."

Ronnie walked out without a backward glance and Jules smiled. All he had planned to do with this visit had happened. Perhaps not the way he expected and certainly not with the beating, but he felt his future was clearer. He got up to gather his things together and after a few minutes he walked out of the flat and headed home.

Chapter 14

Changing Lives

Life was running at a pace. Things were happening. Roly was excited. Since that very day of the terrorist attack when his life changed, which seemed so long ago, Roly had had no structure in his life. He did things at his pace, when and if he so decided and to be honest, he had often decided not to. Even in Cranport, if it had not been for the accidental meeting with Chrissie he would have probably continued to drift. Jamie and Chrissie had been right to challenge him and now he had not only made a start but was determined to drive forwards. He had emailed his 'Vision' document to Kate within twenty-four hours. She had reviewed and revised it sending back a different document, but he had to admit, the same vision but a better document. They were on the agenda for the Planning Committee but they had only five minutes under Any other business. Reviewing the agenda, Roly got disappointed.

"How come we've got five minutes at the end when they are spending up to twenty minutes on other nonsense?" he wailed.

"What is nonsense?" responded Kate.

"Extension of the supermarket car park for one, turning Front Street into a one-way system is another, we even have more time on a Mr Evans who wants to knock down his back garden wall and build a garage. Damn it, none of these things will change people's lives to the extent we want to."

Immediately after speaking, Roly knew he was

wrong. He looked up into the eyes of both Kate and Chrissie and saw disappointment; they knew he was wrong too.

"God, I am such a pompous prat. Who do I think I am? Do I really think that I am better than anyone else – ladies, I am sorry, I apologise. If I ever act like that again promise me, you will take me swimming with my boat anchor."

"Roly, you are just frustrated and want to get on. You didn't mean those things and five minutes in AOB is no bad thing. Let me explain," said Kate.

"Before you do, Kate, let me explain something to Roly. You are not a pompous prat because the moment you acted like one you recognised it – prats don't. You are something a whole less obnoxious; I would call you a temporary dickhead, but the illness is over, so let's get on."

Roly looked at them again and saw the disappointment in their eyes had been replaced with care and support. He laughed with both embarrassment and pleasure that he was surrounded by such individuals.

"OK, what can be done in five minutes?"

"Well," responded Kate, "in five minutes we introduce the idea and get to understand the process they want to put us through. In five minutes, you don't get a yes, but you could get a no. If they were to feel that your plans were not credible they could just say no. Our plan is to get a clear understanding of the hoops and hurdles they want us to jump through and over."

"OK, so what do you want me to say or do?"

"Absolutely nothing; you will not be there. At best, you will be in the public gallery where there is no ability to speak. I will speak for you – that's my job. If we get the recognition that this is an idea or project worth exploring then I am sure that you will get every opportunity to participate more directly."

Roly nodded but his frustration was still present.

"OK, let's see how it goes. Run things as you see fit, Kate. Chrissie, I think we should head back to my flat and call up Jamie. Three days now with nothing from him, which either means he is yet to get started or that he has forgotten about us."

By early evening, they had managed to contact Jamie. Again, even though the telephone their end was put on speaker, the conversation seemed to be all between Jamie and Chrissie and all about how family members were, what the trip back was like, what the weather was like on the coast versus London etc. Roly sat perfectly bemused realising that he, and apparently only he, had a completely stunted ability to make small talk. Was he worried? Frankly, he felt blessed.

"When are we going to talk about something that means something?"

"Oh, look out, Chrissie," giggled Jamie, "the strong silent type has spoken. We must pay attention."

More giggles and insults came Roly's way until eventually they settled down.

"Roly, you wanted me to make some contacts to explore corporate sponsorships."

"And?"

"Well, although I know many senior executives, I was frightened that I might just blunder in and spoil things from the outset. So, I took some advice."

"Jamie, don't drag it out. That's a tease, what have you done so far."

"Ooh, Chrissie, he's spoiling my report because I

have such good news. I went to Jeremy, that's Jeremy Gaul from Coutts Bank, Chrissie. I asked Jeremy how I could get some sponsorship from several companies for a new charity and I know you said that I mustn't say exactly what it is or will be and how it will run…"

"That's because we don't know yet, Jamie," interrupted Roly, "and we don't want them telling us how to do it."

"Yes, but you know Jeremy. He wouldn't answer a hypothetical question. So anyway, I told him what you wanted to do, and he was thrilled. He said so many large corporations need to demonstrate their social citizenship but were too cautious to do it themselves and anxious that standard charities take money and apart from appearing to do well are in his terms 'a low value investment for the efforts'. He said two key things; first he wants Coutts in as a founding company but no operational responsibilities at all, and if you agree to this Coutts will work with us to get in not just anyone with money but the right companies that truly represent the right values. Bottom line, he wants to meet you again. This time he said he'll come to you although when I mentioned Cranport he seemed bemused about where it might be."

"Wow, Jamie, you are just too good. Please thank Jeremy and tell him we would be thrilled for him, or rather Coutts, to get involved. Hell no, we are thrilled that he and Coutts are going to get involved. I know he is a busy guy, tell him whenever he can make it will be good for us. Jamie, bring him down and we'll spend a dinner and night together."

"Roly, where in Cranport would we take a banker for dinner?" piped up Chrissie.

"Chrissie, this guy is one of the good guys. Yes, he has a big job, but he treats all people with respect. Hell, we'll have a barbecue in my flat, your mum can make that infamous potato salad, Jamie will cremate animals that once walked in fields, and I will serve outstanding Rioja. You can glide around looking beautiful and we will all stop Trev from telling naval stories."

"I do not cremate meat, that was a one-off when you talked to me and I forgot about the steaks," bleated Jamie.

That resulted in a most wonderful set of belly laughs amongst the three of them. We are the three amigos, thought Roly, we always end up laughing. What have I done to deserve such people in my life? He let the thoughts drift away as they ended the conversation outlining next steps for their plans.

The Planning Committee meeting was exactly as Kate had predicted. It was scheduled from 5–7.30pm and Roly, with Chrissie, Margie and Trev, all sat in the public gallery patiently waiting their turn. As the agenda topics were tackled, Roly started to clearly see and understand how they ran. The chairwoman was an elderly lady and councillor that just gave the meeting structure by announcing and ending each topic. The secretary, a council employee, simply took the minutes and never even looked up. That left four councillors and a council lawyer. The council lawyer advised when requested or when they felt it necessary to interject with legal advice about both local laws and national laws. Three councillors simply sat there and the only way you could be sure that they had not drifted into slumber was the occasional head nod or "I agree, Chairwoman" statement they made in support of the fourth councillor.

This guy clearly drove everything. He was late middle-aged, with a brush of ginger hair with grey tufts and the clear start of a paunch. He commented on everything; no one challenged him on any point and it was clear to Roly and surely everyone else that he ran this committee. This became even clearer as the Chairwoman spoke.

"Committee, this now brings us to AOB and we have only one item this evening. We have a request from a Mrs Katherine Wyatt, who represents a Mr Roland Johns, for consideration of the council for the purchase of a town owned property, the Harbour Warehouse, for transformation into a holiday hotel. Mrs Wyatt is here, and the outline was I believe circulated to all committee members earlier this week, so if there are questions I would ask you to direct them to Mrs Wyatt after her initial comments. So, Mrs Wyatt."

Kate started to rise when Ginger (as Roly had already decided to call him), shouted, "Point of order, Madame Chair, may I speak?"

"Of course, Councillor."

"Madame Chair, we are talking here about one of the most key, strategic buildings of the town. How can we discuss what is appropriate for this great town of ours in a five-minute pitch from a solicitor?" The last word of his sentence was thrown with a completely disrespectful hand wave towards Kate.

"May I speak, Madame Chair?" Kate tried to interject.

"No," said Ginger, "I have the floor. I want to know how this got on the agenda; I want to know how such a critical topic came to be circulated only twenty-four hours before this meeting."

The chair looked anxiously at the secretary.

"They asked for agenda time, and we had it so I put it on. I didn't know it was such a big deal."

The Chair again looked around bemused and Kate took the opportunity again to get her attention.

"Yes, Mrs Wyatt, you may speak."

And at this, Ginger harrumphed and almost turned his back to Kate like a sulky teenager.

"Madame Chair, we have followed standard council practice. And I formally request, and I am sure you will support this request, that the minutes note two key corrections from the earlier false statements of Councillor Mansfield."

At this, Ginger's interest peaked. "False statements, how dare you. What false statements have I made?"

"Councillor, if you would allow me to continue with the floor, as given to me by the Chair, I would be happy to enlighten not only you but everyone here," said Kate with a beautiful innocence that everyone recognised as a clear slapdown of Ginger's bullying.

"This item is on the agenda because I, on behalf of my client who is a resident in Cranport, wished to follow council process clearly and respectfully. The Planning Committee Secretary has just confirmed that. The false statements – let me clarify. The secretary informed me that each committee member must have an introductory document sent to them forty-eight hours prior to the start of a Planning Committee session for an AOB topic. This was done by email and from the date of the email which I have here" – and at that she reached down and picked up a printed copy of the email – "you can see that it was sent out not two, but four days ago."

Ginger almost started to rise but Kate actually signalled with her hand for him to sit back down and to his own surprise he did.

"Four days, not the twenty-four hours that the councillor mentioned earlier and to confirm, so there can be no doubt, the email was opened by the councillor, or his staff within thirty-two minutes of it being sent."

Now both the committee and those in the public gallery were paying full attention, especially the local journalist who for years had dreamily drifted off during these sessions – yet now he sensed something.

Kate continued: "The second falsehood as spoken by Councillor Mansfield may be open to interpretation. Let me further clarify. The councillor referred to the Harbour Warehouse as one of the most key, strategic buildings of the town. Now this building was a compulsory purchase by the town nineteen years and four months ago. Since that purchase, one wall was demolished, and a rickety wire fence has been put around it. No council work has been done to this building for eighteen years! Now, if the councillor can inform us that this building has been referred to in any strategic planning document over the last eighteen years or if he wishes to confirm formally that in his opinion eighteen years of neglect is the right approach for the planning of such a strategic building, I will happily take back my claim of an inaccuracy. If he does not, I request the inaccuracy be noted in the minutes."

There was a hush in the room until Roly erupted and stood up to shout, "Bravo, bravo." The chairwoman now completely bemused looked directly at Councillor Mansfield for obvious guidance.

With a snarl on his lips, he spoke. "Madame Chair, I accept that I might have spoken a little too passionately earlier and only because I care so much for this town it is easy to make a simple mistake and I thank the lady for correcting me. However, our five minutes is more than up, and I am sure that many of us like me, have other commitments that we must attend to. Can I suggest, Madame Chair, that this topic be given a complete agenda in a special meeting say two weeks from now? We might also welcome any others who have thoughts about this poor building rather than simply considering one person's view of what is best for Cranport."

The chairwoman, with obvious relief, grasped the suggestion of a way to end this extraordinary session and said, "Committee, unless there is anyone in disagreement, I think this is a fine suggestion."

The nodding heads of the councillors all brought the topic to an end and the chairwoman closed the meeting.

They all rushed out of the public gallery and down the stairs to meet up with Kate. As she emerged Roly headed towards her and with a whoop picked her up and swung her around.

"Kate, you were wonderful."

Before he could say anything else, she had prised herself from his arms and grimly said, "No, Roly, that was stupid. Not as stupid as you cheering from the gallery perhaps but today we made an enemy. I should have controlled myself better. Councillor Mansfield will now do all in his power, which is not inconsiderable, to foil us at every point. His influence and contacts are substantial. Today I made the process more difficult and you pay me to make it easy – I'm sorry."

"Who the hell is this guy Mansfield and why was he so hostile to us?" asked Roly.

"That's a discussion for another day; I'm going home to my family, so I'll speak to you the day after tomorrow at ten o'clock in the morning," said Kate rather wearily. She picked up her briefcase and after a hug and kiss to Chrissie she walked off.

"I can tell you about Mansfield," said a nondescript portly man who had been standing in the building entrance close but unnoticed.

"Who the hell are you?" roared Roly. "And what has it to do with you? And why are you listening into our conversation?"

"Let me introduce myself. My name is Mr Gareth Morgan, senior journalist on the Cranport Examiner," he said and held out his hand to Roly who just left it hanging there.

"Mr Johns, not everyone in my trade is low-life pond scum. I saw that TV reporter trying to fit you up a few weeks ago. Your young lady sorted him out. Well done." He turned and acknowledged Chrissie. "Let me tell you all I know about Mansfield and then, no pressure, you can decide whether you want to continue our discussion and even, possibly, shake my hand."

At this, Roly felt embarrassed about his initial rudeness but did not want to completely relent with his antagonism so he, in his mind, compromised.

"I'll give you twenty minutes in the pub over there," he said pointing across the road. "We can all buy our own drinks," he said somewhat melodramatically and realised how ridiculous he sounded when both Mr Morgan and Chrissie smiled.

It was a great investment of twenty minutes. Gareth Morgan told him that Doug Mansfield was the CEO of Mansfield of Cranport Builders Limited, a once honourable business created by his now dead father Harry Mansfield. It was by far the largest and most successful building company not only in town but in the region with an astounding success in competing for local government contracts.

"Doug Mansfield became a councillor over ten years ago. He believes he runs the council, he certainly does the Planning Committee. It is amazing how many approved building plans, both private and public, end up being carried out by Mansfield's of Cranport Limited. Everyone knows it goes on and I have been trying to catch him out now for years, but he is no dummy and he keeps it all nice and tight. I know he's a crook, but I just can't prove it. I hope, Mr Johns, that if your enemy is my enemy then that might make us allies. Perhaps we could share what we have together and remove this weasel from the power base he has created. We could make it fair for all. I mean, for all the people in Cranport not fair just for us."

"Mr Morgan, I thank you for your time and I will shake your hand in future. You can ask me any questions you want, and I will answer them, but I am not joining you or anyone in a campaign against Mansfield. I don't care about him enough to waste my time on it. All I want is my Planning Request to get approved."

"Expect then to either bow down to him or to be tied up in all sorts of diversions for many a month. Unless you give him something out of your project he will be an obstacle. Let's leave it at that for now. I think you need to have some Mansfield experience rather than Mansfield advice but if you ever want to talk then call me." He offered Roly his card, drained his glass, nodded to Chrissie and left them.

It did not take long to start to experience what Gareth Morgan had called "the Mansfield experience". Next evening before he left the flat to meet up with Chrissie at the marina, she called him.

"Roly, did you just see the local news?"

"What news?"

"The local TV station, that TV presenter from before has just been interviewing Mansfield about you and the Planning Committee. It was outrageous."

"What did he say?"

"Look, as soon as it came on and I realised what was happening I hit the video record button – I might have missed a few seconds, but I got the rest. Don't meet at the marina, come here and I'll show it to you."

Roly quickly picked up his jacket, jumped in his car and headed over. When he arrived, Chrissie ushered him into the lounge while Margie was trying to placate a crying Stevie in the kitchen.

"What's wrong with Stevie?" asked Roly.

"Oh, my fault, when I hit the record button, we overwrote his favourite cartoons. I'll get him a present tomorrow and he'll forget it but right this moment I am as he calls me 'Bad Mummy'! Never mind, see this."

Roly sat down on the edge of the sofa next to Trev as Chrissie switched on the tape. The television picture came to life with the reporter standing in front of the Harbour Warehouse fence with Doug Mansfield next to him.

"…disquiet yesterday at the town Planning Committee when representatives of Mr Roland Johns tried to rush through a proposal to buy this building behind me and turn it into some sort of holiday camp. Only Councillor Mansfield stopped them in their tracks. Councillor, there seemed to be some strong-arm tactics employed yesterday but you successfully held off for a special detailed meeting to go through these plans are you concerned?"

"Yes, I am," said Mansfield and then looking into the camera. "And all people in Cranport should be concerned. I mean who is this Roland Johns? No one knows. What we do know is that he has no job, he has been linked with a terrorist attack in London, he left there for some unknown reason and now he lives here in Cranport and already he has been interviewed by the police with his gay friend about an incident with a little girl lost from her poor mother at the supermarket. I'm just asking the questions that Cranport people want answered."

The camera cut back to the reporter. "Well thank you, Councillor, for keeping the focus on what is right for this town, and we'll keep you all at home informed as future developments occur. Now, Jenny, back to you in the studio…"

Chrissie switched off the television and everyone looked at Roly.

"My God, what a… what did the reporter last night call him? What a weasel! Nothing he said was technically wrong, but it was put over in such a wrong way. This is bad, but you know now he has got me really pissed off. I thought he was just an obnoxious jobsworth, but he is far, far worse than that. He's picked a fight with the wrong person. First chance I get I am going to squash him."

The next day, Chrissie and Roly had their meeting with Kate. Chrissie had brought the tape, but it was unnecessary. Not only had Kate seen it but everyone in town was discussing it.

"We have to fight back, Mansfield must not get away

with this, and I will not let him." Roly was still outraged.

Kate brought focus back.

"Roly, our purpose hasn't changed. Do not sacrifice your energies to a testosterone fight with Mansfield. He is not worth it, and you are better than that. We will stay focussed on preparing everything necessary for the committee in ten days' time and I mean everything. Mansfield has no facts or legitimate points to fight us on. However, I do agree it would help if we could get our basic point and premise across to the general public, but no campaign please."

"Kate, so wise; how would I manage without your guidance?" joked Roly. "You are right, we do it your way, but I know a journalist who can help us get our point out, no emotion, just the facts."

Kate nodded and the rest of the session was consumed with agreeing and outlining all they would need for the next Planning Committee.

Later that day, Roly met up with Gareth Morgan. They agreed on an article with photograph to appear in the Sunday paper under the Review of the Week section that Gareth edited. They took the opportunity in an interview style to directly address every innuendo that Mansfield and the television reporter had left hanging out there. With no drama, just the facts, Roly outlined who he was, why he came to Cranport and most importantly, what he wanted to do with the Harbour Warehouse. Only the last question was left open.

Gareth had asked, "Roly, you seem to have upset Councillor Mansfield – why is that?"

"Yes, Gareth, he does seem upset, but you know I find his motives difficult to understand. We have never met, we have never spoken. Read the minutes of the

Planning Committee, it records accurately that we have followed every council process. The committee's secretary put us on the agenda at the end for five minutes. I was disappointed because that gives us little time to outline our ideas and to seek local support. Other people who know the councillor can better answer why he acts in such a strange way. Let's hope that at the special Planning Committee meeting we can all simply get the facts out there and make decisions based on them. I will back up every comment, claim or proposal I make with facts and details, is it not only fair that Cranport expects an elected councillor to do the same?"

The article was excellent and throughout the day he received calls of support from friends and neighbours. Even Kate rang and said she was delighted, he had pitched it perfectly and then as she ended the conversation she said, "But, no more, Roly. That is, until after the Planning Committee."

That evening, the most bizarre situation happened. Roly was in his flat alone, Margie and Trev were going out and Chrissie was with Stevie. The phone rang and Roly got up from his desk where he had been working on some ideas with his laptop. He picked up the telephone.

"Hello, Mr Johns, Councillor Mansfield here."

"You're joking, who is this?"

"No joke, Mr Johns, I've just finished reading your newspaper interview and I thought you're right we have never met, we have never spoken. So, I thought that I should just give you a call."

"Now what makes you think there is any reason why we should talk?"

"Oh, there are always reasons to talk, reasons of

mutual interest even. We don't need to be on opposite sides if we can identify some benefits to all. Why don't we have a private conversation?"

Roly's stomach turned at the oily, sneaky words and phrasing of Mansfield. He wanted to scream "Fuck off" and slam down the phone but instead he simply replied, "When and where?"

"Your place now, why delay such an important conversation?"

"Where are you?"

"Mr Johns, look outside your window. I'm in my car. May I come in?"

Roly pulled the curtain back and Mansfield smiled and waved from his car while still speaking into his mobile.

"Hello again, Mr Johns, a quiet and private chat cannot do any harm now can it? Far better we have this impromptu meeting than arranging to meet somewhere only to find all the local press there waiting to see if we revert to fisticuffs or fall in love."

As he listened and looked through the window, he felt his skin crawl.

"OK, give me two minutes and come over," he said through gritted teeth. He hung up and turned to look around his lounge. He started to pick up papers from his desk and to put them in a folder and out of sight in a drawer. He turned to his laptop and saved the document he had been typing and closed the application. He was just about to turn off the laptop when he saw the video button. He hit it and up appeared a box offering either to watch or record a video. He hit record and saw himself staring at himself. He stepped aside and the camera picture changed to a view of the room, sofa and armchair on the other side of the room. He hit record again and walked out to open the door and beckoned Mansfield into his room.

"Beautiful room, Mr Johns." He almost purred like a cat. "These old buildings are so nice when they have been refurbished." He continued to scan the room, and Roly felt for sure he must have seen the laptop recording, but he hadn't.

"Cut the crap, Mansfield, this is not a social call so why don't you just tell me what you want?"

"Why are you so aggressive, Mr Johns? May I call you Roly?"

"No, may I call you arsehole?"

This was the moment that all pretence fell away. Roly now had a very angry and aggressive Mansfield in his room. Mansfield's stance had also changed. He held himself tall and upright and stepped forward. Mansfield's tone of voice was no longer oily and sickly sweet but hard-edged, with each syllable emphasised with a pointed finger.

"You have to understand how things work in this town, Johns. I run it. You want something I decide to give it or not give it. That's how we do it here. Now you want that old building, it's simple – what's in it for me?"

Roly did not feel physically or verbally intimidated, he surprised himself – he was just ice-cold.

"Mansfield, if you wave that finger in my face anymore, I am going to snap it off and stick it up your arse. Stop talking in riddles. What do you want?"

"I don't give a fuck what you want to do with that derelict building but whatever you do it will need major refurbishment. Let my company do the work for a fair price, well perhaps for a fair price plus say a ten per cent bonus or it could be twenty per cent if you call me an arsehole again."

"How would this work? Why don't I simply rely on convincing the others on the committee? You're just one of five voting councillors. Do you pay them off?"

Mansfield chuckled.

"No need to, you saw them. The old lady is frightened of her shadow and the three clowns barely share a brain cell between them. Pay me an opening bonus of say fifty thousand pounds, put the work out to tender but my company gets all the building work, and I will get you full planning approval within the month. Johns, this town is full of in-breeds, they need a leader, they're happy when they have a leader. I'm their leader."

Roly could take no more.

"You evil little bastard, this town does not deserve this. In fact, no town deserves this, and I would rather give up any plans I might have than end up associated with a creep like you. You would be a stain on everything I ever tried to do. So, Mansfield, the answer is no. No fucking way, never in a million years and talking of time, you have five seconds to walk out of this flat or I will kick you out."

Now Roly stepped towards Mansfield. It wasn't a gesture, it was full of menace.

"Hell, no, I lied," he shouted at a retreating Mansfield, "you don't have five seconds and I will kick you out."

Mansfield ran out of the flat and as he ran to his car he shouted, "You will regret this!"

Roly, standing in the doorway, reached down for a flowerpot of some red bushy flowers and hurled it at the car. It exploded on the back of Mansfield's Jaguar, splattering soil and petals over the car and road as the car screeched off down the street. Slowly, Roly walked back into his flat and stood there shaking. He had almost forgotten about the laptop until he saw it there with the red light still blinking. He walked over and stopped the recording. The file was for seven minutes and thirty-four seconds, but it had seemed longer, much longer. The application asked him for a filename, he typed in 'Mansfield' and the date. Then, still shaken he hit 'play.' It was all there, all of it. The pictures were not the clearest, but they were recognisable, especially when Mansfield had scanned around the room on his entrance. The sound was a little distant, but the words were there.

"I've got him, I've got him. No way will he ever survive this," Roly said to himself. Then realising how absolutely critical this file was he decided to protect it.

He attached it to an email that he sent to both Kate and himself. Now it was on an internet server, in both his inbox and sent mailbox and in Kate's email.

***

He rang Kate. Her husband answered and put Kate on the line.

"Roly, what's so important that it could not wait until tomorrow?"

"Were you busy?"

"Yes, I was painting my toenails."

"What colour?"

"You will see tomorrow. Now that's a word that keeps cropping up – tomorrow!"

"Seriously, Kate, this is important. Sit down you're not going to believe this. Guess who just paid me a visit."

He told her all about it, Kate didn't interrupt but every now and then he heard a "My God" or "Never!" When he had finished, he made one last point.

"Now, Kate, what do we do?"

"With my vast experience in local government fraud and skulduggery and not forgetting the fact that you never had Mansfield's permission to record him, I think I am going to think this through. Tell no one about this. I mean no one."

"Kate, I have to tell Chrissie. She is as much involved in this as me."

"Of course, but please Roly no one else until we meet. Be in my office at nine o'clock."

"This evening?"

"Tomorrow, you fool," she laughed. "Remember that word again, tomorrow."

"How you ever keep any clients when you insult them so much, I do not know," replied Roly and he heard her laughing as she hung up. He called Chrissie and again outlined all that had happened. Where Kate had said My God and Never, Chrissie was more forthright; there were several squeals and shrieks but just one word, Shit, said on various occasions as he ran through the story. He rang off after confirming that he would pick her up in the morning on the way to Kate's office.

By 9.05 the following morning the three of them were huddled around Kate's desk peering at the video. Only Chrissie was seeing it for the first time, yet all three gasped as it unfolded. When it ended, they sat back.

"So, Kate, what do we do?" asked Roly.

"Nothing, absolutely nothing; not until the Planning Committee meeting. If this got out now, the whole council planning process would be cancelled. There would be inquiries, possibly even police inquiries, which could delay everything for months and months."

"But we have to do something surely?" said Chrissie.

"We will, believe me we will. Let me explain, we three tell absolutely no one. I am going to see the Planning Secretary and ensure that we have an agreed agenda for our presentation. The whole town is already talking about this planning application, so we should get your friendly journalist to encourage the public to attend and see the committee in action. We will ensure that they all get to see this and that it is made available to the press and television station immediately after the meeting for further full coverage. I predict that no one will challenge our request after this meeting without appearing to side with this malevolent, obnoxious shit Mansfield."

"Ooh, Kate, you swore," teased Roly and they all laughed.

Keeping a secret is difficult. Knowing something and not telling, or even implying is difficult. It is equally difficult to not let on to anyone that you have a secret but are not telling. But they kept it for the next eight days as they prepared for the Planning Committee Meeting and they did it by keeping busy and preparing in detail all their plans and aspirations for The Water's Edge. The most difficult thing for Roly was not sharing with Jamie, he wrestled with it for three days and never felt good and so he sat down with Kate and explained that he would. He was expecting resistance but perhaps the way he explained to Kate that Jamie was a dear friend and part of the trio she simply nodded in agreement. That evening on the phone with Jamie, Roly explained all about Mansfield. Jamie responded with more "Oh my God" and "he never did" and a whole series of oohs and aahs that were like Kate and Chrissie combined. Roly made him promise to keep it to himself but had to promise in return to let him see the video as soon as he came down.

"Roly, this is like a spy case there's no way I'm missing this Planning Meeting, keep that spare room for me, I'm coming."

A few hours later and Jamie called back.

"Roly, I was talking to Jeremy, and I told him all about Mansfield and when I said I was coming down for this meeting he said he would come also. So, you'll have all our support."

"Jamie, just three hours ago you gave me the most profound promise that you would not tell anyone and now you've been discussing it with Jeremy. My God, Jamie, explain yourself."

"Oops, did I do wrong. Isn't Jeremy on our side? I thought you didn't want me to tell strangers. Sorry, next time you are going to have to be more precise."

Roly simply sighed, at least they only had three days to go, and Jamie and Jeremy were in London.

Kate got the agenda formalised and they were not surprised to hear that there would be a counterproposal from the council itself headed by Mansfield. The project was called Achieving the best for Cranport – Commercial redevelopment of the Harbour District.

"He can't vote on his own project, surely?" asked Roly.

"He may be an obnoxious runt, but we should not underestimate him. No, he will not vote on his project but abstain officially, but clearly, he would have used all his influence before the session."

"Should we be worried?"

"No," said Kate, "we are on first and by the time we are finished he will have no credibility and a whole host of other worries that will take his time and attention."

Roly took the agenda to Gareth, and it was the basis of a front-page article encouraging all Cranport residents to attend. It created great interest; everyone was asking for information, but nothing came out from Roly's side. Mansfield, however, was busy. Almost every other day he was on the local television news programme. Trying to look almost Churchillian with his voice dropping an octave, he warned Cranport residents to ensure they supported what was best for the town and to view with distrust ideas from outsiders who were just looking to make a quick buck. He didn't openly criticise Roly's proposal because he had no further information and if he tried to imply details, he would no doubt have been challenged to provide facts. Either he did not have any or he was equally loath to share them openly before the official day.

That official day eventually came. The meeting was scheduled for four hours in the Town Hall and to start at 1pm. The Town Hall had been scheduled because of the obvious local demand and by 12.30 people were already taking seats in the cordoned off public area. Roly was at the front with Kate. Chrissie and her family were in the first few rows of the public area. Kate was in formal mode and organising her papers and a young council technician was connecting up Roly's laptop that he was going to use for his presentation.

"This will support full video, won't it?" asked Roly.

"Sure will," said the technician. "If it appears on the

laptop screen it will be duplicated on that big screen."

"Yes, but what about sound?" Roly asked again.

"You want sound? No one said sound to me."

Roly's heart took a leap and then saw the kid smirking.

"Don't worry, sir. See all those speakers around the hall, they are all linked in and if you've got some music or words, out they come."

Roly perhaps did not look so convinced, so the kid made an offer.

"You want to try it out now quickly."

"Hell, no," responded Roly, "but I tell you what, if you stay in the room in case I have any problems, I'll give you twenty pounds."

"Do I still get the twenty pounds if it just works and doesn't need fixing?"

"Kid, if you stay in the room, you get the money."

The kid smiled and stayed. Roly's nerves were starting to take over and he worried that he might not be able to control them. Suddenly he heard a familiar sound.

"Yoohoo, Roly, yoohoo."

Roly and it seemed like everyone else in the room looked around to see Jamie dragging in a slightly embarrassed Jeremy into a few remaining empty seats. Jeremy gave a far more modest hand wave and sat down quickly. Roly smiled. How special was Jamie, the man was simply irrepressible, and his simple presence made Roly's spirits rise. He quietly spoke to himself, Roly you are going to do this because it is the right thing to do and because it's the start of you doing even more right things. Time to start changing some lives.

The buzz of all the people stopped as the Planning

Committee Chairwoman entered, followed by all the other councillors, the secretary and town lawyer. Mansfield was all smiles and false bonhomie. He was waving and nodding to individuals in the crowd and backslapping with various members of the committee. Every effort was to demonstrate that he was the good old local guy and at that moment Roly did feel like an outsider. Kate looked over at Roly and reached for his arm.

"It all means nothing, Roly. Have no doubt, we are prepared, and we will do this. Just follow my lead and do what we said we would do."

The chairperson spoke, "Planning Committee Meeting for Cranport and surrounding district is about to start. We have a published an agreed agenda which we shall follow. There will be no comment from the public unless invited to do so from this chair, there will be no interruptions to speakers unless a committee member requests through this chair a point of clarification. Is that clear to everyone – I hope so. Mr Secretary, first agenda topic please."

"Madame Chair, Mrs Katherine Wyatt, representing Mr Roland Johns wishes to present a proposal for the Harbour Warehouse building."

"Mrs Wyatt, you have the floor."

"Thank you, Madame Chair. I have already circulated all necessary background information as requested by Mr Secretary, and he has copies for each committee member. This background detail is the basis of my client's proposal to the town of Cranport and in addition I have an online presentation to emphasise many key points. Can you circulate the copies please, Mr Secretary."

The secretary looked around, bemused. "I have my copy. No one said I had to make copies for everyone."

"There you go," shouted Mansfield, "before we even start, they have no details to share with us. Madam Chair, this is inexcusable. How can we be expected to judge a proposal without the detail and just a few slides?"

The public audience started to grumble and complain when Kate reached down and grabbed a folder from her briefcase.

"Madam Chair, I agree fully with Councillor Mansfield. Just in case there was any slight inefficiency in the secretary's support to this committee, we all know how busy he can be."

At this the public sniggered.

"I took the liberty to make copies for everyone. As I said, just in case."

More sniggers from people, and Roly thought Well done, Kate, you are so good.

The copies were distributed, and Kate got back into presentation mode. She introduced Roly, described his background, referred to his heroic response in the terrorist attack.

"How relevant is all this?" shouted Mansfield. "This is a planning meeting not a hero's parade."

"Two things, Councillor: first, I am surprised that the Chair has not admonished you for interrupting without going through the Chair. Second, I am sure that many individuals here today will specifically remember the Councillor's great verbal concern that he shared on our noble local television news channel, when he said and I quote, 'I mean who is this Roland Johns? No one knows. What we do know is that he has no job, he has been linked with a terrorist attack in London, he left there for some unknown reason and now he lives here in Cranport and already he has been interviewed by the police with his gay friend about an incident with a little girl lost from her poor mother at the supermarket.' I am here, Madam Chair, to tell you who Mr Roland Johns is because Councillor Mansfield said it was important. He was involved in a terrorist attack; he fought them off saving lives of members of the Saudi royal family and was shot in the process of doing so. After hospital and recovery, he decided that he wanted to do something far more worthwhile with his life and came down here to Cranport to do just that. He picked up a little girl who had tripped and fallen over in the car park of the supermarket and returned the child to her mother. Yes, there was a slight misunderstanding, but the police were assured by members of the public of Mr Johns' gallantry and there is no more to say about that."

Mansfield squirmed in his seat and there was a buzz of positive feedback from the public.

"And so, in summary, to answer the Councillor's question, Mr Johns is a man of substantial bravery, willing to stand up against wrongdoing even at personal risk. Someone who cares for people not only in his day-to-day activities but now he is trying to make it a focus of his life. I would suggest that Cranport, indeed no town, would consider that such a resident was not a very good thing to have."

Someone in the public cheered and started to clap, it caught on with others and broke into a most splendid applause. It proved to be a turning point, even for Madam Chair.

"Thank you, Mrs Wyatt, and please everyone quiet

down. Councillor Mansfield, no more interruptions please without going through this Chair. Mrs Wyatt, perhaps we can now actually move onto the specifics of the proposal?"

Kate outlined the vision and the purpose and each time she nodded at Roly he advanced a slide in the presentation, so the key points were shown to all on the large screen.

"The Water's Edge is the name we have chosen for this hotel that we propose to build from the renovation of the old derelict Harbour Warehouse. We are willing to pay the town a realistic price for this ruin that no one has paid any attention to for over eighteen years. It will be a place of respite to unfortunate individuals and their families who, through no fault of their own, have fallen on most unfortunate circumstances and who cannot afford to pay for a short holiday break away from the tough times."

"That will cost millions," shouted Mansfield. "He doesn't even have a job, where is all this money to come from? Tell me that," he sneered.

Now for the first time, the public and even the committee were not on his side. They heard the sneering and they saw him as the mean-spirited person he was.

"Councillor, if you interrupt again without following due process you will have to leave this meeting," roared the Chairwoman.

A completely startled expression came across Mansfield's face and people close enough in the public area actually laughed out loud. Kate was quick to regain the floor and certainly did not want Mansfield to leave, not yet anyway.

"Madam Chair, if I might," and on receiving a nod

from the Chair she continued. "Our plan is to secure corporate sponsorship from national and international companies who feel a heavy desire to support social needs in the countries they do business."

Mansfield just couldn't help himself. "Yeah," he sneered, "how many have you got?"

The Chair started to respond, and Kate actually held up her hand and stopped her.

"Madam Chair, I am happy to respond, I want there to be no misunderstanding. We are yet to secure any sponsorship. It is hard to secure it without having an agreement to even build The Water's Edge."

"It's a pipe dream!" shouted Mansfield. "If he doesn't get sponsorship, he takes this prime property and turns it into something for himself."

Again, the Chair was about to respond when a call came from the back of the room.

"Madam Speaker, may I provide some crucial evidence to this committee?" And standing at the back of the room was Jeremy.

"Who the hell is this now?" shouted Mansfield.

"Shut up, Councillor," said the Chairwoman. "Who is trying to get my attention? Please introduce yourself."

"Madam Chair, apologies for this unexpected intrusion. I only seek this unannounced interruption to take this opportunity to share with the committee the very latest information. Again, sincere apologies, let me introduce myself. I am Jeremy Gaul, Vice-president of Client Services for the Coutts Bank."

Such an elegant interruption had the Chair almost swooning.

"Please, Mr Gaul, do say what you want to say."

"I thank you, Madam Chair. I want to inform you that

Mr Johns asked me a few weeks ago that if he was fortunate enough to gain access to this building and to create The Water's Edge, then would my bank be willing to consider a foundation sponsorship. I can now tell you that if this does occur then Coutts Bank would most certainly wish to be involved. The Councillor with red hair and a bad attitude, again apologies, but I have forgotten his name, is right, this could well cost millions, but I am equally confident that for the bank this would not prove to be a problem. It is a most worthy cause."

These comments brought about whoops of laughter, especially the comments about red hair and a bad attitude, and again spontaneous applause.

"God damn it," squealed Mansfield, "what sort of bank is this?"

Jeremy allowed himself a smile and a dramatic pause. Everyone, committee and public waited for the response and were not disappointed.

"Councillor whatever your name is, most people know us as the banker for the Queen, but we do of course have many clients."

Uproar, laughter and applause from everyone and it took several minutes before calm was re-established. Kate again gained the eye of the Chair.

"Madam Chair," said Kate. "I must thank Mr Gaul for this most welcome news. It does I believe complete our proposal. All that remains is this Planning Committee's process, but I am afraid that this is a very serious concern to my client and me. You see just a few days ago, a very influential person told my client that there are strange, illogical and unfair practices associated with this Planning Committee and it appears that these practices could unjustly block my client's proposal."

183

Everyone in the room was dumbfounded. The Chairwoman just blinked for several moments wondering if she had heard correctly what was being said before she got her voice back in control.

"Mrs Wyatt, the only thing that will severely go against your proposal is that deeply insulting comment unless you can back it up with facts."

Kate had the attention she had played for and responded clearly and clinically.

"Madam Chair, let me share something with you and everyone here. Then you can tell me if my client and I have any reason to be worried."

She nodded to Roly, and he pushed play on the video file. It took most people a few seconds to realise what they were watching. It took Mansfield far less. His mouth hung open as he saw and heard himself in Roly's apartment.

The comments had their anticipated reactions from all. Roly calling Mansfield an arsehole brought laughter, threatening to snap off his finger and to stuff it up his arse brought roars. Mansfield's comments about the various committee members brought silence. His final comments about the Cranport public and his leadership of them brought out uproar. His demand for fifty thousand pounds brought angered shouts of Shame and what a bastard.

Over the mayhem, the Chairwoman shouted to be heard.

"Fifteen-minute recess, fifteen-minute recess. We will reconvene in fifteen minutes." And then she was gone, herding out the committee before her. Journalists immediately went on their mobile phones, people just buzzed with animated conversations amongst those close to them. Jamie, Jeremy, Chrissie and her family all surged down to Kate and Roly.

"Wow," said Roly, "wow."

"I think that went well," said Kate.

"What do we do now?" asked Chrissie.

"We wait fifteen minutes. The committee is in recess; it's not over. They have to come in and explain the next steps. Keep your fingers crossed. Mansfield is finished that's for sure, but we are yet to get approval."

It was twenty-five minutes before Madam Chair returned with all the committee, but there was no sign of Mansfield. There was a hush as everyone waited.

"This has been a most extraordinary meeting. Frankly, never in my life have I experienced anything like it. Mr Johns and Mrs Wyatt, I can assure you that the comments we heard from Councillor Mansfield on your video are inaccurate and untrue. I need to request from you a copy of that video so we can ask the local constabulary to explore all possible wrongdoing. In return for your cooperation, I am pleased to tell you that this committee fully approves your proposal and would welcome an early opportunity to negotiate a fair price for the purchase of this property so that you can, without delay, commence with this most worthy cause."

Chapter 15

Stick to the Rules

Jules' return caused quite a stir. When he arrived home that first evening, his mother took one look and burst into tears. It was a full half-hour of tears, questions and attempts to nurse him before Jules was able to be obnoxious enough to demand to be left alone and stormed upstairs to his room. Later, in the bathroom, he looked at his reflection in the mirror. His nose was probably broken but not too bad. He now had what looked like racoon eyes. Even more ludicrous was that the black and blue around his eyes was turning into purple and yellow. The rest of his body was covered in bruises which were tender to touch but hidden from view, thankfully, by his clothes. The worse by far was his swollen and misshapen big toes. This caused him to limp and that seemed to emphasise his obvious beating.

The next day, when he met up with the gang and Tina, he had to go through it all again,

"Holy fuck!" said Holvey. "What happened to you?"

"Oh, Jules. My God!" said Tina as she put her hands around his shoulders only to be shrugged off. The gang all gathered around to hear what had happened to their leader.

"Three guys mugged me," said Jules. And he was sticking to it, giving very little information away. "I walked around this corner and one guy stopped in front of me. Before I could ask him what he wanted, two guys hit me from behind. I tried to fight them off, but they stamped on my foot. I think my toe is broken, and they ran off with my wallet. If I had not had some cash and notes in my pocket, I would not have been able to catch the train home."

No one disbelieved him. The evidence was clear to see but still, somehow, Jules was diminished in their eyes. Their psycho leader had seemed invincible and impervious to the problems, issues and concerns that everyone else seemed to have to navigate around as they went through life. Only Tina knew why Jules had gone to London. In a quiet moment, he took her aside to update her. He stuck with his mugging story, though. There was no way he would ever tell her of the beating they had given him or the threats of worse if he ever let Ronnie down.

"I made contact, Tina, and they want me to join them. There's a top guy and he has several gang leaders working for him, but one of these guys is a favourite and he's only about mid-twenties. Ronnie, that's his name, and we got on great. You know what, that shit Lawrence wasn't a boss not even a soldier. He was just someone who used to come up now and then and buy or sell things from them. They don't care about down here. They get involved in big stuff in London. Ronnie wants me to work for him. He wants me to join him in a few weeks when we finish school."

"Are you going?" asked a surprised Tina.

"What do you mean am I? Tina, we are both going. This is our break to get out of this place. It's what we've talked about in the past."

"Yes, we have, but not straight after school. That's a surprise."

"You'll love it, Tina. We'll get a place together. We can do whatever we want. No one can stop us."

Tina had taken a step back and looked a bit hesitant.

"You do want to come, Tina, don't you?"

"Jules, I want to be with you but not this. I never thought people would get shot. Every night, every time I just shut my eyes or sit quietly, I see his head exploding over the armchair, and I hear her screaming. I will never get used to that. I don't want to get used to that."

"Well fuck, come or don't come but I'm going," said Jules, now getting irritated.

"No, Jules, I'm coming. Course I am," and she stepped up to hug him. If he could have seen her face as it looked over his shoulder, he would have known she was anything but sure. He may have not seen her face, but he soon became aware of a growing distance between them and it was not just an isolation between him and Tina, it was between him and his old life.

Over the next few weeks, everyone slowly but surely recognised that Jules had changed. First, he said they could not carry on the Lawrence business without the money provided by him. No matter, they thought, Jules was bound to come up with ingenious ideas of other scams and opportunities. They were so disappointed when he didn't. Tina got fed up with Jules starting almost every conversation between them with Ronnie said, Ronnie does, or Ronnie wants. Tina didn't like the hold that this person Ronnie had over Jules. She didn't understand it or want it. What had always attracted her to Jules was that he did not care a fuck about anyone regardless of their clout and position but now he was certainly playing second fiddle to this London guy.

The gang knew Jules had changed, Tina knew he had changed and of course Jules knew he had changed. Gone was the swagger, gone was the drive to do whatever he wanted to do. Gone was the desire to rule and lead this gang of kids. Everyone knew Jules tended to drift off into his own thoughts and that had not changed – the thoughts had. All that consumed Jules now was one question and he spoke it to himself all the time inside his head: What can I do to impress Ronnie? He wanted to do nothing else. It was all down to the fact that he was terrified of doing the opposite. If he ever fell short in the eyes of Ronnie he couldn't, he wouldn't take another beating or, God forbid, anything worse.

So, the gang was drifting, and the brickworks was becoming more and more the hooligan's youth club, just as Jules as once described it. As the weather improved, the gang started to walk the streets aimlessly just to see what was happening and usually nothing was. This particular day, Holvey, Joe and two other kids were just strolling downtown heading towards the supermarket. They knew they would not be able to shoplift there from recent experience. The security guard had actually followed them up and down each aisle the last time they had visited. No, this time they were legitimate shoppers. With the ever-shrinking amount of gang money in their pockets they were going to buy some sandwiches, pies, crisps and soft drinks to take back to the waiting gang. As they wandered across the side carpark, they were in deep conversation about their ability to claim a youth allowance from the job centre after school and how much they would get.

"They've got to give us something, I mean it won't be much but it will be something," said Holvey.

"Enough to get pissed one night a week at best," responded Joe.

As they chatted and wondered how else they were

going to get money without actually taking a job and working, they turned the corner of the supermarket building. At that very moment, Roly was coming in the opposite direction. He had his hands full of plastic bags with a week's provisions and his mind full of thoughts about the plans, commitments, and actions he was in the middle of for the refurbishment of The Water's Edge. Holvey and Roly bumped straight into each other.

"Look out, you fool!" shouted Holvey as his knee made contact with a handful of plastic bags, and as a handle of one of them snapped, the contents scattered over the floor.

"Sorry. Sorry," repeated Roly politely. "Didn't see you. Not paying attention, my mistake." He gave the young man a smile and then looking down at all the shopping on the floor he simply said, "Bugger," and started to bend down. He would have said a lot more if he had noticed Joe's action. When Roly had paid at the checkout, he had put his wallet on the top of the last plastic bag as he walked out to his car. That wallet was now on the floor and Joe saw it first. He simply stepped over it and backheeled it to his mate behind him before joining Holvey and Roly in picking up the goods. Everyone started to help except the lad with the wallet now in his pocket who nonchalantly continued walking.

Holvey managed to distract Roly even further by picking up a broken sugar bag and handing it to Roly saying, "Don't know what you are going to do with that, Mr."

As the sugar spilled out through Roly's fingers, the boys laughed and strolled on. As Holvey turned to go into the store, Joe grabbed his arm and said, "Keep walking. Keep walking." They speeded up and only when they were a good two hundred yards away in the next street did Joe explain to a confused Holvey.

"What luck," he giggled as they examined the wallet's contents. "Must be almost two hundred pounds here and all these credit cards. Fuck crisps and sandwiches, we can buy some booze and have a party. Let's get back to the brickworks."

It would be much later that day before Roly started to look for his wallet. Yet back at the brickworks there were whoops of delight as they all started to discuss about how their newfound wealth was going to be spent.

Jules was only half paying attention to them and Holvey was examining the other contents of the wallet as Joe counted out the cash.

"One hundred and sixty-five pounds for nothing… not a bad day's work, is it?" he announced. "Anything else there?"

"There are some credit cards, can we use them?"

"Nah, if we do, we'd get caught. Best chuck them."

"Wait, this one isn't a credit card," said Holvey holding up Roly's marina access card. "The lucky bastard has got a boat. He must be rich, anyone fancy a trip over to France on Cariad, Pontoon C slip 31."

Jules stood up. "Holvey, give me that," and he reached over for the wallet and after taking it he sat back down and slipped back into his thoughts. The others looked on for a moment before paying him little attention. Frankly, they hadn't now for a few days. So, they were particularly surprised when he stood up and shouted to regain their attention.

"Listen up, OK listen up. Joe's right, we deserve a party. Holvey and Joe, go down to the off-licence in Judd Street. He's sold us booze before so get us some vodka and Red Bull and cans of lager. Get some of that sweet sparkling stuff for the girls. Tina, take someone with you and get some good food in. The rest of you clean up this shithouse. Everyone back here in two hours – we're going to have a party!"

"Yeah," they all whooped. After days of boredom, they were all overcome with the excitement of partying. As they all got organised and moved on to their assigned tasks, Jules picked up the wallet and went into his side room and shut the door.

"A boat," he mumbled to himself, "now how do I use that?"

After being in deep thought he took the mobile phone out of his pocket that Ronnie had given him. Each day since his return, as Ronnie had commanded, he had sent a text. It was always the same. "Hi Ronnie – all's OK." Now Jules had an idea, so he typed, "Ronnie, I got an idea. When can I call you?" After it was sent, he wondered how long he would have to wait for a response. It was three minutes. It would have been much longer if Ronnie had known it was from the kid and he wasn't in such a good mood, but he was just getting into his car when one of several phones he carried buzzed to say he had a message. As he sat in the driver's seat, he fished out the phones to find out which one and who had contacted him. He read the message and smiled, and he immediately called.

Jules jumped as the phone rang and answered. There were no pleasantries, only a barked question from Ronnie.

"What's this idea, kid? Have you forgot already? I have the ideas, you just do!"

"Haven't forgotten, Ronnie, but just wanted to run

something past you that's all."

"OK, shoot, kid, I haven't got all day."

"What if I had access to a boat here?" Jules waited for a response but there was none, so he continued. "I mean, there must be stuff that would benefit from getting into or out from the country without going through the normal channels of airports and seaports?"

"What boat have you got, kid? Stop talking in riddles, will you? Tell me what you got, how you got it and what you're suggesting."

Jules explained the wallet and how they got it.

"For fuck's sake, kid, I told you to stop that kid gang stuff. All it will do is draw attention to you and if you get known I can't use you."

"No, Ronnie, all the gang stuff is finished. This was just a dropped wallet that one of the guys picked up. The point is the wallet belongs to someone with a boat!"

"So, what type of boat? Have you met this guy yet?" asked a frustrated Ronnie, trying to understand.

Jules sighed, and it was heard down the phone.

"Ronnie, I have not done anything yet. I wanted to pass it by you first. That's what you gave me this phone for wasn't it?" All said in a slower, slightly condescending manner and coupled with the initial sigh it made Ronnie smile as he thought, This kid has spirit, it might kill him, but he has it.

"Kid, talk to me like I'm a fool one more time and I'll reach down this fucking phone and rip out your tongue!"

"Sorry, Ronnie." He had the kid's attention now. "I just thought that when I return this wallet to the owner, saying that I had found it, I would get a chance to see the boat and, if we could use it, perhaps we could bring some things in."

"You mean drugs."

"Yes, I mean drugs."

"Kid, this is a big step and we're not going to discuss anything on the phone. Go see the boat then call me, in the meantime no fucking about. In three weeks you're coming up aren't you?"

"Yes, me and my girl. Ronnie, we'll need a place to live."

"When you get here, we'll sort it all out. Just call me tomorrow about five and tell me more about this boat thing."

Ronnie hung up. No goodbye, no nice to hear from you, no well done for thinking about this opportunity. The phone just went dead. Jules slumped back in his chair deep in thought. Was he pleased? Did I do right? What about this boat? How do I get access to it? Can I use it? His mind swirled with all these thoughts and questions, and he lost all sense of time until all these thoughts were interrupted by loud music from the main room.

Within the hour the place had been cleaned up, food laid out on one of the tables and booze and paper cups on the other. Everyone looked young, innocent and excited and they all looked expectantly at Jules.

He looked around and smiled,

"OK, let's party."

As the music volume turned up everyone started. Some went for the booze first, others to the food. A few girls started to dance. The party started on a high and increased. Within a few hours what food was left was over the floor, most of the booze had been drunk, the dancing was becoming more manic because the kids were manic. Even Jules had relaxed and he and Tina, not drunk but both with a buzz on, were happily dancing. Then some of the boys started moving people to the sides of the room as they moved two tables into the centre making an uneven, unstable gangway.

"What's going on?" shouted Jules.

"Step back, Jules, step back, Tina, you're going to love this," said one of the boys.

"Ready," shouted someone as the music switched over to a strong bass beat disco piece. Suddenly, Holvey and Joe, both bollock naked, exploded from the side room. They leapt onto the tables and proceeded to do The Willy Dance which was to wiggle and thrust their hips to make their semi-erect dicks and scrotums bounce in time with the disco beat.

The gang whooped and laughed and pointed and sniggered. Holvey and Joe, oblivious to all but the laughter thanks to the vodka and Red Bull, continued on tiptoes to switch their bums and thrust their hips.

The laughter was good, everyone had wanted and needed it. When inevitably things had calmed down and people paired off, Jules held Tina close and looking over the group said, "This was great, I'm going to miss these guys."

Tina said nothing.

The next day, mid-morning, Jules went to the marina. At the electronic gate that secured access to the moored boats, he used Roly's card and as the gate swung open, he walked down the gangway. He was walking towards Pontoon C, slip 27 when a voice challenged him from behind.

"Now where are you going, young man? I haven't seen you here before." Chrissie's dad was cleaning his hands on an oily rag as he walked up to Jules.

"Hi, Mr," said Jules with a smile and a prepared speech. "I found this wallet and it had no address in it just this marina card and a driving licence for a Mr Johns who doesn't live in Cranport. I thought if I brought it here, I could give it him back. If he's here that is."

"Well, he's not," said Trev taking the wallet, "but he does live in Cranport. Come with me and we'll give him a call."

They arrived at Trev's office a few minutes later and called Roly.

"Roly, have you lost your wallet?"

"Hell, yes, Trev. Have you found it?" asked a surprised Roly.

"Not me, Roly, but a young fellow came to the marina to give it back. It had your marina card in it. Your driving licence has your old address on it. You need to change that, you know."

"Yeah, I haven't got round to it. Is the boy there now?"

"Yes, he is."

"Ask him to wait, I'll be there in five minutes."

Trev turned to Jules as he hung up, "He's coming over, young man. Want to wait here with me?"

"Um, that's good but could I just go and look at the boats?"

Trev hesitated and then said, "Sure, you can go look but don't get on any. OK?" and he walked back to the gate and opened it letting Jules in. Well, he thought, no harm done; after all the kid is returning a wallet, he must be a good 'un.

Jules spent the few minutes it took Roly to get to the marina walking the pontoon. While he glanced at them all he paid particular attention to Roly's Cariad. He knew nothing about boats, but it was clear that this motor boat was designed for the open sea.

"It will do nicely," he said quietly to himself as Roly appeared on the pontoon and waved with a smile and a pleasant greeting.

"Hi there, you are the young man I need to say thanks to," he said holding the wallet. "Where did you find it?"

"It was down the side of a stack of rubbish bins by Judd Street."

Jules' prepared explanation was spoken in a relaxed manner accompanied with a boyish smile that defied any suspicion on Roly's part. Jules continued, "I just went to throw my chewing gum away and I stepped on it. That made it muddy, sorry about that, Mr...?"

"Don't apologise you've saved me a lot of trouble. Replacing all these cards would have been a pain. I suppose it would have been asking too much to get the cash back."

"Hey Mr, there was no cash in it. You can ask my mum if you don't believe me."

Roly realised what he had said and quickly responded, "No, no. Please don't misunderstand me. I am so very grateful to you. I think I know how I lost my wallet at the supermarket. Some other kids stole it. I am very grateful to you and your mum. You, young man, deserve a reward."

As Roly put his hand into his trouser pocket, Jules played his planned trump card. He stepped forward and held Roly's trousered hand.

"No Mr, I don't want a reward. I'm just giving you back something that's yours."

Roly looked at him somewhat bemused. He did not know what next to say. There was an uncomfortable pause. Jules took the opportunity and turned around to look at Cariad.

"This is a beautiful boat, Mr. What type is it?"

Roly leapt at the chance to dispel the uncomfortable moment and launched into a description of the boat. As he spoke, he put his hand on Jules' shoulder and invited him aboard to look around. At the chart table, Jules asked all sorts of questions about GPS and how they knew where they were. Roly demonstrated the chart plotter and gave a quick basic lesson in longitude and latitude. He got caught up in the boy's excitement and as the lesson ended Jules sighed, "One day, I'm going to get a boat if I can."

"You like boats then?"

"Oh yeah. It must be so great to be out on the open sea in something like this."

Roly smiled and responded just as Jules had anticipated.

"OK, kid, this is what we do. As a thank you, I will take you out on the boat for a day. How about that?"

"Wow, Mr, are you sure? That would be fantastic. I'll have to ask my mum but I'm sure she won't mind."

"Look, kid, first what's your name? Mine is Roly."

"It's Danny, Mr. I mean Roly."

"OK, Danny, tell your mother that it is a seaworthy boat, and we have all the safety features we need. We have lifejackets, VHF, life rafts and I'm fully qualified and if she wants to, she can come as well."

"No, she can't," said Jules a little too quickly. "She's not well, she rarely leaves the house. Can I call to arrange it after I've spoken to her? I am sure she will be

OK with it. When do you think we could do it?"

"Well, if the weather is OK, not tomorrow but how about Thursday?"

Jules nodded with apparent excitement and Roly reached down for a pen and notepad from the chart table and wrote his name and telephone number.

"Call me later today or tomorrow and we can sort it out."

Jules grabbed the page and with a big smile said, "Thanks, Roly." He stepped down from the boat onto the pontoon and with a wave almost skipped along as he left the marina. It may have appeared to Roly and others watching that it was just innocent boyish enthusiasm and excitement but inside Jules was far more cold and calculating. He was developing the plan, he was thinking about the next call to Ronnie. He had been told clearly to stick to the rules but within those rules there had to be room for his big plan.

Chapter 16

This Big Plan

As commanded by Ronnie, Jules rang him later that day.

"It's a great boat, Ronnie, just what we need. I'm not going out on it until later this week, but I think it is going to work out."

"You think! Jesus, kid, you don't fuck around with these sorts of things unless you are absolutely sure. Do you remember what I said to you about what happens to people who don't deliver what they promise?"

"Yeah, I remember, Ronnie, but look, I will find out more and you explore what we could do your side without commitments. If everything firms up, then and only then, we commit but it doesn't stop us from planning, does it?"

"Kid, that almost sounded like you were telling me what to do," chuckled Ronnie. "OK, you explore the boat and I'll explore options here. When and only when I say that I am happy with this big plan do we act. Not a word now to any of your kiddy gang and call me after you have been out on this boat."

Ronnie hung up as he always did with no goodbye or well done or any spare chat at all, but Jules felt great. Ronnie had said this big plan and it was Jules who had brought it to him. Jules felt energised and focussed once again and he did not intend to let this drive drop over the next few weeks.

Jules as Danny, made sure that he was Roly's best friend. The first trip was such fun for both of them that they ended up going out on Cariad almost every other day. Jules was like an obedient Labrador, always willing to grab a line, wash the deck, learn about the boat, how to steer, how to set a waypoint course, how to read the wind and waves. Roly felt like a big brother and thoroughly enjoyed teaching Danny, who made steady and quick progress. After several trips they had fallen into a comfortable relationship with Danny always at Roly's elbow asking questions or offering to do things.

"What's that thing?" asked Danny as Roly set the boat up to re-enter the marina.

"When a boat is going very slow, like now as we head into our berth, the wind can blow you all over the place especially on a day like today with fifteen to eighteen knots of wind coming in from the southwest. You see, the hull acts like a big sail but this little switch is your secret weapon. It's called a bow-thruster. Under the waterline on the front of the boat there is a little tunnel the size of a porthole and mounted in that hole is an electric powered propeller. Push the switch here and the bow goes left or port as we call it; push it back here and the bow goes right or starboard. So, you come in slow and use this to always make sure the bow is pointing where you want to go. There are no brakes so as you come in you use reverse to stop."

"Can I have a go?"

"Danny, I think I made it appear too easy. Lots of judgment calls to be made and if you get it wrong you can be all over the place or worse bouncing around the marina like the ball in a pinball game."

"Oh, Roly, go on. You can stand right by me and stop me from doing anything wrong. You can take over at any time."

Roly just could not think of any more objections and smiled as he stepped aside.

"OK, Danny, let's give it a go."

Danny had not only brought the boat smoothly and unhurriedly into berth, but he stopped the forward motion with just the right amount of reverse thrust. He ended the job with an athletic teenage leap onto the pontoon and wrapped a bowline around the cleat before shouting, "Tarrah!" and stood there taking his mock bow to Roly.

"My God, Danny, you are a natural. That's better than I sometimes do."

Jules beamed, he now felt he was all set up and ready.

While Jules was acquiring his boating skills, Ronnie was hesitantly exploring options with Mr Hopkins. He was anxious and quite rightly so because the initial response was not pleasant. He had tried to pick a quiet moment and during an afternoon session when Hopkins and about three other guys (he was never alone) were just chatting about nothing in particular after a pub lunch and a few drinks.

"Mr Hopkins, I need to discuss something with you. Is now a good time to talk?"

"Sure, Ronnie, what's up? You got a problem?"

"No problem but possibly a good opportunity."

"Spit it out, we could do with some opportunities." This last comment was said with a smile and a friendly pat on the shoulder but proved to be the only kind and friendly interaction that afternoon.

"Remember that kid that I brought on board several weeks ago?" said Ronnie returning the smile.

"Yeah, that little Al Capone kid who shot those people in the hotel. What a kid he was, but you sorted him out didn't you. Isn't he one of your soldiers?"

"Yes, he's coming up in a few weeks and as you said he is a smart kid. I think I am going to be able to develop him over time."

"Good, Ronnie, that's good but that's not the opportunity you wanted to speak about, is it? What's on your mind?"

"Well, it is really because the kid has brought a possible opportunity our way. You know he lives on the south coast. Well, he has access to a boat. He has asked me if there is a chance to use it to bring in some goods."

At this Hopkins sat up straight and while Ronnie waited for him to speak, he almost felt the temperature in the room drop sharply.

"Jesus Christ, Ronnie! You are talking about a kid. Where the fuck is your brain? You disappoint me, I told you this kid was going to be trouble unless you controlled him and now, he's leading you a merry dance with kiddie ideas of being a big gangster."

"No, Mr Hopkins…"

"Shut the fuck up when I'm talking to you. You know the rules even if your schoolkid thinks he's running you – you know I am!"

"Yes, Mr Hopkins, I'm sorry," and Ronnie stopped and looked down at the floor and waited for the next comment. Hopkins let the silence hang there and after the significance of the pause had sunk in, he started to speak again.

"Ronnie, you know how I do business. It is always well planned, only with people I trust, and it always comes good. My old man was a carpenter and he always said, 'Measure twice, cut once'." At this profound point all the other guys in the room nodded sagely. "I've never had anything more than a parking ticket and even then, I had some guys to break the fingers of the stupid arsehole who wrote the ticket." He chuckled and so did the others. "We are careful, we plan for all eventualities, and we make good money. You make good money. Now why would we want to risk things getting involved with some kid with a rowing boat? Why, for fuck's sake?" He paused and then said, "Ronnie, now it's time for you to talk."

"Mr Hopkins, I agree with every word you said. I am not doing anything with this kid right now, I wouldn't. All I am doing is asking you for advice and guidance. Not for doing a job with this kid but for doing a job with me. If we had some contacts and wanted to bring some things in and if it looked like a profitable venture, then and only then, would I personally get directly involved and to make certain the plans are in place to ensure success. That is what you taught me, Mr Hopkins. My mistake was to start off by telling you that we had an opportunity. Let me start again by saying, I believe I can get access to a boat. If I could, and we did it with all our normal planning, do we have any contacts out there that would make it a sound business opportunity?"

Mr Hopkins spoke quietly now, thinking of his words almost one by one. He was cold and menacing but was exploring the opportunity just like Ronnie had wanted.

"I know people, people on the continent, Spain actually. These people are weird little fuckers, though, they bring in dope, skunk, coke all that stuff from Africa and then distribute it around Europe. We get small amounts of stuff through the ports and ferries or even the tunnel now and then and yes it can be very profitable, but we have never considered a big one-off deal with them. Remember, I said they are animals. Once you are dealing with them it's like a marriage only no chance of a divorce. Ronnie, this is a big step. I am not sure that I want to get directly involved, I'm not sure that I want you directly involved. There is no way I would want to introduce this kid to them. Let me think on it. Let's talk more in a few days but in the meantime, you get direct control of little Al Capone. He needs to understand that he needs your approval even if he wants to fart!"

On that happy note the conversation ended and Ronnie did not expect it to return, yet only three days later Mr Hopkins pulled him aside.

"Ronnie, I have been thinking about you and Al Capone." It looked like the kid had now got himself a nickname for life.

"Yes, Mr Hopkins?"

"It's not for me, Ronnie, but if you think you can pull it off, I have a telephone number for you. Just remember two things. First, you don't fuck around with these guys, make sure they understand it is a one-off and then get out of there. Second, I will expect a ten per cent introductory fee and if you need financing, and I'd be surprised if you didn't, then that would be another fifteen per cent. Now, you think on it and get back to me say by the weekend."

"Hey, Mr Hopkins, that is really very good of you, I appreciate it," said Ronnie reeling from the immediate loss of twenty-five per cent yet taking a hundred per cent of the risk. "I understand that you don't want to be in yourself, but I hope I can still rely on you for advice and guidance?"

"Always, Ronnie, always."

That day was a changing point for Ronnie. He had always been happy enough to be recognised as Hopkins' man and the up-and-coming kid for some time in the future, but now he saw himself in truth. He was nothing more than a tool to be used as Hopkins saw fit. Hopkins was never going to give up power and authority, it would be taken from him either by God when he died or by someone like Ronnie. The question started in Ronnie's mind, who was going to be first, God or Ronnie? Sure, as hell was hot, Ronnie was not going to let any other goon take his prize – but that was for another day, sooner than he had ever thought but realistically not today. Today was the time to start the planning in detail with young Al Capone. If there was to be a future, this needed to work. This would be the start of him building his independence.

"Jesus, I hope this kid knows what he is doing." Ronnie surprised himself as the comment was spoken aloud and he looked around quickly to see if anyone had heard him but no, Hopkins and his older colleagues were already in a deep discussion on some other point. Ronnie signalled his departure with a nod and left them to it. He walked out into the pub with a clear determination developing in his mind.

"Hello, Ronnie, are we leaving now?" asked Laurie, who was his driver from time to time.

"No, Laurie, you're free for today, but I need you early in the morning. We're going down to the seaside and if you're good I'll buy you an ice cream. Pick me up at eight-thirty, OK?"

Laurie nodded, looking a little bemused as Ronnie walked out still deep in thought.

Later, he called Jules. When the mobile rang, Jules literally jumped and grabbed into his pocket for the phone.

"Ronnie?"

"Kid, be ready to meet me tomorrow." Again, as usual, no greeting, no introduction, just gruffly straight to the point but still it thrilled Jules. "I'll be down in your area about eleven o'clock in the morning; we need to meet and discuss this boat plan of yours. Where do you want to meet?"

"Sure, Ronnie, no problem. We could meet in the pedestrian area outside McDonald's in the High Street. I'll be there but do you want me to bring anything?"

"Just your brain, kid, and I will want to see this boat."

"OK, Ronnie, see you about eleven. Anything else?"

"No." The phone went dead, and this time Jules smiled. Ronnie had rung him. Ronnie wanted to discuss his plan. Ronnie was coming to him. It seemed a little unreal but God, he was excited.

***

At 10.45 the next morning, Jules was walking up and down outside McDonald's. He constantly looked in turn up the street and down the street for Ronnie. It was 11.05 when a car pulled up at the far corner and out stepped Ronnie as the car pulled away. Jules had to stop himself from running towards Ronnie but even though he smiled and waved and walked slowly towards his visitor he still could not avoid appearing like a spaniel puppy excited at his owner's arrival.

"Hi, Ronnie, welcome to Cranport."

"Yeah, sure," said a grumpy Ronnie. "Anywhere

close for a coffee?"

"Well, we could do McDonalds."

"That's like drinking shit, there must be a better coffee house around?"

"I don't know for sure but if we walk up the street there must be someplace."

So, they did, no talking, just a quiet amble through the pedestrian precinct until they came across a small café on a corner where they could sit outside under a glass canopy.

"Get me a regular black coffee with one sugar," growled Ronnie as he sat down. Jules stood there feeling embarrassed.

"Ah, Ronnie, I didn't bring any money with me. Sorry, but I didn't think we were going to the shops."

"Jesus, kid," laughed Ronnie. "I come all the way here to visit you and I have to buy my own coffee." At this he handed Jules a tenner and as Jules hustled into the café quickly, Ronnie looked out and around the pedestrian area. All these people, popping into and out from shops. Carrying their goods in brightly coloured canvas bags, they wished each other hearty Good Mornings and Bye after a chat. All with some purpose to their actions but Ronnie just could not see it or appreciate it. For him, it just seemed so bloody pointless.

"Here you are, Ronnie," said Jules. "I got myself a diet coke, that's OK, isn't it?" Jules handed back the change.

"Kid, I need to be back by early evening, so this is what I want to do today. I have the chance to contact some people if I believe we have a serious plan to act upon. This plan has to be completely foolproof because my name and your life are dependent on it. Now is not the time for kid stuff. I want to go over your idea step by step. I want to see the boat. I want to ask all the questions and I want nothing but the absolute truth from you. Kid, understand this one thing, it would be far better for you to tell me that you don't know something when I ask or that you are not sure when I ask than to simply tell me what you think I want to hear. Do you understand? Right now, we can always walk away with no hard feelings – not every idea turns out to be as good as first thought."

Jules looked at Ronnie and for once said the right thing and more importantly, said it in the right way.

"OK, Ronnie, let's talk it through in whatever level of detail you want. If I have got it wrong then fine, we call it off, but I think we have a chance here if we create a plan together that you are fully comfortable with."

"How do I see the boat?"

"Well, we can't go to the marina, that would raise suspicions, but the marina is on the side of a river just before it enters into the open harbour and then the sea. If we go on the other side of the river we can look over and you will clearly see the set-up for the marina, the pontoons and Roly's boat."

"Roly is the boat owner?"

"Yeah, he is a nice guy. It was his wallet I returned and as a result we've become friends, at least he believes we are. I have been out with him on the boat now about six times and it's not difficult. Let me explain."

"Not here, I'll call up the car and we can go and take a look." Ronnie took out his mobile and called his driver. "Laurie, pick me and the kid back up in five minutes from where you dropped me."

They strolled back and although Jules hoped to

continue the conversation, they walked in silence and as they sat in the car Ronnie said, "Kid, tell Laurie where we are going."

Jules leaned over the back of the front passenger seat and gave simple directions to the driver. It was left here, right there, second exit of roundabout and Jules almost enjoyed being a human GPS. On the other side of the river opposite the marina was a housing development of expensive homes and they had more land and open spaces and halfway up the hill on a broad road was a most convenient layby. It even had an old bench looking out over the river and there Jules and Ronnie sat, leaving Laurie in the car. Ronnie looked quizzically at Jules.

"See the river, Ronnie. Just around that headland you enter the town's old harbour and once through that you are into the open sea. All told, that is about three quarters of a mile. In the boat, it takes about twenty minutes from leaving the marina to the open sea."

"So where is this boat?"

"OK, let's concentrate on the marina. First, see the big open car park," said Jules pointing across the river. "As you can see, during the week and especially out of season it is often quite empty. If you head down the car park towards the building, there are four sections. The marina office is the first part. There they hold all the boat keys and where owners and boat tradesmen check in to do work or whatever."

"How do you get the keys?"

"Let me come to that in a moment." Ronnie did not react to this, and Jules continued. "Next to the marina office is the chandlery shop where they sell all the boat stuff that people need. Above these two sections on the first floor is the café and bar. They do simple breakfasts, lunches and dinner and a small bar where marina members meet to chat and plan their trips. The building next to it is the marina workshop and as you can see it opens onto the water so boats can be taken there if the marina boat mechanics are going to work on it. Finally, the first floor of that building is the wash house. There you can use the toilets, showers and even do your laundry."

Even through all this trivial detail, Ronnie's eyes followed Jules' hand gestures as he pointed in various directions.

Jules continued, "Now to the pontoons, see there are five of them all named A, B, C, D and E and the whole area is fenced off with a security gate. Our boat is on Pontoon C. From the start on the marina side, you count out eleven boats. See our boat, it is the motorboat with the white hull with a blue stripe across the top and wooden cabin top."

Ronnie raised a finger, "How do you get onto the pontoon?"

"You use a marina card, or you type in a pin number. I gave the marina card back to Roly when I returned his wallet. However, once when I was going out with him, I told him I needed to go to the toilet. Now the boat has a toilet, but people don't use it unless they have to because eventually you have to have it all cleaned out. So, if you are in the marina you use the washrooms. Roly told me to use them and that the pin number was 1957. Now I use it whenever I come down. It never changes." Ronnie nodded and so Jules continued. "I have become close to Roly. When we plan to go out, he always checks his diary to find a convenient date when the weather is good and when he can get away from his other duties. He is in the middle of developing a hotel in town. For example, I know that today he is in London talking to sponsors or something, but he said we couldn't go today but we can tomorrow. So, all I need to do is to find a day when he will not be around." Another finger from Ronnie and Jules waited.

"What would people do if you turned up on a day when the owner was away?"

"Look at it, Ronnie. This is not Fort Knox, it is a sleepy little marina where everyone knows that I am Roly's sidekick and that I am always down there. They will not even think twice if I just casually arrive and go down to the boat and if they did, I would just smile and say I left something on the boat." Ronnie nodded but not quite as emphatically as Jules would have preferred. "Ronnie, there is no one around. Just look out there now. A great boating day and no one is around."

"Now answer my question: how do you get the keys?"

"OK, I do not need to get them from the marina office. All boaters live in constant fear of dropping things over the side. So, for things like engine and boat keys they often have floating key fobs or spares. Roly has both. Under the navigation table in a drawer is a complete set of spares. To get into the cabin is a metal latch screwed into a wooden batten. A small jemmy bar and you can rip it right off in seconds."

Ronnie now nodded more enthusiastically. He then continued, "OK, you are on the boat, you can start the boat – can you sail it?"

"It's easy, Ronnie, like driving a car really."

Ronnie humphed and snarled. "Don't be a dick kid, you can't drive a fucking car!"

"Sorry, Ronnie, let me explain far more clearly," said a chastised Jules. "Ronnie, I have been out with Roly now at least six or seven times. Roly has really enjoyed teaching me what to do and when to do it. Under his guidance, I have taken the boat out, sailed all day and returned it to the berth all directly under my control. He has taught me how to read the sea in terms of waves, wind, tide and currents. If you enter a GPS address into the automatic steering system, the boat will literally take you to within thirty feet of where you want to be. The GPS is like a postcode, only it is a principle of longitude and latitude. Getting out of the marina and getting back in can be tricky but you just have to take your time and use all the various features that this boat has. The main feature is called a bow thruster; it is just a little switch that you push left or right to always make sure the boat is pointing in the direction you want to go and then the main engines drive you either forward or in reverse. You use reverse to stop." Jules stopped to see if his explanation had been accepted by Ronnie. There was no reaction but no further questions, so Jules assumed he was OK.

"So, you go out to sea but where do you want to go?"

"We need the people who are dropping off the stuff to do it about ten miles offshore. At that distance they will be beyond the horizon from shore and beyond where the fishermen leave their pots for crabs and lobster or even nets, but they could even just do it at night. They can just drop stuff off beneath floats and if they tell us about the address on their GPS we can sail to it and do the pickup the following day."

"So, they leave the stuff for us to pick up. How do we pay them?"

"Well, we could leave the money where the drugs were, and they could come back and pick it up?"

"No, kid, this is a lot of money. We're not leaving it floating in the sea." Ronnie paused and then continued. "Leave that with me. So, you pick up the stuff and bring it back to the marina?"

"Yes, I suppose. To be honest, I haven't thought that bit through." Ronnie nodded in appreciation of his honesty and joined Jules to think over that point.

"Kid, I think that you bring it back here and I will have a car waiting to pick it up from you. I don't want you taking it home and your mum wondering why you have all these wet suitcases. If I have a car in the area, you can call on the mobile when you are entering the marina."

"Yeah, when I am about three miles out, I can still get a mobile signal because Roly has taken calls out there. That would work but it is important that no one enters the marina car park until I am back in the berth or that would be noticed."

"You get the stuff back, kid, and you can jump in the car with the cases and we'll give you a quick lift home."

"How many cases, Ronnie? And how much does it weigh? We need to know that."

"Leave that with me," Ronnie nodded before continuing almost as if he was simply thinking aloud. "It will not be that heavy. I was talking to a guy the other day. He tells me that fifty kilos of pure cocaine has a street value of about five million pounds and a cost of about eight hundred thousand. I need to get funding and to work out how I distribute it and all that costs but we should be able to walk away with between two and two and a half million pounds."

Jules immediately picked up on Ronnie's use of the word 'we'. He knew he was not an equal partner, but he stood to realise more money than he had ever thought possible.

"One more question, kid, the risks are all here at the marina. Why don't I simply buy you a boat?"

"Ronnie, sorry but you are not thinking this through. If I had a boat then we would need it put somewhere, like this marina. People would want to know and understand how a kid could afford it. We would have to register it with details that would be checked. If we got caught, and that is always a possibility, immediately they got me. Here it is different. No one at the marina knows me, I am just the kid that often supports Roly called Danny. If I got caught on the way out, I am just a kid taking liberties. Coming back, when you see me coming in the car arrives and we load it immediately and I jump in the car, and we're gone!"

Ronnie looked on pensively and eventually shrugged before he continued.

"Let me work out all these details. Kid, there are big risks here but so are the rewards. We can either commit now and run with it or walk away and do other things. Shall we do it, kid?"

With nothing more than a considered smile Jules replied, "Ronnie, let's do it."

"OK, kid, you do absolutely nothing until I call you. Go and play with your girlfriend or play with yourself, just keep well out of trouble. I will call you in a couple of days."

Ronnie rose and walked over to the car. If Jules had done nothing, he would have been left sitting there on a bench on the other side of town but he didn't.

"Jesus, Ronnie, are we on the same team or what? Can't you give me a lift back to town?"

A surprised Ronnie gave an almost innocent giggle. "Sure, kid, sorry about that, just get in. I was deep in thought. Laurie, take us back to town we have to drop off one of our guys." With that he leant back in his rear seat again going into deep thought but not before ruffling Jules' hair like a big brother.

Everything went quiet for the next few days and Jules was starting to wonder if it would actually happen when again he got a call from Ronnie. It had been anything but calm for Ronnie. He had received a name and number from Mr Hopkins but when he rang the person answering claimed he had no idea what Ronnie was talking about and insisted on checking with someone before they called back Ronnie back. The discussions followed and seemed straightforward with a few exceptions. First, they had no idea where Cranport was and would have to get back. Second, they did not have a price list of any kind – there was no standard charge per kilo or anything. They wanted to know how much Ronnie wanted and he wanted to know how much it would cost. They ran around this circle for several minutes until Ronnie said he was thinking of about half a million pounds worth. They promised to get back quickly. They did but the request was clear; he had to pay them the money upfront, and they would drop off 44 kg in two submerged suitcases held up by floats. They would text him the GPS coordinates when they had made the drop. It was up to him to pick it up because they would be paid upfront. Ronnie had money, in fact for a young man he was quite well off, but he certainly did not have £500,000 to give to a name at the end of a telephone line or indeed about the same again to process it into street cocaine and distribute it in the capital. This was when Ronnie had to go back to Mr Hopkins.

"Ronnie, this is a big deal, and I wanted no part in it except my normal fee for introduction. Now you want me to not only fund the drop but also to fund the setup of a distribution system. Sounds like apart from you letting Al Capone steal a boat, I'm doing all the work here. How the hell did that happen?"

"Mr Hopkins, I am doing the work. I want you to lend me the money. Give me the money for three months and I'll pay you fifteen per cent."

"I give you a million, you turn it into five million and I get a lousy hundred and fifty thousand. Are you insulting me, Ronnie?"

"Absolutely not, Mr Hopkins. Look, what do you want? I am sure we can figure this out fairly and respectfully to both of us."

"Ronnie, this is it. I give you one million. You give me two million back in three months. This is your deal. I want nothing else to do with it. As far as I am concerned, I am lending you one million pounds for three months. What you do with it has nothing to do with me. Are you clear on this?"

"OK, Mr Hopkins," said Ronnie with a sigh, "but how do I get the upfront five hundred thousand to the guys in Spain?"

"Jesus, Ronnie, you are like a child. Send one of your girls on a weekend break down there and stick it in their suitcases. It really is that simple."

So, it was all arranged. This was to be Ronnie's big deal, but Hopkins had made him feel like shit. He sucked it up, but it hurt. He swore to himself, if this was as successful as he anticipated he would never go cap in hand again. This changed him from a lieutenant to a player.

Ronnie's call to Jules mentioned none of this, just the basic facts.

"Kid, it is all arranged. When we say go, I get the money to Spain and three days later the drop-off happens. I do not want this stuff floating out there for long so if they drop it on a night, the next day you pick it up, right?"

"Sure, Ronnie, but we have to pick the day when Roly is away."

"When will that be?"

"Well, I don't know yet. I haven't been in touch with him since we last spoke. You told me to do nothing, remember?"

The first hint of frustration came to Ronnie. Sure, many things could go wrong but if he had to, he would take a couple of guys down with him and take this boat owner out to pick up the stuff. He played along with Jules.

"Kid, get back involved. You need to give me a date at least one week out that we can plan against. Call me when you have that date." The line went dead.

Jules, with a mixture of fear and excitement, shuddered. It's going to happen he said to himself before ringing Roly and arranging to see him back on the boat.

The big plan was in place.

Chapter 17

Realising the Purpose

Roly was pleased to get a call from Danny. While he had been busy and surprisingly successful in establishing the plan for the creation of The Water's Edge, it had not been without the stresses and worries that came when you drive yourself hard to achieve a life's goal. He had made great progress but as always, he was hard on himself and impatient. Sponsorship had been the easiest, with Jeremy's help his bank was in from Day One. Other sponsors were all lined up to join the moment The Water's Edge was a reality. Operational costs weren't going to be a problem and if his estimates of running costs were accurate then they would also be able to plan for future buildings. He had an architect who had also brought in an engineering Project Manager. Kate had brought on board an accountant and he was acting like a Director of Operations. The building design had been straightforward. Upstairs they would have twenty double rooms and about eight family rooms, all with their own toilet and bathroom facilities. Downstairs had been kept simple with a restaurant, a corner bar, a laundry room and a communal TV lounge before opening up onto a partially covered terrace. The grounds would have open lawns with a small pool and a short walkway in front of the harbour walls. All, according to the architect and Project Manager, could be done in fourteen months. The old building had looked decrepit but apparently it was all mostly cosmetic and with some sympathetic building work and decorating all the wonderful old features could be preserved.

Planning permissions were needed for everything individually; sewer plans, window designs, wall refurbishment, even gate entry and harbour wall refurbishment, but surprisingly the local council enthusiastically approved everything with a smile, a nod of approval and signed paperwork almost overnight. Décor involved discussions full of open debate between the architect, Jamie, Chrissie and Roly. Roly knew what he wanted but could not describe it. He wanted classy but certainly not ostentatious. Guests to The Water's Edge would be people of simple means and Roly wanted them to feel comfortable but not in awe of the surroundings, but also to feel they were somewhere special, an escape from the day-to-day grind in their normal lives. Chrissie, with Jamie always nodding, mentioned that it had to be easily cleaned. The architect talked of colours and materials. Together, they all ended up agreeing on something that made Roly well up inside when he saw the first design documents. With the help of those that he loved and trusted they had turned feelings in his head into plans for a reality.

However, as pleased as he was with his team and progress, he was tired and stressed and the chance to go out with Danny on the boat was just the break he needed. They agreed to meet the next day.

"Hi, Captain" said Danny, as he walked up the pontoon.

"Nice to see you, deck swab, come aboard," replied Roly. The humour in their chatter was something that had started almost from the beginning.

"What you been up to, Danny?"

"Just hanging around really."

"But you're up for a trip today, though?"

"You bet, Captain."

Roly smiled, "Danny, you don't have to call me Captain. Just call me Roly or anything else."

"OK, Admiral," giggled Danny.

"OK, Danny, but if you call me a Rear Admiral, you're going over the side for some keel hauling."

At this they laughed together and neither themselves nor an outsider could have believed that this was anything but a genuine, happy relationship.

"Where to today, Admiral?"

"How about a run across the bay? We will have the tide with us for at least the next two hours and then a slack before it will turn in our favour for the return. I have some food and drinks on board so why don't we just get out there and let the wind blow away all our worldly worries."

"Yes, Admiral," smiled Danny, and even Jules inside felt the genuine desire to just cruise and forget all concerns.

There were no more comments and they each got on with their normal duties. Roly checked the engines and instruments while Danny set the lines up for leaving the berth, stored unneeded fenders, and tidied up the canvas cover. Within just a few short minutes they were heading out of the marina and down the river. As they turned the bend the open sea beckoned, the sun came from behind the clouds, and it seemed like there was a golden path on the water leading the way forwards. They did not speak but they did glance at each other and smile contentedly. As they left the river Roly opened up the engines and Cariad surged forward in an elegant response.

They made their return several hours later, after a lunch of store sandwiches, mugs of tea and the sharing of a chocolate bar.

"Admiral, this is so good. Are you getting too busy now to do it that often?"

"Things are busy, Danny, but we have to find time for days like this. You know, you only get so many of these days in a lifetime. God forbid that we waste them."

"You're right, I love them, but my dad wants me to start helping him out at his business." Danny started on the rehearsed and planned story.

"Well, that's good, isn't it? Working with your dad I mean."

"Yeah, but I don't want to miss out on days like this. Do you think we could plan them? I mean, set up some sort of schedule so I can plan my time with Dad. I mean if I knew when you couldn't make it, I could plan to be with Dad or even start looking for a proper job. You know I leave school in two weeks."

"Sure, we can, go into the cabin and bring up my satchel."

Danny skipped to it and a few moments later Roly had his desk diary opened up on the cockpit windscreen shelf and they were discussing dates.

"Days out of town, like next Wednesday, are often scheduled a few weeks in advance. Local meetings are often more flexible but not always."

While this conversation continued, Jules was memorising the three out-of- town days he could see in the coming weeks.

"Great, how about trying to make it a regular Tuesday and Thursday?" suggested Danny.

"Yeah, conditional on the weather and meetings I

cannot re-schedule. let's do that. Don't forget weekends as well. You have my number but give me yours and then if anything does crop up, we can keep each other informed," said Roly.

With the agreement made they were quiet for a few minutes before Roly started up a new line of conversation that almost made Jules forget why he was there in the first place.

"Leaving school in a few weeks then, so what do you plan to do? You said you were going to look for a job; what sort of job do you want?"

"Oh, I don't know. Dad wants me to go into some sort of office job, but I would hate that. Some of my friends are looking to be tradesmen, you know, electricians or plumbers. Others are going into factories. Mum says she just wants me to be happy whatever I do, but I have no idea."

"Well in my opinion your mother is right. I did a job for decades that I didn't like, it never brought me happiness. So, what makes you happy?"

"This, just this," said Danny, reaching out and pointing with both arms out over the front of the boat. There was another pause as Roly tried to digest an emerging thought.

"Danny, do you know what I do?"

"You've never said, Roly."

"I'm opening up a special type of hotel in town. It will be a holiday hotel for poor and unfortunate people who are having some sort of tough times through illness and circumstances. These people cannot afford a holiday of their own."

"So how do they pay you then?"

"That's it they don't. It is free to them. I get large

companies to sponsor the hotel as a charity so we can offer these people some help."

"Wow, that sounds like a good thing, Roly, but I don't want to work in a hotel."

"No, I'm not thinking of that. When the hotel is all set up and ready to go, I will have a berth for Cariad on the harbour walls. I intend to use Cariad to take people out for days like this. You could help me with that."

"Oh wow, that would be great," said Danny with a genuineness supported by Jules.

"Look, it isn't that simple," said Roly trying to dampen down an escalating enthusiasm. "There are all sorts of regulations that need to be fulfilled. I need to modify Cariad so she can take on seated passengers and wheelchairs. I need all sorts of safety systems put on board. The captain and crew must be qualified to take passengers by passing all sorts of marine examinations. The boat would not be used eight hours a day, fifty-two weeks a year, so I need people who are flexible. I need someone whose principal job is the boat but who is also willing to help out with not only boat maintenance but frankly, anything else that needs to be done around the hotel and I mean anything, from blocked toilets to decorating, from trade work to office work. The hotel is too small a set-up for staff to just do one thing. If you are interested, we can talk more but I would pay you the going rate for an apprentice learning a trade. I would support your training for the boat skipper and anything else we need you to do." At this Roly stopped because he saw that Danny's mouth was hanging open.

Roly continued, "Say nothing now, just think on it and discuss it with your parents. If they want to talk to me tell them to call. We can discuss it more next

Thursday if you like."

"Oh, Roly, my God, I don't know what to say."

"Well, you don't listen, that's for sure. I just said say nothing." And with that Roly smiled and ruffled the boy's hair. "Time to get ready, river is coming up. Who is taking her in, you or me?" Roly was in no doubt how Danny would respond to this point.

"I'm Captain, you deck swab. Get the fenders and lines out we're coming home."

They set to their tasks and soon they were berthed; Cariad had been washed down and they were walking along the pontoon.

"Danny, think on what I said about a job now. There is no rush, the hotel won't be up and running for many months yet and that takes us into winter. If you are interested, we can start soon and be ready for next summer."

Danny nodded and they parted company at the car park. As Roly climbed the stairs to the marina bar, and hopefully meet Chrissie, he looked over his shoulder and acknowledged a last wave from Danny as he walked out of view. He felt closer now to realising his purpose.

Chapter 18

Time for Action

As Danny reverted to being Jules and headed back to phone Ronnie with his target date of next Wednesday, he could not help but be moved by Roly's offer. In fact, he could not remember when anyone had made such a positive impact on him for a very long time.

By evening, Danny had disappeared, and Jules was in full command. He rang Ronnie and was surprised that Ronnie answered almost immediately as if he had been waiting.

"Hi, Ronnie, I've got a date." Ronnie sat up straight, said nothing and waited for Jules to continue. "The boat owner is out of town next Wednesday, a business trip to London. So, if you can get your contacts to drop the stuff on Tuesday night I can go out and pick it up." It sounded so ordinary, such a normal activity but it fooled no one. In the stomachs of both Ronnie and Jules the tension throbbed.

"Are you sure, kid, this is the point of no return. Up to now we have just been talking about things; if we go now, that's it for both of us."

Jules picked up immediately on this; up until now the threats were always directed to Jules, now it seemed like the threat was being shared openly with Ronnie.

"Ronnie, we've talked this all through before and we were happy with it. Now we have a specific date, so we have only improved the plan. We go."

"OK," said Ronnie who, for once, failed to see that it

was Jules making the decision. "I'll call you when we've passed on the money and then again when they send me the coordinates. Kid, when we've done this, things will change and trust me it will be for the good. You get back to me immediately if anything changes your side. You did good, kid." The line went dead.

Jules sat in his room and smiled. When he and Ronnie were running things together, he would educate him on telephone etiquette. A Hello to start a call followed with a Bye for now to end them would not go amiss. He lay on his bed, he had Friday, the weekend and Monday and Tuesday to wait. How would he pass the time? He had no idea. He had no stomach for joining the gang down at the brickworks, his prediction of it declining into a hooligan's youth club was absolutely spot on. He also had to recognise that he and Tina had never been more distant. She did not want him as much as she wanted to be with the gang leader. No gang to lead and no Tina. He felt disappointed but not too upset.

"Should have shagged her though," he said to himself with a smile and a shrug. He heard his mother downstairs and decided to go down and see how she was. While he surprised himself with this decision it had an even bigger impact on her.

"Hello, Julian," she said through arched eyebrows. "Are you hungry?"

Though early evening they ate and chatted together. Simple topics that allowed Jules to have his own internal conversation while responding to her. He wondered how she would manage when he left. He wondered if he would ever return. He did care and he would make sure she was not short of money, but he could not stand being with her when she started to whinge and whine. She, he decided, was quite happy to be a victim of life. She did nothing to improve her situation, in fact complaining about the unfairness of her position seemed to be the main point of her existence. He wondered what she had been like as a young girl or even a young wife and mother. While he hated his father and had no desire to ever see him again, he had to give the man the recognition that he had a drive and energy and was no one's fool. It looked like he got more from his father's side than his mother's.

"Julian, did you hear me?"

Jules looked up and shrugged.

"I said what are you going to do after school? You know you could stay on and work towards university. Your father would have to pay, and he would."

"I want nothing from that man," said Jules with a snarl.

"He's your father, it is his duty. I'll call him tomorrow and sort it out," she replied.

"Hell no, don't you realise he has moved on; I have moved on when are you going to?" shouted Jules.

His mother crumpled and started to whimper and this further infuriated Jules.

"God, I'm going to my room," he bellowed like a sulky teenager and slammed the door as he left the room.

The weekend passed quick enough, he slept late, wandered around and he did visit the brickworks. Everyone was friendly but in a distant sort of way. It was clear to the gang that Jules was into something different now; what it was they had no idea, but it was not them. They didn't look to Jules for decisions anymore; they didn't act like a gang anymore. All of them were moving slowly but surely into being unemployed teenage jobseekers with very little future potential or expectations. He said his farewell and moved towards the door just as Tina and two girls wandered in. Tina and Jules looked at each other and it was embarrassing to both.

"Hi, Jules," she almost whispered as the other two girls hurried away. "You haven't called me, I wondered what's been happening."

"You haven't rung me either, have you?" said Jules, a little harshly.

"No, that's true. I guess I haven't."

"Tina, I don't feel we are close anymore."

"Neither do I," agreed Tina.

"What changed?"

"You changed, Jules. This was our gang, our town, our time. I feel you want something so different. All this means nothing to you, does it?"

Jules just stared back at her with no emotion in his face. Then he spoke quietly and directly, "You did once, but be serious, look at all this. It's a derelict building; it's a small, decrepit seaside town and it's full of people going nowhere."

"Where are you going, Jules?"

"Somewhere better but I guess without you."

"Yes, without me. Don't be angry, Jules. We had some fun but now it's time to move on."

"Same question to you, where are you going?"

"Oh, Jules, I'm not like you. I am not trying to conquer the world. I like my little world. I want someone to look after me. I want nice things, go out to nice places." She caught a sneer on Jules' face. "Yeah, and I want to get married and have kids and a nice house. I want to remember my fun teenage years, not be terrified of them. With you, Jules, I would always be terrified."

"I guess we're different." He stepped aside to pass her, and she caught his shoulder.

"Jules, I did care at first and I worry about you. Please take care and I hope you are happy."

"I'm happy." He started to move and then stepped back and gave her a chaste kiss on the cheek and then left quickly before she saw his eyes start to water.

Sunday evening, in his room, Jules was not paying attention to the television programme, but his ears picked up when the weather forecaster spoke: "The South looks like it is going to have a very unseasonable summer week coming our way. If you look out in the Atlantic on this chart you can see a very clear and I should say, very strong, low that has formed and it's coming our way over the next two or three days. As you can also see, the isobars are close together so that means high winds. So, enjoy Monday because you are going to need your brollies and raincoats for later in the week."

"Shit," said Jules and he opened up his laptop to study further weather implications. He visited specific marine weather websites and found predictions of 25-30 knot winds from the southwest, wave sizes of 1.5-2.0 metres with poor visibility and heavy rain. He had never been out in anything like that and although he was confident it would not be a problem for the boat, he knew it would be uncomfortable for him. Should I call Ronnie and get it rescheduled? he thought and decided that perhaps the best approach would be to discuss it with him and let Ronnie make the decision. He shrugged and shook his head. Ronnie knew nothing about boats he would ask Jules what to do. Also, if they were going to do a pickup on Wednesday then this weekend Ronnie would have paid the money. The last thing he now needed was Ronnie screaming down the phone at him. He could almost hear him saying I don't care if the fucking boat sinks, I've paid the money just go and get the stuff. OK, it was going to be rough, but he would just have to do it. You didn't get anything in this world for nothing.

He spent the remainder of the evening trawling the internet and found a US website with video instructions about boat handling in storms. In one video covering 'Man Overboard' situations there was a commentary running while the picture showed a man on a boat like Cariad leaning over the side with a boathook trying to catch a person in the water. The voice chilled Jules as it spoke: "As you can see, even in a modest swell with waves of about one metre, it is difficult for the person to give the helmsman the right directions to bring the boat aside the MOB. If he gets it wrong, they either miss the person entirely or they hit him with the boat. Even worse is the chance to damage him with the propeller."

For the second time that night Jules reacted. "Shit, I'm going to need someone with me."

He sank back into his bed and his mind raced – Who can I get to come who can handle the boat? No one, just me. Who can I get to handle the boathook? Ronnie? Never, he is not a boatman. One of his goons? No, they would not listen to me. I can't ask Ronnie for help, this is my plan. Must be one of my guys but who? Holvey or Joe? Joe would be better, more reliable and he can keep a secret. Yes – I'll see him tomorrow! Should I tell Ronnie? – no way he'll go apeshit! My plan, my Joe, I'll pay him well.

He lay on his back and closed his eyes. He opened

them again to switch off the light, but he did not have a good night's sleep.

Mid-morning, he was up and out and heading back to the brickworks. Of course, he should have known it was far too early for the gang to be there. He felt foolish in the old building all on his own and so with haste he left to walk the streets. He was looking for people he knew, someone he could ask about Joe. He walked the high street, the pedestrian zone, looking into café bars but all for nothing. It was as if all teenagers had abandoned Cranport.

As the day passed, he felt desperation rise and he realised that he had cut himself out of Cranport before he had established himself anywhere else. He had been wandering aimlessly now for quite some time and as he turned the next corner, he surprised himself. Perhaps a quarter of a mile away as the road crested the hill and turned down towards the other side of town was Lawrence's old filling station. He walked slowly towards it only to find that the fuel pumps were no longer functioning and the main 'Petrol Open' sign had been smashed.

Edie's shop and cashier building was boarded up but two of the maintenance bays were still open and two or three guys seemed to be doing things to ever more battered cars. Those maintenance bays, mused Jules, seemed to be in some sort of time warp. He had never seen cars go in or cars come out. The guys worked on and on almost oblivious to what was happening in the rest of the world. Their life never changed but realised Jules, his had and would forever after this week.

He shrugged, turned, and headed back.

If he had started to despair, it had now turned into a

resignation. This resignation now rose on a crescendo to determination; he could not live in Cranport, he would not live in Cranport, he was different to others, he needed to be different.

Now mid-afternoon, he headed back towards the brickworks and smiled to himself when he heard laughter and Holvey's voice in particular,

"There's nothing worth nicking is there? I mean how many vacuum cleaners do you need? In a week me mum would have enough cleaner bags to last a lifetime."

The others laughed and Joe's voice piped in, "So, did you get the job?"

"Nah, the foreman said that if I could not get there on time for the interview there was little chance of me getting there on time to work. I mean, I was only twenty minutes late!"

"So, what did you say?"

"I told him to stick the job up his arse and came out. I did attend so they can't stop my youth employment benefit, can they?"

It was a question left unanswered as they all turned as Jules came in. The pause was ended by Joe who walked over and clapped Jules on the shoulder saying, "Hi, Jules, where you been? You should have been here earlier and hear Holvey describe his first failed job interview." And he laughed, with the others joining in.

"What was the job, Holvey?" asked Jules.

"It was a warehouse packer at a vacuum cleaner company. All the bits come in bulk and you have to put them together in a box ready to be shipped to the stores. What a boring job. I'm not doing that."

"So, what job are you going to do?" asked Jules with a big smile. He wanted to join in with this playful banter even if it was for a short time.

"Fucked if I know, but it must pay well. I have a lifestyle to protect."

More laughter and Joe built on it, "How about a brain surgeon?"

Jules added to it before Holvey could respond, "Hell no, Holvey has to build on his strengths. He could be a brain damager. He causes the brain damage in people and his partners the brain surgeons repair them. He could be on commission!"

"Yeah, that sounds right," hollered Holvey and the rest just whooped, jigged, and laughed. Jules found that it felt good. Soon the teenagers drifted into smaller groups and separate conversations and Jules looked for an opportunity to talk to Joe. He didn't have to wait long.

"Hey, everyone, I got to go. My elder sister is moving flats and I promised to help." As Joe started to say his goodbyes and move towards the door, Jules joined him.

"Hold up, Joe. I'll walk with you."

As they left the brickworks through the old broken fence and stepped onto the pavement, Jules grabbed Joe's arm.

"Joe, I've got a job for you. I need you Wednesday. It will pay very well. Are you interested?"

"What is it, Jules?"

"Are you available Wednesday?" repeated Jules.

"Sure, what is it?"

"Look, I can't tell you all of it, but this is a big deal that I'm in. I'm working with some guys from London and I'm taking a boat out from the marina on Wednesday."

"Shit, you're stealing a boat?" exclaimed Joe.

"No, you goon, I'm just borrowing it. I need to head out and pick up some stuff floating in the bay, and I need an extra pair of hands. Help me and it will be the best-paid day of your life."

By now Joe had stopped listening and only had more questions. "What stuff? Where's it floating? How do you know it's there? Who are these London guys? My God, Jules, you've become a real gangster, haven't you? I mean we were all just playing at it but its real for you, isn't it?"

"Joe, are you in or not? If you're in, I can answer your questions. If you're out, then I can't."

"For Wednesday I'm in," said Joe excitedly, "but tell me more."

"How much time do you have? When do you need to be at your sister's place?"

"Fuck her, this is far more interesting. Look, let's talk in the library."

They turned together and walked about four hundred yards to the old corner building that was the town's library. They often went there especially when it rained because it was quiet and just filled with old men reading free newspapers and magazines and with a few geeks on PCs in the corner. They walked up the stairs to the first floor and headed over to the corner reference section. It was chosen because it was the quietest, empty spot in the building. They pulled together two old wooden chairs into the bay window and with their heads close together Jules explained the plan.

"You know I've been going out on the boat with that guy whose wallet you nicked? Well, he thinks we are friends and I've been going out two or three times a week now over the last month. I know all about the boat and how to get in and start it up and even sail it out on the sea. It's easy really. Well, I mentioned it to this guy I met in London, you know the last time I was up there."

"The three guys, the ones that beat you up?"

"Hell no, don't be a prat. The reason I was up there was to meet up with the guys that used to do business with Lawrence."

"Oh, I see. You met his partners."

"He didn't have partners, he was just a soldier. He took things to them, and he bought things from them. These are big guys doing big deals. When I suggested that I take over from the deceased Lawrence they couldn't give a fuck. They told me that Cranport was nothing to them but if I had any bigger ideas to let them know."

"So, this is your deal then?"

"Well, yes. I mean it was my idea, let me explain." Jules cleared his throat and took one last look around before he explained the deal to Joe, who sat there with his mouth open, nodding like a toy dog as Jules went through it.

"So, the guy in London, and I'm not mentioning names because you don't need to know, has paid a large amount of money to some people in Spain. They in return are dropping off some drugs in cases under floating buoys about ten miles offshore on Tuesday night. I will get a call telling me the GPS coordinates and on Wednesday I just go out and get it. When we get back, I hand it over to the guy in London and a few weeks after it has been processed, I get a big pile of cash. Joe, you need to know that I'm going to London to work with this guy permanently, but I will make sure to look after you. I promise you at least a thousand pounds, possibly more."

"Holy fuck!"

"I operate the boat, you just enjoy the trip and when we get there you lean over with the boathook and pull it in. You then enjoy the trip back and, in a few weeks, I'll get the money to you. You must never speak of this because these guys would not forget or understand. These people will kill if they have to."

"Did they kill Lawrence?"

"I don't know, possibly, but you don't ask these guys that sort of question."

Joe nodded as if he understood but the truth was, he had no conception of such people.

"Jesus, count me in, Jules. This is the most exciting thing I've ever done. I wouldn't miss this for the world. What do you want me to do?"

"Keep Wednesday free and talk to no one. I expect a call soon, this evening or tomorrow and then we can sort it out. I don't want you at the marina. They know me but not you, but outside the marina entrance there is a visitor's berth where boats tie up when they visit. On the way out, I will pick you up from there. I'm thinking it will be in the morning sometime. Give me your mobile number and here is mine. For now, just keep quiet and not a word to anyone."

Again, Joe nodded, "OK then, done. Now I had better get to my sister's or Mum will create merry hell with me. See you, Jules, and thanks for thinking of me for this." With that he got up, smiled, shook his head still in amazement and left.

Jules wondered if he had done the right thing but as flaky as Joe was, he was the best of the bunch and sure as hell he needed help. Five minutes later he too was walking home when his mobile rang,

"Hi, Ronnie," Jules answered.

"Kid, the money has been paid. It's going ahead. I'll get a text with the coordinates, I'll forward them to you. How long do you think you will take?"

"Ten miles offshore, say about four hours there and back."

"Good, because when you go, I will make sure I'm waiting for you on your return. Listen, kid, make sure you always have your mobile on. No flat batteries because when we hear you go, and you can also ring me when you're coming back. I don't want that stuff floating in the English Channel for a minute longer than necessary. We've paid so it's ours now."

Ronnie hung up. His complete lack of telephone etiquette was now so very amusing to Jules, he laughed out loud and walked on. As he headed home, he thought, All the planning has been done, now is the time for action.

Chapter 19

The Day

Jules heard nothing all day and evening on Tuesday. He monitored the weather forecasts, they did not change. Tuesday night and Wednesday into Thursday were going to be rainy and blustery but so be it, he thought. Why worry about what you cannot control? It was late and he was thinking of sleep when he got his first of two calls.

"Hey, Jules, what time are we starting tomorrow?" asked Joe.

"Heard nothing yet but I expect to have heard by the time we wake up. Stand by your phone, sailor, and await my command," joked Jules in a poor mimic of a navy officer's voice, but it was enough to get a snigger out of Joe.

"OK, Jules, just call me anyway in the morning. If you haven't heard, we can also wait together."

"Sure, good night now," and Jules hung up.

"As he was reaching over to his bedside table to put the mobile back down it rang in his hand and made him jump.

"Hi, Ronnie."

"I haven't heard anything. They said they would drop the stuff Tuesday night."

"Ronnie, it is now Tuesday evening, late evening I grant you but for most people Tuesday night runs until Wednesday morning. There is plenty of time yet. They will want to do it in the middle of the night is my guess. If you want to worry, then start worrying if you haven't heard by mid-morning tomorrow."

Ronnie chuckled, "Kid, you and me are going to get on fine. You're right but don't make a habit of it. Is your phone fully charged? I'll call you in the morning, bye."

The phone went dead, and Jules giggled again. My, what progress, I actually got a bye out of him. Surprisingly, a calm, relaxed Jules turned over in bed and fell into a deep sleep.

It was 7,10am when Jules was awoken by a call on his mobile phone.

"Morning, Ronnie."

"I've had a text. It has the coordinate numbers on it. Have you got a pen ready?"

"Ronnie don't read out the numbers, just forward the text to me. That way there is a less of a chance of making a mistake."

"How the fuck do I forward a text?" asked an exasperated Ronnie.

It was now Jules' turn to laugh. "Jesus, Ronnie. What type of mobile do you have? Is it the same as the one you gave me?"

"Yeah, I've got several of them, so what?"

"OK, when you have hung up, go to the text message and at the bottom you will see a little green arrowhead. Click on that and it will ask you what number you want to forward the message to. Type in my mobile number and hit enter. That's it, easy."

"OK, call me back in ten minutes to confirm you have it." The line went dead. It was a further five or six minutes before his mobile beeped signalling receipt of a text. Jules opened it and there was the text and more importantly the coordinates. The text read,

50* 32' 34.66" N 2* 54' 56.97" W. Bon voyage, mon ami.

As Jules digested the information his phone rang.

"Yes, Ronnie?"

"Kid, I told you to call me back."

"Jesus, Ronnie, it just arrived. I was reading it when you rang. No worries, it's all there. I have all that I need."

"So, what are you doing in bed, kid? Get your arse in gear and go and get our future."

Again, Jules picked up on it immediately. This was not just a deal, it was the future, and not just Ronnie's future but their joint future.

"How long do you reckon, kid?"

"OK, it's just gone seven-thirty now, so if I get to the marina by nine, I could be there and back by two pm. Is that, OK?"

"Yes, I'm on my way. Call me when you are arriving. We meet in the car park. Don't forget, any problems just call." The line went dead.

Jules jumped out of bed and was about to call Joe when he realised that to call at such an early time would have been ridiculous. He washed, dressed and had breakfast before calling around eight-thirty. Still early and it had to ring for quite some time before a groggy Joe answered the call.

"Yeah, what?"

"Joe, it's Jules. Are you up?"

"Are you mad? It's still the middle of the night," protested Joe.

"Nah, it's time to go for a boat ride. It's always better in the morning. How quickly can you get down to the marina, Joe?"

Much more awake now Joe replied, "See you there in an hour?"

"That's fine," said Jules before realising that this already put him behind the schedule he'd quoted to Ronnie. "Don't go in, I'll meet you about a hundred yards from the entrance and then I can show you how to get down to the public visitor's pontoon."

"OK, see you there."

Joe was waiting there as expected and Jules went over and gave him a hug. They both felt the importance of what they were doing that day.

"Look over there, Joe," said Jules pointing to a gangway leading to a small pontoon with room at the end for two or three boats. As usual, it was completely empty. "See that marina wall over there," pointed Jules. "I'll come around there in about ten to fifteen minutes and when I do just run down to the end of the pontoon. I'll come in close and stop the boat, but we won't tie up, you just jump on and we'll be away. Don't stand and wait down there, though, it might catch someone's attention. OK?"

"Sure, Jules. When I see you, I'll come down."

Jules slapped Joe on the back and left him there and walked down the lane until he reached the main marina gates. From the top of the almost completely empty car park, Jules could see that it was as deserted as he had expected. Five minutes later, he had crossed the car park, entered the pin code into the pontoon entrance gate and was walking as casually as he could towards the boat. Glancing around while trying not to look too hard, he could not see anyone about until, that is, he reached Cariad. There were toolkits on the finger berth and loud whistling coming from the boat. Jules looked over the side and saw the big floor panel had been removed. He tried to back away, but Trev saw him and said, "Hello, young Danny. What are you doing here? Roly is away today. Didn't he tell you?"

"Yes, he did, sir" replied Jules, immediately falling into his planned explanation. "I've lost my mobile and I thought I might have left it here. Mum will kill me if I don't find it, I lost one before. Can I come on and have a look around?"

A puzzled Trev looked up. "Sure, but if I had not been here, how would you have got into the cabin? They wouldn't have given you the keys from the marina office?"

"No, I know that but look, I got my friend's mobile," he responded quickly, "I thought if I called from here then I might hear it ringing."

"Well go ahead, young fellow, we can both listen."

Jules typed in a fictitious number and pretended to listen as did Trev. Jules looked down at the phone in his hand and said, "Nothing, it's not even ringing now. It was before but I guess the battery has run down."

"Well, come aboard, son, have a quick look around but make sure you don't fall into the engine bilge."

Jules hopped in and went down into the cabin. He pretended to look around but soon gave up. As he came up the stairs onto the cabin deck he spoke again to Trev.

"Nah, nothing around that I could see. I bet I left it somewhere else, but I can't think where. If Roly finds it, will you tell him it's mine?"

"No problem, lad."

"So, what's wrong with the boat? It was fine last time when we took it out."

"Nothing wrong with this lady, my lad. She's just getting an oil change and a general fifty-hour service. Roly wants it done while he's out in London."

"So will it take all day?" asked Jules, peering into the engine bilge trying desperately to be a curious child.

"No, everything is open and easily accessible. Not like these new plastic boats you get today," said Trev casting his hand around all the other boats in the marina. "They all have these little hatches, and you have to be like a midget with six feet long arms to tunnel in and do the job right. Here we just pick up the floor and as you can see it's all open and easily done. I'll be gone from here in about two hours. Just in time for lunch," he chuckled.

"Well, that's great, sir. Tell Roly to look out for my phone but I've got to get on. See you next time."

And with a wave he left the boat and casually walked back up the pontoon, out through the security gate and across the car park. All this was done without giving in to the terrible urge to look back over his shoulder. As he entered the lane, he could see Joe peering over the short fence down to the visitor's berth. As he got closer, he whistled and as Joe turned around, he signalled for Joe to follow him as they left the lane and entered the main street.

"What's up then?" asked Joe.

"Fuck, there's a maintenance guy there changing the engine oil and stuff. He's going to be working on it all morning. Jesus, Ronnie's heading down, he'll go nuts. I'll have to ring him."

Joe did not fully understand what was going to happen, but he saw the anxiety in Jules and decided now was not the time to ask. As they turned the corner the wind and rain hit them, so they ducked into a bus shelter. Jules sat down on a seat and rang.

"Hi, Ronnie."

"What's up, are you on the boat?"

"No, that's why I rang."

"Explain quick, kid."

"When I got to the boat, there was a maintenance guy there. He was doing an engine service on it."

"Jesus, kid, we've got millions floating in the fucking sea. I'm halfway down to that piss-hole town you call home, and we have no boat. This gets better." As Ronnie paused for breath, Jules took the opportunity to explain.

"Listen please, Ronnie, it's no big deal. I talked to the engineer. He said he'll be finished by lunchtime. So, what we got is a slight delay nothing more.

I'll head back about two, if I get on the boat by then I can still be back by about six. We've waited this long surely a few hours more won't hurt."

"Kid, this is too big to fuck up. If we don't get the boat this afternoon then me, you and my guys are going to take any boat we find and go get our stuff. I only left London about forty minutes ago, so I'll head back. I want a call from you by two-thirty saying you're on board or all hell breaks out." The line went dead.

"So, what do we do now?" asked Joe.

"Have you had breakfast?" Joe shook his head. "Thought so, let's head into town and have a late breakfast or early lunch. Everything is delayed until this afternoon."

They headed down the street into town but there was no further conversation because the wind had picked up and the rain grew stronger.

Later, sitting in a café, Joe swallowed a mouthful before asking, "Weather's bad, Jules. Is it going to be safe out on the sea in this storm?"

"It's not a storm, it is a bit blowy, and it will rain, so

are you willing to get your hair blown and get a little bit wet for a few hours for a grand?"

"Yeah, I was just asking, is it safe?"

"It's a big, comfortable boat, most of the time you can be in the cabin out of the weather. It might rock and roll a little but that's all. I'm not going to drown either of us." At this they both laughed, and Jules changed the subject,

"Now look, I need to get back down there but I cannot go until the maintenance man has finished and gone. He can't see me again without getting suspicious. He said he would be finished for lunch, so I'll leave it until one-thirty. If I leave it any later my London contact will be down here with his goons and all hell breaks out. You, Joe, mustn't be around then. He doesn't know I have you to help me."

"But he'll see me when we get back, what then? He might finish me off like Lawrence!"

"Don't be a prat. When we get back, we'll have the stuff. He'll be happy then. I'll tell him you and I are together. No sweat, we'll be alright."

They sat quietly for a while and then Jules moved on with the new plan for the day.

"OK, this is what we'll do. We go back for one-thirty. I go on and if he is on the boat, I tell him that I found my phone and just leave. If that happens, you clear off and I'll sort out my London guy somehow. If he is not there, I start up the boat and pick you up as before and we do the job just a few hours later than expected. OK with that?"

"Yeah, I don't want to meet the London guy unless it's after, that's for sure. So, one more coffee each and we can walk back."

That's what they did but even walking slowly they got back a good forty-five minutes early. They tucked themselves back into the bus stop to get out of the strong wind and constant drizzle. They chatted a little but mainly stared out across fields and houses. Five minutes before one-thirty Jules stood up.

"OK, time to do it," he said. "We've got five minutes to walk around the corner and then you wait for me where I said this morning. I'll either be back with a boat or back down the lane and you're free to shoot off. Ready?"

Joe just nodded and they shuffled out and up the lane. As Jules left him to walk into the marina, Joe felt that perhaps the best option for him was the no boat option. This had started out as a fantastic bit of fun; suddenly, it was deadly serious.

For the second time that day, Jules walked across the car park, entered the security pin number, and walked as casually as he could down the pontoon. As he walked down the finger berth to his enormous relief no one was there. A quick glance and he had vaulted over onto the boat. He knelt down to be as out of sight as possible. Then, he pulled a flat twelve-inch steel bar from his inside jacket pocket. The latch into the cabin was a little loose. It was easy to slide the bar under it and with a quick heave the screws holding the latch into the teak wood surround broke free with a loud splintering crack. The noise surprised Jules and he quickly looked around, but nothing moved. He caressed the broken wood. It gave him no pleasure to damage Cariad. He pushed open the cabin door and entered. Quickly he secured the spare engine keys, turned on all the instruments and leapt back into the cockpit to start the engine. Power on, turn of the key and Cariad's engines throbbed alive. No red engine warning lights came on, so all was well. Now he looked up and around – with the grey clouds, blustery wind, and heavy drizzle, no one was to be seen.

"Let's do it," he said aloud to no one. He left the boat to release the two bow lines, the spring and stern lines and climbed straight back on board. Even in the twenty seconds this took, the wind had started to move the hull around, and they bumped awkwardly against the finger berth as Cariad floated free to the influence of the wind. Jules engaged reverse and backed out. Within a few minutes the boat was moving slowly but surely towards the marina exit.

Trev was leaving the marina bar after having a beer and sandwich for lunch with Chrissie. He heard the engine and looked over to see the tail end of the boat leaving the marina.

"What the hell?" he grumbled and went down the steps and walked towards Pontoon C for a clearer view.

By now Jules was rounding the marina wall and he waved for Joe. As planned, Joe ran down the walkway across the short pontoon and stopped at the visitor berths. Out of the marina, the wind had picked up and as Jules reduced power the wind continued to blow Cariad to the dock. Realising too late, Jules hit a hard reverse and the boat lurched to a hard stop but still they hit the deck heavily.

Joe jumped back and shouted, "Jesus, Jules, you almost ran me down."

"Just get on and quick."

Joe clambered on board as Jules maintained reverse to back away. Soon he had enough space to engage drive and head down the centre of the river.

"Wow!" shouted Joe. "Bloody fantastic." Jules was far quieter. The weather conditions were far different from anything he had experienced, so he was going to have to concentrate.

"Joe, take the wheel."

"Are you mad? I can't steer this thing."

"Just keep her in the middle of the river, and don't touch anything else. Call me if you are worried."

Joe was worried but he did as he was told. Free from the helm, Jules was down below using the chart plotter to set up a waypoint for the coordinates he had.

"Shit," he said out loud as the electronic charts came up telling him the course direction he had to take and more importantly the distance. "It's twelve and a half miles and two hours and twenty-seven minutes." Then he realised that this was based on their current speed on the river. Once they were out on the sea, they could go much faster. He scrambled back up to the helm and took the wheel allowing Joe to duck in out of the wind and rain.

While all this was happening, all hell was breaking out in the marina. As Trev went up the pontoon, he quickly saw that Cariad had gone. Turning and heading back to the bar, he entered shouting for Chrissie.

"What's up, Dad?"

"Is Roly back?"

"He's in London today, you know that. Why?"

"Either he or someone has taken his boat out; it's gone."

"He wouldn't take it out on a day like this and he wouldn't go out without saying at least hi to us. Call him on his mobile." She handed over her mobile and Trev rang.

"Hi, Chrissie, what's up?"

"Roly, it's not Chrissie it's me."

"Hey, Trev, how's the boat?"

"Just going to ask you the same; are you on it?"

"What do you mean? I don't understand."

"Where are you, Roly?"

"On the train heading back, about five minutes out of town but I was going down to the solicitors. What's up?"

"Someone has just taken your boat out of the marina."

"What, are you sure? Who the hell would do that?"

"I think it's the kid, Roly. That lad Danny was there this morning when I was doing the service. When I asked him what he was doing he said he had lost his mobile and thought he might have left it on the boat. It didn't sound too bad then, but I did tell him I would be finished in a few hours. I reckon he has come back and has taken the boat."

"Danny, no, never... why would he do that? Where would he go? Was he alone?"

"No idea, Roly, I just saw the stern of the boat as it left the marina."

"When?"

"About ten minutes ago now. What do you want me to do? Call the police or coastguard?"

"Do nothing; I'm coming straight from the station by taxi. I'll be there in twenty minutes."

As the phone went dead, Trev turned to Chrissie and as he handed it back he said, "Roly is coming straight here. He'll be here in twenty minutes. We think it's that kid Danny."

While Trev was calling Roly, Jules called Ronnie. It was a short call.

"Ronnie, I'm on the boat."

"Well done, kid. What time back?"

"About six but the weather's bad so it might be a little longer."

"No worries, kid, just do the job and I'll be waiting."

As the phone went dead the boat left the river and entered the bay. With the wind blowing the open sea had had the chance to build up quite a swell and Cariad started to roll and plough through ever-increasing waves.

"My God," said Joe as he held on fast as Cariad bounced again through a wave.

"It's nothing," said a white-faced Jules, "go down into the cabin if you want to. I can handle this."

Joe nervously nodded and went down into the cabin and tried to wedge himself onto a bench seat behind the cabin table. Jules checked their course and added some more engine power and headed directly for the waypoint.

Twenty-five minutes later and a taxi pulled into the marina with Roly on board. He stepped out and ran up the stairs to the marina bar. He entered and stood there in business suit, collar and tie, raincoat, and polished shoes. Chrissie and Trev rushed over.

"Any news?"

"Nothing here," replied Trev. "You told me to wait."

"Yes, of course but this is a hell of a day to take a boat out for a joy ride."

"Shall I contact the marina office? They'll call the police and coastguard."

"I don't know what Danny is up to. He's a great kid. Hell, last time we were out I offered him a job. No, don't call anyone yet. I need to know what's going on. Where is he now?"

"I don't know, just saw the boat leave. Can't even

confirm that it is Danny."

"Well, we can't just wait, we must do something. What if I tried to make contact on the VHF?"

"If you do everyone will hear, but you have given me an idea," said Trev. "We have the marina tender, it has a small VHF, GPS and AIS system."

"That old metal dinghy with the fenders all around it that moves boats around the marina? Why would you put a GPS and AIS chart plotter on that? Even you, Trev, will not get lost in the marina." Roly's attempt at humour fell flat.

"That tender has multiple uses, the marina offers a standard service. If you are within ten miles of the marina and have an engine problem, we'll come and get you. For a price of course. The GPS and AIS tells us exactly where they are. If whoever has taken Cariad has turned on the instruments, we can see exactly where they are."

"Great, well let's go get my boat back. If it's not Danny, we can call the coastguard on the VHF. If it is, well, we can sort that out later."

As Trev turned to leave, Chrissie said, "Roly, you can't go out in those clothes. Look at the weather."

"It'll have to do; at least it is a raincoat, and I am sure Trev has an extra lifejacket." Roly looked at the concern in her eyes. "Don't worry, we are not going to do anything daft."

Roly left and quickly joined up with Trev who was carrying a canvas bag and two life jackets. The Tender was moored up outside the maintenance area and as they jumped in Trev started checking out everything.

"Full tank of petrol, here… put on this lifejacket, and this little gadget box should be what we need." He unzipped the bag and pulled out a set of wires, plugs and aerials. He gave a running commentary.

"This is the GPS and clips in here. This VHF Aerial clips onto the bow, by keeping them apart we reduce interference. And then when we plug them into the box here the screen should light up." There was a brief pause before he continued. "Yes, here she comes and there it shows us in the marina." He turned to Roly with a childlike smile on his face.

Roly fought down his frustration and exasperation before speaking, "Trev, great, but I know where we are. Where the hell is Cariad?"

"Patience, young man, you've spent too much time in London. I'll sort that out in a moment. In the meantime, do some work. Let go the lines, start up the outboard and get us moving."

Duly chastised, that is exactly what he did. In short order the Tender was motoring down the river somewhat faster than the regulation six knots. Trev continued fiddling with the system while hunched down on a seat using his body to protect as much as possible of the equipment from the driving rain. He set the chart plotter to five miles and the system ran through a cycle identifying every boat within that distance that had their GPS system on. Nothing but a fishing boat returning and a ferry boat running across the bay. He set the plotter to ten miles, and after examining the results for a few moments, he shouted, "There she blows. I've found her. Running SSW at eight knots, we can do better than that. Charge up that engine, Roly, and take a course of 210."

The light Tender accelerated and bounced hard as it skipped over the choppy waves but within minutes, they were registering fourteen knots. It was very uncomfortable and sometimes unstable. Trev hunkered down, Roly forged on. Too harsh and noisy to talk so every five minutes or so, Trev gave Roly a hand signal. Often just a thumbs up now and then, a signal to adjust direction.

The day was getting grey and angry but stoically Roly drove on. Stoic was not the way to describe the situation for both Jules and Joe. Jules, sheltered by the windscreen, was avoiding the worst of the weather but it still concerned him. Constantly glancing at the chart plotter, he was frustrated by two things. First, he found it almost impossible to steer in a straight line and second, the slaloming course was taking them far longer than he had expected. Joe was experiencing far worse. Being tossed around inside the cabin even when he held on to every grab point available had done nothing good for his stomach. He needed some fresh air, so he came up into the cockpit. He gave a weak smile to Jules and sat in beside him behind the cockpit screen. He looked around, the sea had sharp rolling waves and each crested with white water from the wind. Any chance he had of settling his stomach was lost due to the increase in anxiety. He swivelled sideways and threw up over the cabin floor.

"Jesus, Joe, over the side, you stupid bastard," was the only comforting comment he got from Jules.

"Sorry, Jules, sorry," whimpered Joe and as his stomach complained again, he tried to comply. He staggered to the side of the boat intending to throw up over the side. He grabbed the lifelines and as he leaned over, the boat rolled heavily. His feet slipped on the vomit, and he fell forward and head-butted the top of the lifeline post. Jules had seen it as if in slow motion and watched in silence. Joe gave out an almighty groan and collapsed in a heap on the floor. He slowly turned around and his expression was matched by the horror on Jules' face. Joe's forehead had been sliced open. As he put his hands to his head, blood poured through his fingers.

"Oh fuck," said Jules. Then he let the helm go and shot down into the cabin and grabbed the first aid kit. Soon he was by Joe's side.

"Joe, Joe, are you alright?" There was no response, nothing but moans from Joe. "Let me see, move your hands." He pulled Joe's fingers away and saw his savagely sliced forehead. He ripped open the first aid kit, grabbed a big square plaster and daubed the central padded area with some antiseptic ointment. Then, again pulling away Joe's hands, he quickly wiped away the blood before slapping on the plaster. He used a bit more force than he intended, and Joe groaned and rolled into a foetal position on the cabin floor.

Jules looked at him, "That's it, Joe, can't do any more right now." He turned back to the helm and aimed the boat back onto the waypoint.

***

Roly was closing but slowly.

"Where are they now?" he shouted.

"They seemed to go off course for a while but now back on. They are only about three miles, perhaps a little more, ahead. If it wasn't for this weather, we would see them. Keep on and keep your eyes open."

Roly's jaw tightened and he drove on and all the time his mind was racing.

Is this Danny? Why is he doing this? Could I have been so wrong? Was this planned from the start? He was like a kid brother or nephew (he knew he avoided the word son). Something is up. Where's he going? He's just heading out to sea. Why? This is not the type of day for a joyride. Something is up.

It was a further fifteen minutes before they saw the boat. Still a couple of miles away but it was clearly Cariad.

"I see her, Trev, I see her!" shouted Roly, and Trev jumped up to see for himself.

He glanced from chart plotter to horizon and back again before responding, "That's her, and she's slowing down. We'll be there soon. Stay with it, Roly, keep your eyes on her."

Just as Roly peered towards his boat Jules peered towards his waypoint. They were close now, less than a mile. He turned towards Joe.

"Get up, Joe, get up and help. We need green flags. Look damn it look. Stand up and look."

There was no response at all from Joe and Jules cast him a glance to confirm it was a lost cause there. As the boat got closer, he slowed her down, the slower they went the more severely the boat rolled. Yet Joe curled up around the stem of the cabin seat on the floor and held on in complete fear.

"I see it, I see it!" shouted Jules, but there was no one to listen. Engines were now ticking over as he tried to manoeuvre towards the small green buoy and flag that was lost from sight every thirty seconds when it was in the trough of the waves. Jules frantically grabbed for the boathook, slipping and sliding across the cabin floor. The boat had turned sideways to the waves and as she rolled a larger wave swamped the cabin floor and deck.

"We're sinking, oh fuck we're sinking!" screamed Joe, but Jules knew they weren't.

He put on more power and circled the flag and then tried to set it up to drift onto the flag.

Jules was oblivious now to everything else. He did not even realise that Roly and Trev were no more than two hundred yards away and approaching fast.

"What the hell is he doing?" shouted Roly. "My God, he's trying to pick something up – get me in there, Trev," and he handed over the tiller while he positioned himself to the side.

"We cannot raft up in this weather. This little Tender won't stand being bashed against your boat. I'll get you in close as close as I can and as we pass on the lea side you have to decide if you can jump aboard. For Christ's sake, be careful. If you fall between the boats, I won't be able to stop you from being crushed."

Approaching the wildly rolling Cariad at about five knots, the little Tender was bouncing like a cork. Roly waited for a brief moment of contact and leapt. His foot slipped and his shin was skinned on the hull's side but with all his strength backed up with fear he scrambled aboard.

Jules had only seen them for the last few moments, and he was struck dumb and frozen with the boathook in his hand. The pause lasted no more than a second or two and as Roly clambered over the side, he brought the boathook down in a wide swipe over Roly's back. Stung but not hurt, the anger rose in Roly.

"You little bastard," he snarled and grabbed the boathook and slapped Jules across the face with the back of his hand. Jules staggered backwards tripping over Joe and joined him in a heap on the floor.

Roly grabbed the boathook, signalled to Trev who was now about ten metres away that he was OK, and looked over the side. There resting against the boat was the green flag. Deftly in one smooth action he caught the line and pulled on board some sort of box and parachute anchor attached. He hauled everything aboard and it came onto the cabin floor with the boys. Turning now to the helm position he engaged the engines and turned into the waves to maintain control. Five minutes later he had turned the boat to home, and they were running with the wind instead of against it. The journey for once was far more comfortable and calm even though the weather had not changed. He hand signalled to Trev for a VHF call, then called him on the normal channel sixteen.

"Calling. Trev Tender, calling Trev Tender, this is Cariad, over."

"Cariad, Trev here, are you OK, over."

"Trev, everything fine and heading home, how about you, over."

"Cariad, lot of water on board but better now, running with the wind. I'll head back in front of you if you like, over."

"Trev, that's perfect, over and out."

The wind blew and the rain fell but Cariad was now on a gentle roll as Roly followed Trev back to the marina. Roly set the course and secured the wheel before turning to the boys.

Joe was obviously in some sort of shocked trance and Jules was mumbling to himself at his side.

"What the hell were you thinking, Danny? What's in the bag?" He pulled open a cockpit drawer and pulled out his boat knife. He thought he knew what was in the bag, but he was still shocked as he cut into it to see all these white powder bricks wrapped in some sort of cling film of plastic. He stabbed a brick and the powder spilled over his hands onto the cabin floor.

"Using my boat Cariad to bring in this evil stuff, God knows you are a nasty piece of work. These should not be left for recycling."

Roly slashed the drug bricks one by one before tossing them over the side. He watched them slowly but surely dissolve into the sea and sink.

Jules also looked on and in horror he mumbled, "Oh fuck, I'm dead, I'm dead," and seemed to join Joe into a stupor.

The calm after the chase descended onto Roly and even though they were going slower than when they went out, before too long the river entrance was in sight. Trev was ahead by about fifty metres, and they entered the protective waters of the outer harbour and turned up the river towards the marina. He glanced over to the boys but there was no change, they didn't even seem to recognise that they were almost back. Roly manoeuvred the boat into the marina and was pleased to see Trev waiting to take a line as he entered his berth.

"What now, Roly?" asked Trev. "Should we call the police? These lads have been up to bad stuff. You should have kept the drugs, the police will want them as proof."

"I guess so, I just didn't want it on my boat."

They secured the lines and wearily walked up the pontoon towards the marina offices, each supporting a shocked boy. Trev held Joe and Roly had Danny.

Just as they got out of the secured area it all happened.

A big Mercedes roared from the top end of the car

park and accelerated towards them with headlights on full beam. It made a hard stop just before them. The doors flung open and out stepped Ronnie and three big thugs – all, except Ronnie, openly carrying guns.

"Good evening, sir. I believe you have something for me."

"What do you mean?" asked Roly.

"Do you know who I am, sir?" asked Ronnie calmly.

"No, I don't," replied Roly.

"That's good because it is the only thing keeping you all alive," he said confidently and received with a chill by everyone. "I want what you picked up."

"The drugs sank," said Roly. There was a pause.

"What a pity," replied Ronnie. "In that case, I'll take him."

A terrified Jules came to life. "No please don't let him take me, please," he begged as one of the guys came and grabbed him by the collar and dragged him backwards towards the car. "No, please, no!"

It was the last sound they heard as the big car accelerated away.

Trev and Roly were left just standing there unable to speak. Joe started to sob. "They'll kill him just like they killed Lawrence."

Roly looked toward Trev. "We need to talk to the police, I think." As they turned and looked up towards the marina bar they saw Chrissie staring out of the window. They headed up the stairs and phoned the police. In his head, Roly still heard Danny's screams. He knew that this was a day he would never forget.

Chapter 20

Everyone Struggles To Get By As Best They Can

The call to the police was the start of chaos. They came within minutes and cordoned off the entire marina while they took statements and asked questions. Roly, still with Danny's screams in his head, tried to get their attention.

"They took the boy; they are in a dark Mercedes somewhere. Can't you put out a call or something? Roadblocks even, God I don't know but just don't sit here and ask questions." He got no support, they had a procedure to follow and that's what they did. The police were, as Trev predicted, upset that the drugs were sunk but there were sufficient traces all over Cariad's cockpit floor to provide evidence. They declared the boat as evidence, and no one was allowed back on board for several weeks until the eventual court case for Joe.

As far as Roly knew, nothing else came out of it. He found out that Danny was Jules and that some guys in London had contacted him and according to Joe these Londoners had already murdered some local criminal called Lawrence.

These Londoners and Jules were missing and not traceable, so the police proceeded to charge young Joe with boat stealing and drug handling. In the court case both Trev and Roly had to give witness testimony and Joe ended up with an eighteen-month sentence to some juvenile detention centre.

Roly was so upset, down and depressed, it seemed such a poor end and a waste and he still heard those screams. If he had known how it really ended it would have probably been worse.

As the Mercedes roared back to London, not too fast to gain attention but fast enough, Jules was pinned in the back between the thugs. They showed their irritation to the discomfort by giving him a regular elbow now and then but apart from that no one spoke. The destination was Ronnie's gang flat and there Jules was thrown into a bedroom and left. In the living room Ronnie paced up and down trying to work out what he should do. Not what he should do with Jules, that was not the issue, he now owed Hopkins one million pounds and he had no drugs! Recognising the eventuality of it he knew he had to ring in, so he dialled a number and waited.

"Hello, Mr Hopkins, sorry to bother you in the evening but I've got a problem."

"Problem, Ronnie? What problem?"

"The sea pick-up went wrong, we lost the drugs. The kid was followed by the boat owner. He was supposed to be away, but I guess he wasn't."

"Sorry, Ronnie, you say we lost the drugs. Don't you mean you lost the drugs? It has nothing to do with me."

Ronnie sighed; he knew what was coming.

"Yes, you're right. I lost the drugs."

"And the kid?"

"I got him here."

"Really, well that's for you to deal with, I hope this won't have any impact on our money agreement. You owe me two million in three months' time."

"Hey, Mr Hopkins, be reasonable. I borrowed one million for an operation that now isn't going to happen.

Two million was if I did the drug processing. Can't we strike a more reasonable settlement? You know I'm good for it, Mr Hopkins, but I might need some time. Can we discuss this in detail, say tomorrow?"

"I tell you what, the million I gave you was also for processing and distribution. I guess you don't need that now and I'm sure you have some funds of your own. How much could you pull together now, Ronnie?"

Ronnie was stumped by the question and stumbled as he tried to answer.

"I don't know, I guess I have half of it still for the operations and my money... well, I suppose I could pull together about three hundred grand."

"Get it, Ronnie. This is a hard lesson for you I know, but I did warn you."

"I can't get the whole lot by tomorrow, Mr Hopkins, that's unreasonable." As soon as he said it, he knew it had been the wrong thing to say.

"So, I'm being unreasonable, that's an interesting viewpoint," said a much colder voice. "Ronnie, tomorrow afternoon I'm sending Terry over. Get what you can." The line went dead.

Ronnie was in trouble, and he knew it. He paced the flat for a further ten minutes deep in thought before he shouted at the two guys in the room.

"Look after the kid, no beatings, no nothing. Take it in turns and I'll be back tomorrow at midday."

That's what the guys did, nothing, absolutely nothing. Jules emerged just briefly to use the toilet and to take the opportunity to drink water in the bathroom. He saw no one, he talked to no one. He waited, just waited. He even did not dare to think what he was waiting for.

Ronnie returned late morning. He looked smartly

dressed and elegant as usual, but his actions gave him away. He was close to losing it. His plan was to take what humiliation came his way, just suck it up and if he was lucky, he could slowly build back his reputation.

At one o clock the door banged. Everyone looked up and Ronnie nodded at one of his guys to go and answer it. He waited, hearing the steps of several men climbing the stairs.

"Hi there, Ronnie," said another young fellow, dressed almost like a twin to Ronnie. The same smooth-cut, tailored suit with clean, shiny shoes and the inevitable crisp shirt and silk tie, a young businessman who would not look out of place in the city. Ronnie glanced at Terry, he knew him and did not like him. A year or two younger, and everyone knew he saw Ronnie as a threat.

"Mr Hopkins asked me to pay you a visit."

All the unsaid implications of that little phrase were understood, and it so irritated Ronnie. Suck it up, Ronnie, just suck it up, he thought to himself.

"Where's the kid?" Ronnie nodded again to his guys and Jules was dragged into the room and thrown on the floor in the room.

"So, this is Al Capone, is it? Ronnie, he's a schoolkid for Christ's sake." Ronnie almost rose to angrily reply when Terry held up his hand and continued. "I'm to call Mr Hopkins." He took out his mobile and made the call. "We're all here, Mr Hopkins. What? OK," and he handed the phone to Ronnie.

"Ronnie, how much money did you pull together?"

"Mr Hopkins, I've got about seven hundred and twenty thousand in cash," said Ronnie as he tried to turn towards the wall and speak quietly to preserve some dignity. It didn't work. They all heard.

"Give it to Terry and just one last thing, Ronnie, shoot the kid."

"What? I mean, OK," said a startled Ronnie. As he looked up Terry was standing there smiling and offering a pistol in one hand. Ronnie took it and paused for a moment and then simply turned, took a step forward and shot Jules straight through the chest. The sound of the shot startled everyone, and Ronnie's guys jumped up from the sofa.

"Ronnie, Ronnie," called Mr Hopkins, his words, breaking the silence.

Ronnie put the mobile to his ear. "Yes, Mr Hopkins," he said with a flat voice.

"Ronnie, is it done?"

"It's done."

"That was a hard lesson for you, Ronnie, but in future you must remember to listen to those that give you advice. Now give the gun back to Terry and put him on. That's all for now."

Ronnie handed over the gun and mobile. "He wants to talk to you now," he said.

Terry held the phone to his ear. "Yes, Mr Hopkins?"

"Terry, shoot Ronnie please."

"Sure, no problem." Terry turned to Ronnie, smiled, and lifted his gun to shoot him point blank in his face.

"Anything else, Mr Hopkins?"

"No, Terry, that's all for now. Do pop in with the money, though, won't you."

"Of course, Mr Hopkins, I'm on my way."

He turned to the two terrified ex-Ronnie guys.

"I suggest that you two lose these bodies somewhere really good. Then take a couple of days off, come see me towards the end of the week. You know where to find me." And he turned and walked out.

***

Moving on was what Roly found difficult to do. He had support from Chrissie, Trev and Margie. Even Jamie announced he was moving down and introduced them to his new friend Derek, a waiter from Fulham. The plans and work schedule for The Water's Edge progressed but still, Roly was like half the man he was when he, Chrissie and Jamie had dreamt up the idea and purpose they shared for the future.

Chrissie and Jamie spoke almost every day; they were so concerned about Roly, and so it was decided that they would all meet up for dinner in their old bistro and somehow talk him out of his depression.

"So, come down tomorrow afternoon. I'll book the restaurant and if you text me when your train is arriving, I'll even pick you up," said Chrissie.

"Do you think I can bring Derek? Would Roly mind?" asked Jamie.

"Jamie, there is nothing you could do to upset Roly, he's been looking forward to getting to know Derek better and you can both stay in the spare bedroom; Roly and I will be in the other one. We'll try not to make a noise if you two promise also." She giggled.

"Oh, you cheeky girl," laughed Jamie. "Yes, it would be a nice break and a great chance for Derek to see the town again before we move down permanently. That's only another two weeks you know. But let's not forget, our objective is to build Roly back up, God knows he needs it. See you tomorrow, girl."

Later that day, Chrissie told Roly.

"Great, but why? He's moving down here in a few weeks." He looked again at Chrissie. "What's up? You've been planning together, haven't you?"

"Well, we wanted to do a bit of planning for The Water's Edge Promotion Day and Jamie wants us to get to know Derek better. They are a committed couple now you know. This is not just a dalliance."

"A dalliance, where did that word come from? Look, I'm thrilled for Jamie, and Derek seems just right for him. OK, let them come, let them all come, it will not distract me from my dalliance with you, my girl. Come here," he giggled and reached out. Chrissie pretended to escape his clutches but made sure she was caught.

Roly had meetings in the afternoon and by the time he got back to his flat, Chrissie, Jamie and Derek were all there. There was a family atmosphere built on respect, love and fun. It was intoxicating and Roly breathed it in deeply. Derek was much quieter than Jamie, reserved and lacking in confidence but then Jamie had enough confidence for both of them. They were a well-balanced couple of opposites held together with common values, love and respect. In a quiet moment before they left for dinner, and while Chrissie and Jamie were giggling and gossiping together in the bathroom like a pair of teenagers, Derek approached Roly.

"Roly, am I intruding? I know Chrissie, Jamie and you are so close. I would hate to intrude you know."

Roly looked at the quietly spoken man in front of him and smiled.

"Derek, you are so wrong. Chrissie, Jamie and I are not close, we are family, and every now and then, on very special occasions, families get a new member.

Welcome to the family. It is now Chrissie, Jamie, Derek and Roly."

He reached over and hugged him and smiled to himself when Derek bowed his head to avoid Roly seeing tears.

"Thank you, Roly, you have no idea how much I have dreamt of being in a family." At this there were screams and screeches of laughter from the bathroom. Derek raised his eyebrows and smiled, "Mind you this is a special kind of family," and he joined in with the laughter.

The fun and laughter were almost non-stop until after dinner as they drank the last of the wine and sipped coffee. Roly saw it coming when Chrissie nodded to Jamie and he cleared his throat to speak.

"Roly, we're here for a purpose you know."

"Aha," shouted Roly with a giggle, "I knew you two were plotting something. Out with it, out with it."

"It's not a joke, Roly, you know we love you, but Jamie and I have seen you looking down and despondent for weeks now. You really haven't recovered from that awful boat incident. I mean, you got Cariad back from the police over two weeks ago and you still haven't been back to it yet. We're worried, Roly. This should be the best time of your life; you are about to launch something really special and you're sad and hurting inside. We want to help but we don't know how and please be honest, you hate to ask for help. What is it, Roly? How can we help?"

As Chrissie finished, she and Jamie reached out over the table and grabbed his hands and a fraction later, Derek joined them.

"It's the kid, it's the kid," whispered Roly as he

desperately fought to maintain any emotional control. "I let him down. I should have done more. I just let them take him. I was frightened. I still hear his screams, he said, 'Don't let them take me.' Even in the car I heard him. 'Don't let them take me,' and I did nothing." At this, Roly's head slumped down on the table, and he sobbed, great big, shoulder-heaving sobs. There are times in your life when five minutes is over in a flash and other times, like this moment, when it seems like a lifetime in its own right. For five minutes no one spoke or moved and slowly Roly regained control.

"Yes, I know, you will tell me I'm wrong. I did all I could. You may even be right, but if that's all I could do it was not enough. I promise you three here now, that will never happen again. I may have failed Danny, or Julian or whatever his name was, but I will not fail others. You're right, time to move on, time to drive on with our vision, our purpose. I promise you that I will try to get beyond it. How can you help? Never stop supporting me, stay close, always tell me what you think. Just all be you, the most wonderful people in my life."

It was a wonderful evening but not the start of recovery for Roly. It didn't banish old horrors, but it did seem to give him a way of recognizing them.

The Water's Edge Promotion Day rushed upon them. This was the day they were to announce the venture as a charity. They were to share the vision with all the media they could attract. They had many guests; they had sponsors, the main hallway had been partially refurbished and covered with large pictures of designs trying to show how it would be when finished in about a year's time. All last-minute activities were tackled in a frenzy. Trev took control of parking, Margie set up tables, Jamie and Derek set out chairs and small tables with table lamps and Chrissie ran the corner temporary bar for refreshments. Roly ran around checking this and that, suggesting this and that, but generally was ignored by those who understood what was needed far more than him, and as confusing as it seemed, it slowly but clearly fell into place.

There was to be a celebration and speeches with a VIP list of Council members: Jeremy Gaul and other corporate sponsors and the inevitable news and media folk.

The flags were flying outside on two flagpoles; one was white with a picture of the building and around it in blue, the words Welcome to The Water's Edge. The second, designed by Chrissie, had a green cloth with a shining sun high in the sky and in the middle two hands cupped around a stick figure representation of a family – two parents and two children – and the simple words: We care.

At two o'clock that afternoon, with many people milling around, Roly rose to speak. Everyone clapped and cheered as Roly went red as he tried to calm them down.

"Now, everyone, calm down. I don't know why you are clapping you don't know what I am going to say." They laughed and as it died away, they got ready to listen. "For me, this is the most important day of my life because from today I am committed to doing all I can to help others while surrounded and supported by those I love and friends and associates who share similar values. We cannot take away all the hurt and unfairness that sometimes life throws in a random direction at people.

What we can do is give them some respite, a chance to relax and hopefully enjoy a well-earned break. It's not much but I know it is desperately needed. We don't need religions to tell us to be good and, God forbid, we don't need politicians to tell us what is needed. We know. When we see someone stumble, I think all of us want to reach over and give them a steadying hand. It is that simple and that is what we intend to do here."

Applause erupted and there were even shouts from the audience. He heard a "Bless you, Roly" and a "You are so right, Roly" but he calmed them down to speak again.

"Before the speeches end, I want to introduce to you our foundation sponsor: Mr Jeremy Gaul, Vice President of Customer Services for Coutts Bank. When we first had this idea, we needed corporate help. Jeremy and his bank were first in; they recognised the vision we had and simply shared it. We would not be here today without them. Over to you, Jeremy."

Jeremy walked to the front and shaking hands with Roly he turned and spoke to the audience.

"In the corporate world it is not uncommon to find an executive board that would like to give something back to the society in which they trade. There are many charities out there and I am sure they all intend to do what they believe to be important, but Roly is right when he says doing good must be simple and straightforward. That is why I am proud to say that Coutts Bank stands behind Roly's Purpose." At the mention of this Roly looked up, surprised, yet he looked even more surprised when Jeremy nodded across the room to encourage Jamie and Derek to enter carrying what looked like a rolled carpet on brass poles and they joined him at the front.

Jeremy continued, "As a small gesture of our ongoing support, Roly, I would like to present you with this little gift."

At this Jamie and Derek unrolled a most magnificent tapestry and leaned it against the big empty wall. The tapestry read:

The Water's Edge

Roly's Purpose

To help those who, through no fault of their own, have fallen on hard times.

"We will, of course, pay for the tapestry to be mounted on the wall. Not even Coutts Bank would expect Jamie and Derek to remain standing there for ever."

The audience laughed and looked at Roly, who simply stood there with his hands over his mouth. Eventually, he said, "Look, I'm proud of this and proud of everyone who has been involved, but let's not get carried away here. We haven't done anything yet; the first guests don't arrive for just under twelve months. So, before they come, before the hard work starts, let's just enjoy this moment. We have some little treats to be eaten and some cheap champagne and fruit juices to be drunk. All prepared by dear Jamie, Derek and that foxy woman over there called Chrissie. You must all know that when I stumble, those three pick me up. I am so very grateful and lucky to have them in my life. Now please, no more speeches just enjoy."

As the crowd moved towards the drinks, Roly grabbed Jeremy's hand and shook it.

"Jeremy, now that was a surprise. Only this morning I was in an argument with Jamie and Chrissie saying that this big, flat, empty wall needed a picture. You know they convinced me I was wrong, I am never going to trust them again. My God, I don't think I can take any more surprises."

"Well, I hope you can, Roly. I have one more." Placing his hand at Roly's back he led him towards the hotel's entrance. "Please forgive me but I took the liberty of informing someone of your plans and progress and he wished to join you this day." Roly was already walking out to the large limousine that was parked in front. As he arrived a young, able chauffeur jumped out and opening a rear door invited Roly in.

"Hello, Roland."

"Hello, Old Man," replied Roly, grasping his hand.

"Roland, Jeremy has been updating me on your progress. I do hope you do not mind this intrusion on my part."

"Of course not."

"I can see your progress now and I understand your purpose. Roly, are you a more complete and happier person than last time we met?"

"Oh yes, Old Man," smiled Roly. "This is a start, it is not the end. If we do it right, we can have these sorts of places all over the country. Hell, why just this country, people need help everywhere. Your support, your money has made this start possible, but I have also found others who I love and treasure and without them I could not have done it. I am sure you understand, you cannot be happy if you just have money and nothing else."

"Yes, I do think I understand. Have you been happy recently? I sense you have had your own crisis."

Roly leaned back and in a quiet voice told the Old Man about Danny and how he had failed him. The Old Man listened and nodded and simply let Roly finish before speaking.

"Roly, if a man helped a thousand people, would you regard him as a great man?"

"Well, yes but…" The Old Man held up his hand to stop Roly speaking. "If that same man who helped a thousand tried to help one more and failed, would he no longer be a great man? Even a failure?"

"Well, no," acknowledged Roly.

"Roly, life is a struggle and not all battles are equal. Sometimes you fall short, but the measure of a man is if he continues to struggle or gives up."

"You know that is so similar to what my closest friends said to me. They said everyone struggles to get by as best they can."

"Roly, I can see you are surrounded by wise people, keep them close. So, you are doing good and enjoying it. Now go out and do more good. The money is unimportant, it will always be there, so use it as you see fit."

The conversation was over. Roly stepped out of the car and waved as it moved away. As he headed back into the hotel all he could think of was what remarkable people he had by his side and that was all he needed.

Chapter 21

Roly Has Changed

The following few weeks passed in a blur of activity. All those around Roly were so pleased to see him back to normal. He was engaged in everything, his focus and energy were back. The Promotion Day had been an outstanding success and with such prestigious sponsors the media made it national news. Everyone wanted to interview Roly and so he was not surprised when he got a call from Gareth Morgan asking for a chat. They had not been in touch since the disgrace of Councillor Mansfield, and Roly was happy to meet him again. They met in the same town pub as before.

"This time, Mr Morgan, I hope you will allow me to buy the drinks."

"Indeed, Mr Johns, that would be a pleasure."

Roly returned with the drinks, and they sat down, still smiling.

"So, what is Councillor Mansfield up to these days?" asked Roly.

"Oh, he is a very busy man."

"Really, that's not what I expected."

"Oh, he is very busy. Unfortunately for him, not on building work; the police are going through each and every business file examining them for corruption. He has no building work to do; even those projects underway, if they are council work, they have been suspended. The only bad thing is that he has been laying off staff."

"Those guys will get other jobs I'm sure, apart from that it couldn't happen to a nicer guy," said Roly smugly.

"Roly, I didn't come to talk to you about Mansfield or even The Water's Edge. It was something else."

There was a pause in the conversation and Roly realised that whatever Gareth wanted to say it was going to be a difficult topic.

"They found the boy, they found Julian. I mean, they found his body."

He let that sink in before continuing. "I have been contacted by a colleague in London. A few days ago, two bodies were found in a drainage ditch somewhere in Suffolk. They were able to identify a man as a London criminal and they believe the younger boy is Julian or Danny as you knew him. It is going to hit the headlines tomorrow; my colleague wanted me to provide some local background information. I just didn't want this to be a shock for you."

"How did they identify the man?"

"His girlfriend had reported him missing and he had a criminal record so they could trace his DNA. The boy is just an unknown, but they believe that he will be identified by his dental records."

Roly was almost in another world as he whispered, "His poor mother, she must be going nuts. Who was this other guy?"

"Oh, they know all about him. His criminal record was for adolescent stuff, but my contact tells me that he has been on the police radar for years. He is or was a lieutenant for some big criminal. Things go on but the police have never been able to prove anything against the big guy or his troops. I use that word specifically,

Roly, because that is organised crime. It's like an underground army with a hierarchy and orders flow down, things happen but it is so difficult to track anything from outside."

Roly found it hard to take it all in and as he sat there, he heard inside his head Danny shouting again, don't let them take me, don't let them take me.

"Gareth, keep me informed of developments please."

"Roly, I know so little. This is all happening up in London."

"Yeah, of course, look I need to be getting on. Nice to see you, Gareth, stay in touch."

Roly stood up and drained his glass and with a nod left and walked outside in need of some fresh air. He breathed in heavily as he walked in no particular direction and then his anger started to grow.

"It's not right, it's not right," he muttered as he walked.

Just as Gareth had predicted, the next day it was both national and local news. 'Local boy working with London gangsters found dead' was the main headline of the local newspaper and in the report, it was mentioned yet again that the boy Julian had tried to steal Roly's boat for drug smuggling. Added to this, the local television news channel had footage of Cariad at the marina and Roly simply felt that there was no escape from it. However, this time, Roly did not try to escape it all. He simply withdrew into himself and brooded.

"Are you alright, Roly?" asked Chrissie.

"How's things, young man?" asked Trev.

"Roly, can I help?" asked Jamie.

It seemed to Roly that everyone just wanted to question him. He could not recognise the concern in the voices from those that loved him.

Two days later in his flat, on his own in the early evening, he called Gareth.

"Gareth, this colleague of yours in London, yes, the one that was researching all that stuff about organised crime, do you think he would be willing to meet with me?"

"Roly, he would love to but understand all he wants is a story and if he could link in someone like you it would add stars to his report."

"Why for God's sake, this has nothing to do with me?"

"You don't even recognise it; you are becoming a person of national interest in your own right. You save a member of the Saudi royal family, get shot in the process, leave London for Cranport, set up a new charity with the Queen's bank and get your boat stolen by a kid who ends up murdered by the London underworld. Yeah, your story is of no interest to anyone."

"I just want to try and understand it all."

Roly's voice and body slumped. Gareth tried to pick him up.

"OK, this is what we do. Let me talk to this guy and set up a meeting. I will tell him that you will provide some local information in return for him outlining the criminal world the kid got himself involved with. I will ask him to respect the fact that you just knew this kid under the alias of Danny and that you had had an almost brotherly relationship on your boat and that you have been shattered by the reality."

"Tell him that because that is exactly what the situation is like. Gareth, set it up and any time you like. I need to do this. Call me when you have something."

Two days later, Roly and Gareth were driving up to London to see the journalist. As they drove in silence, Roly was thinking, this was the motorway the Mercedes must have driven on.

Roly had not got away without concern. When he announced to Chrissie, Jamie and Kate that he was going to London for a few days and that they had to hold the fort and pick up all his commitments, he had to explain. His explanation was received with an initial shocked silence. To a person, they were not happy. Kate talked about commitment to the plan being more important. Chrissie said that Roly must look forward not backwards. Jamie said he was frightened of Roly getting involved with bad people. Roly listened to no one, he said he was going, and he went.

***

Gareth and Roly arrived in London and booked into a small hotel just up from Great Portland Street. That evening, Roly made vague excuses to Gareth of meeting up with some old friends and left to walk the streets alone. He was in no mood for taking in the sights of the capital or carousing in a pub or even fine dining in a restaurant. Roly knew he had to get his head straight and the inside voice started again to ask the questions.

What do I want? What am I trying to achieve? Why am I here? What difference do I possibly think I could make?

As the questions came so did the anger rise but anger added to frustration is a potion that leads to misery. That stayed with him throughout his walk and only lifted when he turned the last corner into the street where his hotel was. On the corner was a local pub. Outside, on this fair evening, were small groups of young people. As he approached, he heard small talk, he heard people laugh and jest and it reminded him of Jamie and Chrissie. He could not help but smile as he entered the hotel and headed to his room and an early night.

The following morning, Gareth and Roly met with the journalist at the newspaper offices. They met in a small conference room off a short corridor that led to a large open office area. The hustle and bustle were simply continuous as everyone seemed to be on the move with a purpose, moving from one place to another to briefly chat before heading off in a new direction. It was impressive and Roly stared for a brief time before being ushered into the conference room.

Before Gareth could do an introduction, the journalist reached over to shake Roly's hand.

"Mr Johns, welcome. I am so pleased to meet the national hero who fought off the terrorists. Glad you could come; Gareth says that you can help me with my project."

In the seconds it had taken for this to be said, Roly recognised that the journalist was purely interested in his own agenda. It was a slight compliment followed by a straight jump into his topic; Roly knew that his welcome was not open but dependent on his ability to provide information. The false bonhomie and speedy enthusiasm were difficult to accept so he did not and replied,

"I'm sorry, your name is?"

The journalist looked puzzled and looked at Gareth. "Mr Johns, I am Mike Stevens," and turning to Gareth, "I thought you had explained everything?"

Gareth was on top form and smiled.

"Yes, I did, Mike, to both of you. Roly, Mike wants some input on the boy and in return, Mike, you are going to explain to Roly what you know about this underworld that the kid got caught up in. So, why don't we just sit down and start again?"

They did just that. Sitting around the table Roly was questioned by Stevens about Julian or rather Danny as Roly found himself incapable of calling him by any other name. At first, the questions came fast and furious and focussed on the boat episode and the drugs pickup but as the questions ranged wider Roly simply could not answer. Local crime, family situation, past adolescent misdemeanours, the link into London, the murder of Lawrence... all these questions were received by a simple shake of the head from Roly.

Just as Stevens seemed to be realising that there was no more information to come his way, Gareth intervened.

"So, you see, Mike, Roly knew the kid simply as Danny, a kid who loved boats and particularly Roly's boat; now we know why. OK, time to change things around. Roly, you have questions and hopefully Mike, you have some answers."

Roly paused as he tried to work out what questions he had and then in a softly spoken voice he said, "Mr Stevens..."

"Call me Mike, please."

"Of course, and you call me Roly."

Again, a pause as they all recognised Roly's awkwardness and the fact that he had already been referred to as Roly for the last half hour.

"I'm sorry; I'm not normally this obtuse. I just can't seem to get my head around all this. To me Danny was a good kid and as time passed, he became almost like a younger brother. I must accept that he was just playing me. He obviously always knew what his objective was, but why?"

"Roly, your description of the amount of cocaine he was trying to smuggle in is estimated to have a street value by the police of over one and a half million pounds. That is some sort of motivation to a kid who finds himself stuck in a small town with nowhere to go."

"But he would not have got that sort of money if he was dealing with these characters in London, surely?"

"You are right there, the way it tends to work is that someone has an idea and takes it to the top guy not only for approval, although that is important, but also for funding. The criminal economy is just like ours, no different, there are worker bees and there are King bees – sorry for mixing up my metaphor but rarely are there Queen bees in the Underworld. Anyway, these Kings or gang heads control areas or types of crime – often both. You need their blessing to do your crimes and they will want their cut. If you need it, they will provide you with funding but again they will want payback and the rates are slightly higher than the banks in the high street. You don't pay taxes but if you fail to pay back their cut these crime bosses have you pay in other ways. That seems to be what has happened here. The drug smuggling failed so there was no street value to be gained. Failure can often be fatal."

Mike stopped to see if Roly was taking it all in. Roly was and he engaged in the conversation with more energy.

"But how do these crime heads get to be in such control? Don't others fight them or reject their demands?"

"Yes, it happens but let's go back to what I said earlier, this is an economy just like ours but with slightly different rules. When crime bosses fight each other, it is expensive, high costs and nothing coming in. Everyone prefers a quieter life. As long as the demands are not too high, criminals accept it and regard it as a cost of business – just like taxes. Now, over time the more successful build up a reputation of success and one of two things happen; either they become adopted by the current head as some sort of successor or they are allowed to branch out on their own. In this case, the younger guy who was found with your boy Danny seems to have been a prospective future boss of a current crime head called Hopkins. Obviously, something went wrong."

After a slight pause Roly said, "Hopkins, he's a crime boss? We know his name, we know what he does, how come we don't do something about it?"

"Roly, everything I have told you I sincerely believe to be absolutely true but not one single fact backs this up. Courts will not pass judgement on supposition, which by the way is a good thing."

"So, these people hide up somewhere and run a criminal business that takes in the weak, preys on the weak, play by their own rules…"

"Hide? Hell, no," Mike interrupted. "They don't hide. Some of them are local celebrities surrounded by sycophants from our world who regard them as people of stature. Danger is very attractive if it doesn't come too close. Hopkins runs the northeast side of London from a pub. I could take you there now and you would see people in the pub nodding to him, smiling at him, standing up to shake his hand if he comes close. Sure, as hell, he is not hiding."

"Take me there. I want to see it."

Roly's comment hung in the air and Mike leaned back in his chair and looked across at Gareth.

"Roly, this isn't a game. I told you, these people hurt people. Especially if they think that you are some sort of threat to them. They are not some sort of tourist attraction."

"Mike, I know that I do understand but as you said it is a pub. Why don't I take you to lunch for something to eat and a few drinks?"

Mike rolled his eyes and breathed hard before responding, "When I write a report, I keep it vague not because I don't want people to know detail but because I don't want the characters in my report to know I have information. That way I get something out there without it threatening me and my family. This is not a game."

"Fair enough, I understand. You take me to lunch, but you set up the rules. All I want to do is understand where and how it all works."

"Look, no one might be there. They are not standing around doing nothing waiting for tourists to visit."

Mike looked across the table and saw Roly leaning forwards with a little smile on his face.

"OK, we go out for lunch. We do just that, lunch and small talk between us three. You are coming, Gareth, aren't you?"

"Hell, yes. Mind, if they spot us," he said laughing, "I'm on the first train back to nowhere and out of this corrupt Metropolis."

"OK, small talk between us. No attention-seeking activities just lunch which, by the way, Roly, you are paying for. Let me pick up my coat and we'll go by taxi."

Fifteen minutes later and the taxi was pulling up outside the pub. During the taxi ride Roly had tried to ask more questions but had been shut down quickly by Mike. It was clear there were going to be no open conversations in front of the driver.

They entered the pub and glanced around for a place to sit. It was quite empty and it was easy for Mike to guide them towards a corner table. Mike sat down with his back to the pub regulars, allowing Gareth and Roly to sit facing him but looking over his shoulders to take in all the pub activities.

"Just get me a pint of lager and some sort of sandwich, this is not a cordon bleu establishment," sneered Mike as he seemed to shrink lower in his chair.

"Same for me," said an animated Gareth who could not stop himself from continually peering around the bar.

Roly returned with a selection of sandwiches, crisps of various flavours and the inevitable three pints of frothy lager. They sat hunched around the table in a conversation of whispered comments.

Mike had explained that the work meetings were held in rooms down the passageway and that an uninvited visit would gain uninvited attention. Soon the conversation started to dry up and it was clear that no new information or understanding from this visit was going to come Roly's way. Yet, as they finished their crisps and passed some half-eaten sandwiches to the side and prepared to drain their glasses, it happened.

The atmosphere in the room changed. It did not get colder, the lights did not dim, the conversations did not stop, but Roly noticed it all. Coming down the passageway was Hopkins. He conversed with another old colleague with two younger men walking behind with purpose. In front, another young man walked ready to open doors or fend off unwelcome attention. It was almost a caricature of the local gang boss from an old film, and it was this ridiculousness that just struck Roly. It caused a nervous smile, a stare and then to the horror of both Mike and Gareth, Roly stood up.

The front guy had already passed to open the outer doors but Hopkins, his associate and the two young toughs, saw it and they all stopped.

Roly continued his stare and slowly smiled. "How do?"

Hopkins looked and after a short pause simply nodded and as Roly sat back down continued on his way out through the doors.

"Are you mad?" came an almost whispered shriek from Mike as Gareth fought to regain control of both the size of his eyeballs and the height of his eyebrows.

"Let's get out of here." Mike grabbed his coat off the back of his chair and tried to usher out a stunned Gareth and an exceptionally calm Roly. It was to get worse as they exited the pub. There by the kerbside stood Hopkins, still talking to his older associate while one man held open a car door and another sat in the driver's seat.

Again, Roly stopped and stared. Mid-conversation Hopkins also stopped and gazed back at him. He signalled to one of his men to accompany him as he made his way toward the stranger.

"Do I know you?" asked Hopkins.

"No, but I know of you, Hopkins."

"What is this? Who the fuck are you?"

Roly ignored his questions and said, "You, Hopkins, are simply an evil bully. You support the criminals and the thugs as long as they work for you. You frighten and take advantage of the poor and timid. You set yourself up like an evil dictator and everyone bows down to you because you have enough money to buy young muscle and you are ruthless enough to use it."

"Impressive analysis, perhaps I ought to use this; what did you call it, ruthless young muscle, to rip out your tongue?"

The young man almost stepped forward before being stopped by Roly simply holding up his hand.

"You see, Hopkins, if you come across someone who has more money than you, a better ability to buy power and force than you and someone who is happy to be just as damn well destructive as you, but only against the bad guys, well then you become reduced to just some old bastard who deserves all he gets."

"Perhaps I should spend some time thinking about what you deserve to get. I'm afraid I missed your name?"

As Hopkins was speaking Mike and Gareth were glancing around the streets and then Gareth saw what they needed, not a taxi but a police car, and he ran out to wave it down just as the young bodyguard had regained enough composure to realise that he should do something. As the police car arrived with a screech, Roly's arm had been grabbed and he was trying to avoid being pulled to the floor.

"Stop that, stop that," said the policeman. "What is this all about?"

As the policeman spoke, Hopkins had started to walk to his car only to be met by the second policeman who escorted him back.

"Anyone here going to answer my question?"

repeated the policeman.

It was Hopkins who took control.

"Just a misunderstanding, officer, a mistaken identity. This man thought I was someone else. Nothing to concern yourselves, officers, and all over now."

"And who are you?"

Hopkins smiled, "Just an old, retired businessman out for lunch with some old friends. Hopkins is my name," and then pointing at Roly, he continued, "but I have no idea who this fellow is?"

"Who are you then?" repeated the policeman, completely unaware that he was carrying out Hopkins' request.

Roly looked at Hopkins as he spoke to the policeman, all done in a calm voice and a simple smile. "My name is Roland Johns and…"

Gareth cut in, "Yes, officer, and we are out of town and lost. We would be ever so grateful if you could escort us away from here to somewhere where we could get our bearings back."

The obvious request for help was received and understood by the two officers, who now looked more seriously at Hopkins, who merely returned their gaze and smiled.

"Well, officers, thank you for your support and I'm so pleased that any confusion has been resolved. I'll be on my way." And as he turned, he spoke to Roly. "And, Mr Johns, if we ever bump into each other again, and these things do happen, at least we will have the benefit of knowing who we are after this introduction."

The police officers shrugged and then herded the three men into the back of the police car and then drove off.

Just minutes later, they were dropped off at an underground station with a gentle warning not to get involved in any more pavement altercations. Mike was the first to speak and he spoke with no hint of friendship.

"You are one crazy bastard, Roly, remind me never to go socializing with you again." He then stepped into the tube station and disappeared. It was now Gareth's turn to speak.

"Why did you do this, Roly? What can you possibly hope to achieve? He now knows who you are; you might not be afraid, but I am and everyone who is close to you should also be afraid. This guy is a monster."

"I know what I want to achieve. I'm going to take this evil man down but right now we need…" – and as Gareth's eyebrows danced again at the use of the word, we, Roly corrected himself – "I mean, what I now need, is to get back and prepare for my campaign."

They hailed a taxi and headed back to the hotel to pick up the car and drive home.

Deep in thought, Roly realised what he had to do although no idea of how to do it, but the comfort was in realising he had changed.

Chapter 22

The Campaign

That evening as they had arrived in Cranport, Roly knew that his first stop after dropping off Gareth was across to Chrissie's home. He had been welcomed as a member of the family in that, after a few hugs and kisses, family members had reverted back to whatever activity they had been doing prior to his arrival.

All that is except Chrissie, her concern for Roly was clear and her relief at his safe return equally obvious. He grabbed her hand and led her into the back room. There he explained his encounter with Hopkins. Chrissie listened without interruption excepting the occasional "Ooh" or "Ah" and a "you didn't" or a "he never". Roly had already learnt that for Chrissie that was as close to silent as she ever was. As his trip report came to a close, he spoke of his clear objective.

"Chrissie, he is an evil person feeding on the weak and vulnerable. There may be many like Hopkins around but this one has impacted me, and I am going to get him. I do not know how or when, but the campaign starts now."

"Roly, this would not be a fair fight. He may well be willing to do things to you that you would not do to him and if you did do the same things to him, it would change you. You would become a bigger him. Why risk everything you have here? Can't you just move on? Put it behind you."

That thought from Chrissie hit home and he pensively

leaned back and sank into the sofa. He had initially thought that he would hire some bigger and stronger security guys that could more than match Hopkins' goons. Could he ask his men to shoot, club and maim like Hopkins would? No, it would have to be a different way – but which way?

When he looked back at it many months or even years later Roly would always remember this moment. As he lay there struggling with how to launch a campaign against Hopkins without becoming a Hopkins, suddenly there was a scream of delight and a whoop of happiness from the other room. Obviously from Margie, but still strange enough for both Chrissie and Roly to look at each other puzzled before rising and walking into the family room.

"They got him, they got that nasty little bastard," said Margie as she skipped around the room.

"They got who?" queried Roly.

"Chrissie, you remember," continued Margie, "just a few days ago someone mugged that old woman from just a few streets away." Margie looked at Roly. "Roly, she is eighty-two years old, and she was heading back from the Post Office with her pension when this thug knocked her to the ground and mugged her. He hit her in the face and the pictures, oh the pictures of this beautiful old woman's face all swollen, blue, and purple. All she could remember was being hit and as she fell down a hand grabbed her bag. She told them on the local television she had no idea what he looked like but that he had a tattoo of a flying bird on his right hand between the thumb and first finger. Well, there was nothing from the police until a local girl started some sort of website asking for people to name locals who had such tattoos on their hands. Thousands of people locally, thousands locally" – Margie repeated in her excitement – "came forward with names. Many names the same but all passed to the police. Within twenty-four hours they had interviewed many of them and the news programme has just said that a Cranport youth with a history of drugs and thievery had been arrested and admitted the mugging. Wait, wait," said Margie interrupting only herself, "listen to the news summary."

They all remained silent as the news reader of the local channel summarised the major headlines.

"And finally, thanks to the focus of Cara and the website and the support from so many thousands of local people, today a thug is behind bars where he belongs. I will let the Police Chief Superintendent have the last word."

The television picture broke to a smiling policeman giving a press break.

"We could never have moved on this terrible crime so quickly without Cara and, more importantly, all the people that responded to her website. It just goes to show," and with this he raised a clenched fist in the air and matched it with a bigger grin before closing with, "Power to the people."

"My God, that's it, that's it," said Roly. He kissed Margie, hugged and kissed Chrissie and then shouted out a loud, "Goodnight, everyone," and he was out into his car and heading home.

In the morning, before Roly had even had time to think further, he received another call from Gareth.

"Roly, I'm sorry, have you seen any newspapers yet?"

"Not yet, Gareth, kettle is only just filled for coffee.

Why, what's up?"

"It's The Independent Times. It's about Mike Stevens. I'm sorry."

"Sorry for what, Gareth?"

"I guess he needed a story, and you gave it to him. He has a frontpage article headlined: 'Police intervention stops Gangster challenge from Terrorist hero'."

"Read it to me, Gareth."

"'Yesterday afternoon your correspondent accompanied Roland Johns as he insisted on visiting a location in Northeast London that he believed to be the base for criminal activities.'"

"Wait a minute, I believed it because he told me it was."

"There is more. 'Mr Johns, with no facts or figures, challenged a Mr Hopkins and his colleagues on the pavement outside a local hostelry and it was only the fortunate passing of local police that stopped there being a physical confrontation. Afterwards, Mr Hopkins stated that he had no idea why he was so rudely challenged and he was only there for a regular monthly meeting with his old retired friends. Mr Johns was unavailable to comment.'"

"Yes, unavailable because the bastard did not even try to get in touch. What I do not understand is why he portrays Hopkins as the good guy and me some sort of psychopath; whose side is he on?"

"No side, he is simply a commentator. Whatever provides newspaper lines is what he is after. God, sometimes I hate my profession."

That heartfelt complaint from Gareth hit home with Roly and he rose to the occasion.

"Gareth, you are a better man than him and let me

explain to you why. Not before my coffee, though. How about over lunch? What do you say, same pub, same drink, but different sandwich?"

"What time?"

"How about 1pm?"

"Done and again, Roly, I'm sorry."

All that morning Roly focussed on what was becoming an even clearer understanding of what his campaign was to be. He had contacted Kate, Chrissie and Jamie to announce that he was back, but he needed just one day at home to get organised before he would be back to normal. He was not sure that was an accurate description but it was what they all wanted to hear and so it protected him from further interruptions. By the time he entered the town pub and saw Gareth already there, he knew all the various points he would be making.

"An offer of a free pint and you're here early. Gareth, have you been waiting long?" said Roly holding out his hand in friendship.

"Just arrived and bought the pints. I reckon if I had taken another free drink from you, it would question my integrity but not enough to make me buy the sandwiches, which you can get at the second round."

All said and received in good humour, they both sat down and took a drink.

"About Stevens," Roly said.

"Yes, I'm so sorry about that but…"

Roly interrupted, "Listen, Gareth, forget it. It has nothing to do with what I need to discuss with you. The only good thing about Stevens is that it shows us how not to proceed."

Gareth looked confused. He took another drink as

Roly continued.

"You see, I am still convinced that we can get Hopkins and people like him. The police are struggling, the free press is struggling and if we use the same methods that he uses we become like him. So, think for a moment, why does he succeed? It is because all he does is done in the darkness. All threats and agreements are in the shadows where no one can question him. Did you see the local news last night?"

This quick, unexpected question surprised Gareth and he hesitated to answer.

"What about the news?"

"That story about the eighty-two-year-old woman and the mugger."

"Oh yeah, that was a good ending, wasn't it?"

"Did you see that police officer on the news?"

"Well yeah, so what?"

"That's the way we are going to break Hopkins and if it really flies, many others."

"Roly, are you sure this is your first drink of the day? What the hell does an eighty-two-year-old woman being mugged have to do with Hopkins?"

"Everything, Gareth, everything. Just listen and I'll explain. The policeman said that without the support of the people via that website it would have taken so much longer to solve the crime. He even went on to jest with a Power to the People chant. Now what if we create a website, call it peoplepower.com or something, and it has just one purpose. That is, it is a means for the public to share information about crime in their area. This information would be gathered by our professional journalists and presented back publicly for all to see. It would not challenge the law; it would not break the law or libel individuals. Innocent until proven guilty must be a premise we live by but if multiple sources all share similar information, we make it public and invite the authorities to take it forward. What do you think? You see if we do this right, we deny people like the Hopkins the value of the murky shadows. We bring in sunlight and openness. This light will, I believe, be like a disinfectant to organised crime. So, what do you think?"

"Well, it is certainly new; it is what the newspapers were supposed to be when they were first created but times are different now. Perhaps this is something we need, to provide not only that focus but to gain the support from the public. But, Roly, something like this if you start small would have little impact. If you start bigger, say national, then the organisation of it is enormous. It would take quite some time and how do you fund it? The costs would be... the people skills to organise would be..." Here Gareth paused as he started to come to terms with the vision that he was now grasping.

Roly quickly interrupted, "You organise it, set it up as it needs to be, I will fund it and together we'll launch it. What do you think?"

"Are you mad, I have a full-time job. Just because I agree to meet you on occasion for a lunchtime pint does not alter the fact that I am very busy. I couldn't take this on; this is a full-time job itself."

"I agree."

When Roly said no more but simply sat and smiled, Gareth realised what he was saying.

"Wait a minute, you want me to give up my job, forget about my pension and start something new that is going to threaten all the bad people in this country."

"Yes."

Roly offered no more comment and allowed the pause to reinforce his point to Gareth.

"Oh, this is just mad. We would have to hire staff, keep things private to stop individuals being approached by those threatened. We would have to establish a national programme but ensure it was tackling local issues if we want the public to identify with it. All input would have to be anonymous, or the public would not participate. We would have to ensure that everything was legal and above board. A lot of the input would be gossip and we have to be able to recognise that and not react. The police need to see us as on their side not against them. The free press would inevitably see us as a threat and so we need to bring them online. The quality of staff is critical, if we do a bad job the public would never forgive us. We would…"

As Gareth paused to allow his brain to catch up with his words, Roly took advantage. "Yes, we would," he said and smiled. Roly reached over and hugged him. He had never doubted that Gareth was the right man for this job, his passion, his belief, and integrity made Roly realise that he was about to add Gareth to his team of very special individuals. Gareth would fit right in with the others.

Gareth was coming to terms with it all. "OK, this is it. If you get me a beef and onion sandwich with the next pint, I'm all yours," and he laughed out loud at the ridiculousness of the situation.

***

That day was the start of Roly's two-pronged drive. The

Water's Edge was not to be ignored or forgotten; it was always to be there to give rest and support to the needy, but this new initiative was to engage the people in a fight back against the bullies and thieves who wanted to profit from them by keeping a shining light on their devious activities. It would take time; it could not be launched overnight, but that day Gareth and Roly made a start on the campaign.

Chapter 23

The Fight Back

Never had Roly started an initiative with such energy and drive. Never was he so convinced that what they were doing was what was needed. Never was he so wrong.

Roly was pleased that his gang bought in with an equal enthusiasm. They were more than willing to keep The Water's Edge initiative rolling forward almost under its own momentum while accepting Gareth into the team and launching this new idea, which took a lot of energy and drive.

First, they needed a website name and so many were already taken. No "Power to the People", which was first choice, no "Let the People Speak", second choice. Many an evening was spent with the gang bouncing back and forth ideas until they ended up with TTSO.com for "Time to Shout Out", but they were equally thrilled with Jamie's alternative definition of the acronym meaning: "Turn That Shit Off".

The website had to be set up so that it protected anonymous input from the public. It had to be set up so that it could tackle local and national issues and so it was organised around postcodes, city and town names and regions.

Likewise, Gareth was hiring people on a regional level. A mixture of old journalists, some retired, and young enthusiasts wanting to get into something new.

Everything that people submitted, if deemed possible

content, had to be examined and backed up by fact. They were going to be relying on the general goodness of people. If they saw or knew of things that were wrong, then they would be encouraged to send it in with as many facts and pictures as possible.

Anyone could access this information and when they provided a postcode it allowed the website to cascade information down in a meaningful way. It was organised so that on the first screen you saw all that was happening in your area, then your town or city then your region and finally nationally.

Two months into the campaign and, after a review by the full team, Roly felt positive. The website looked good, and it clearly outlined both purpose and rules for all to understand. Of course, pre-launch it was empty, so Roly and Gareth committed to launch it and went on both local and national television and newspapers to inform the public of this brave new world they were introducing.

It was at this point that things started to go unexpectedly badly. The police objected strongly. They regarded it as a direct threat to themselves. They claimed it would encourage vigilantism. Equally, the newspapers regarded TTSO as a threat. As Gareth had pointed out in the first place, the newspapers thought this was their role. The television news programmes invited them in to speak, not because they supported them, but because it simply offered a good story. It seemed to culminate in an evening national news programme where Roly and Gareth debated with their police and newspaper critics.

"Yes, I am concerned," said an invited senior policeman. "Where is the control? Do we simply accuse people and publicly shame them? Some crimes are of high emotion; if I call someone a paedophile for walking through a park and smiling at the playing children, do you think that person is not going to be regarded as guilty until proven innocent? If that person is under threat, will he look to the police for safety or TTSO?"

"Exactly," sneered a newspaper editor. "TTSO is encouraging the people of this country to be gossips. We all know how some people like to spread nasty innuendoes about their neighbours, but do we really want to turn this into a national pastime?"

With a large sigh and a quiet voice, Roly tried to respond. "Have either of you two even bothered to read our rules on the TTSO website? This is ridiculous; we are not looking for neighbourly gossip. We do not publish every input that we receive. This is a professional set-up. Everything that we receive is available to the police. Everything that we publish has been scrutinised for fact and relevance by a staff of professional journalists. We operate at the highest standard."

Gareth intervened. "We certainly would not publish unsubstantiated gossip. Let's consider the source and accuracy of all the gossip diaries in today's newspapers." Leaning forward angrily he pointed at the editor, "My God, man, you are such a hypocrite!"

"Innocent news, we are not claiming people are criminals."

"Exactly," the policeman responded. "That is the role of a police force. We collect facts through an organised procedure and present them to the Criminal Prosecution Service for their consideration. They then take it through the justice system. It has worked well for hundreds of years and now is not the time to shortchange it."

"All we do is to give you a better access to input. We don't want to do your job, we want to help you do your job."

"Frankly, Mr Johns, you think too highly of yourself. We haven't asked for your help, and we do not want it."

That is how the programme ended and to say that Roly and Gareth were miserable and down as they travelled back to Cranport would be a complete understatement.

"So, what do we do now?" asked Gareth.

"We continue and launch. There is no way we are ever going to convince them that we are right. We start and let the public decide if TTSO is of value to them."

They launched later that week and so began their campaign and the public decided. The world did not change, criminal society did not fall apart, but some people did slowly start to use the system. One month after the launch, Roly and Gareth sat down to review what progress had been made. It was a miserable meeting; they had a garage that was fixing the mileage of second-hand cars, they had pictures of dogs crapping in public places with the owner not picking up, they had pictures of home extensions without planning permission.

"They were right," sighed Roly, "it is just a small step above gossip."

"People are just trying it out; it is too early for them to have built up trust yet with anything more substantial," suggested Gareth.

"So how do we gain their trust?"

"I'm sorry, Roly, I don't know. I just don't know."

"What about all your regional staff. What do they say?"

"Frankly, Roly, they are more dejected than us. The young ones saw this as a chance to get into a high-energy new era and the older ones saw it as a chance to truly bring about change, but now…" Gareth paused and let his words sink in.

"So, what do we do now?"

"Staff are leaving or thinking of leaving. If, or perhaps when they do, it will sort itself out. We cannot hire anyone of any true journalistic skill, so if we cannot review input we cannot publish, and viewer access will decline. It's like a dried-up pot plant. Each day the leaves will get browner until they drop off."

"Fuck it, let's go for a drink," was the only positive suggestion that Roly could make.

That evening, Roly updated Jamie and Chrissie. The website performance was not a secret to anyone but still they were concerned that Roly was so down. Unable to offer any solution to his problem they tried to lift his spirits.

"You tried, Roly. So many people just don't try," said Chrissie as she hugged his shoulders.

Jamie added. "Chrissie's right, Roly, there is no shame in trying to do good even if it does fail. Anyway, why don't you come to London with me tomorrow? You know I am going to a school reunion. I was going to take Derek, but he doesn't want to come. He feels out of place with all my public-school friends. I don't know why because he is better than all of them, but he feels a bit self-conscious. You wouldn't though, Roly, would you?"

"Yes, Roly," Chrissie jumped in. "Go and have some fun. You need a break; it has been a long time since you have just gone out with no other objective than to have fun."

Jamie and Chrissie looked at him with smiles on their faces and waited for a response.

"Will Jeremy be there?"

"Possibly, if he can get away from work."

"OK then, but remember if there is music, I am not dancing with you. If you dance, you are on your own."

Chrissie and Jamie laughed out loud and both hugged Roly as he quietly smiled. As Jamie started to leave, he whispered loudly to Chrissie to ensure Roly also heard, "Give him a few drinks and he will dance. I'll take some pictures for you so you can see an old man dancing." They giggled together as she walked to the door with him.

So, the next day they both travelled to London on the train and booked into a small hotel in West London where the reunion was scheduled. Roly's spirits were lifted somewhat, and he committed to have fun and to ignore the small ache that seemed to be held deep inside his chest.

It was certainly a night to remember. There were about fifty to sixty people there and half of them were guests of the old school students. Jeremy did not make it and sent his apologies to Jamie, while Roly was slightly concerned that Jamie might be surrounded by people who had bullied him in school. However, Jamie gave him a running commentary on each person they met; it was clear that at least four or five old students were fond of Jamie. Roly had to keep denying that he was not Jamie's partner, just a close friend, and he was conscious of the growing smiles and giggles from Jamie as the question came up each time. They all drank a lot and ate a little so within a relatively short amount of time they all started to feel it. Slowly but surely the large party split into smaller groups of close friends. They were sitting in a corner with two of Jamie's ex-schoolfriends and their partners. While Jamie chatted and giggled with the wives and girlfriends, Roly was questioned by the others. He had to explain how he met Jamie and his introduction by Jeremy who was his banker but the whole conversation seemed to head towards one simple foundation question.

"So, what do you do, Roly?" asked Ivor, an ex-military man who was now entering the city after a brief regimental officer career.

"Oh, at the moment I'm trying to set up a charity holiday hotel thing on the coast to help those people who have major problems. It's just something to give them a break and a helping hand."

"Roly, you always undersell yourself; let me tell Ivor what you do," interjected Jamie who had broken off his chat with the women. The drinks were having an effect on everyone. "The thing that always frustrates me," he mumbled "Roly here is such a special person, but he always plays it down. Can I tell them my view, Roly?"

Everyone looked at Roly, and he just shrugged, leaned back and waved Jamie on. All eyes turned on him and Jamie sat up straight and started with his version of the truth in a manner that suggested it had been in his mind and heart for some time.

"First, Roly is a hero. Remember that attempt by terrorists to kidnap that little Arabian boy. A royal prince he was, and Roly saved him getting shot in the process. Then his evil little witch of a wife who had left him tried to come back for a reward and he fended her off. Next, he has bought an old property on a harbour in Cranport, Dorset, and he is turning it into a wonderful, holiday hotel free to those who as he says it 'through no fault of their own deserve a free holiday'. Now if that was all, he would be a hero in anyone's book but no, he has tried to do more. A young kid in the town got in with some bad people in London and tried to use Roly's boat to bring in drugs. Roly stopped him and brought him back only to be held up by the baddies in the marina and the kid was kidnapped. He was found later murdered. My God, you would have thought that was enough, but no. Roly started up a website TTSO – 'Time To Shout Out' or Turn That Shit Off as I called it."

They all giggled but quickly leaned forward to hear more.

"Yes, I read about that," said someone, "how is it going?"

"Well," continued Jamie, "that's it, it isn't. Roly set it up when he found out that the person who was involved in the drugs thing and the killing of the boy was a big gangster in London. This person organises everything through his gang, but the police cannot touch him."

Up until this time, Roly had just been quiet but now he wanted to speak.

"You see, that's the problem. This guy goes through life untouched. The idea of the website was to let people anonymously tell of all these bad things that were going on but all we got were neighbours publishing photos of other neighbours allowing their dogs to shit on the pavements or those that parked in disability spaces in supermarket car parks. It just fell apart. That gangster is still untouched and in his hometown, he is even thought of highly, a socialite. No one knows and perhaps they don't even care."

Roly slumped back with a big sigh.

"Who is he?" asked Ivor. "Do you know his name and where he lives?"

"I won't share his name with you, but I know it. He lives in Thurley Street, Basildon. A big, affluent, white house and each morning he travels into Northeast London to carry out his dealings in a pub."

"Well, do you have any evidence? What are the police doing about it?"

"That's the problem, the local police and people are untouched by his crimes so don't look too closely. In London, he is a thug, and everyone pays him either in money or in physical pain and he controls all within North London. Of course, he has his gang and if things ever go wrong, they silently take the blame because his punishments are far worse that the courts."

Roly stopped and looked around at his audience. Ivor looked shocked. After a brief pause, he said, "Roly, I live in Basildon, I know Thurley Street but I know nothing about this person. Are you sure?"

"Ivor, how long have you lived there?"

"About eighteen months now; it is cheaper than the city... the start of the countryside and a train straight into the city of London. I thought it was perfect."

"I'm sure it is but it is also perfect for those who do other things in London. Look, let's get back to enjoying ourselves and not focus on these bad things tonight. This is supposed to be a celebration for all you old school friends not about my issues."

They all sighed, and Jamie said, "Well, if we are going to talk about other issues, let me start." They all giggled and soon the conversations were bouncing back and forth in full party mood.

The evening was full of fun, and it was clear that

there were many old friends happy to catch up but even happier to remind each other of past escapades and thrills. With talk of an early start the next day, it wasn't too long before people were ready to excuse themselves and head off to bed. Roly nodded to Jamie, and they began to head upstairs. Roly waved a hand to all and shouted, "Goodnight," but of course Jamie took at least another ten minutes to hug and kiss everyone with promises to keep in touch before he got away and to his room.

The haphazard meetings at breakfast were different; everyone was quieter, many in a rush and some slowly trying to handle hangovers. Jamie sat down at the corner table where Roly had already started.

"That wasn't so bad, was it? Did I embarrass you?"

"Jamie, it was terrific. It must have been such fun for you to meet up with old friends and you could never embarrass me – well, you could if you really tried but let's not go there. It was a good time and thanks for taking me."

"Well, we don't have to head back early, do we? Why don't we do some shopping in the city and after lunch we can head back. What do you think?"

Roly smiled and nodded, and after shopping and a pub lunch in Fulham, they headed back before the start of the rush hour.

That evening, they had a far more normal evening at the Marina bar updating Chrissie. Jamie had to admit that he'd never got Roly to dance but they were all clearly in far better spirits. So relaxed and somewhat content they all went home. For the moment all was forgotten about fighting back.

Chapter 24

A Focus on Hopkins

That was not the same for Ivor, as all that following day his thoughts strayed away from the job at hand and lingered on Roly's comments. On the train back he decided he had to see for himself. It was not too far out of his normal ten-minute walk home to divert down Thurley Street. He strolled and looked either side for the big, white affluent house Roly had described. All the houses were well-to-do, but he knew he had found it when he saw it. It was just that bit bigger and whiter than the others with a wide, gated driveway and a white painted wooden fence around the front garden that did not allow a view in from the pavement for anyone under six feet tall.

He stood for just a moment but even in that short time he saw a young, fit man walk to the gate and look across at him. Ivor wrestled in his pockets as if he was looking for something before hurrying on.

As he arrived home, his two young children ran out of his more modest home and jumped into his awaiting arms and his wife smiled and waved from the kitchen window. The family dog even woke up from an afternoon sleep to waddle over with its tail wagging. Ivor could not help but feel how incongruous it was to have two such different homes so close together. After dinner, and after updating his wife on the old school get-together, even though it was dark and getting late Ivor announced he was taking the dog out for a walk. He left through the back door and as he walked around to the front he stopped in his garage. In a few minutes he left carrying a plastic bag.

It was not long before he was outside the house in Thurley Street. All was quiet, and a quick walk past the driveway allowed him to see inside. No cars and a room light on in the back. He turned around and walked back to the white fence. Reaching into his plastic bag he pulled out a pot of green outside paint and a thick brush. Within moments he was painting. He just splashed on his comments and shortly was able to back off to the other side of the road to read his words:

"GANGSTER'S HOUSE" in large two-foot capitals and underneath smaller but still easily read, "Know your neighbour, he's a gangster and thug!"

Pleased with his efforts he glanced around and seeing it was all clear, promptly placed the brush and paint can back in the plastic bag and wandered home, the bemused family dog following by his side.

"I'm in bed," shouted his wife. "You took a while?"

"Yeah, I just wanted a bit of fresh air. I will be up in a moment."

In the kitchen, he scrubbed his hands to remove as much paint as possible and then sat down with his laptop. He had just one more thing to do for Roly. He entered the Essex BBC website and using their contact details for news he typed in an anonymous message suggesting that they check out Thurley Street.

The following morning, before the wife and kids were up, Ivor left the house and walked along his normal path to the station. He felt pleased with himself. At least he had ensured that the people of Basildon now knew who lived amongst them. For Ivor this was a small but important local issue. He had no idea what he had sparked.

That day was a slow news day. BBC Essex had received Ivor's anonymous note and decided that they should at least send someone down to Thurley Street. A young journalist paid it a visit in the very early hours of the morning. Even in the night-time with the streetlamps providing a dimmed light, he saw Ivor's fence message. He stood there and called back to the office.

"Stay there and wait," was the message he got. With no other news topics threatening to burst out, the news department looked into who owned the house. At 4am the regional news groups update the national news groups. At this point, the relevance of Mr Hopkins became clear as did recent news stories. The storyline was escalated and by 6am a full news van with audio, cameras, presenter, and full crew arrived. It is extremely difficult to keep secrets within the various news channels and the escalation within the BBC caused attention within the others. By 6.30am, two more news van crews were there outside Hopkins' home. Everyone there knew each other; they chatted and tossed coins for who was going to go into the town for coffees and snacks, but they all agreed that they had no idea what they were going to do or were even supposed to do. But sometimes these events create their own content. That is what happened that morning in Thurley Street.

Five minutes before 8am, a young well-built man walked around the corner. George, a young thug who was Hopkins' personal bodyguard and driver, was arriving for work. He was half asleep and not paying any real attention to the world except that he would be in trouble if he was late. The sight of the various news crews was disorienting. Confused, he pushed past them and tried to get to the gate. The moment the news people realised he was more than a passer-by, they pounced.

"Who are you, mate? Do you work for Hopkins? What do you do? What about this message? Is it true? Do you work for a gangster? Is Hopkins a gangster? Is the fence message right?"

There were many questions directed at George. He was a bit slow – not too slow to allow anyone in through the gate but far too slow to respond to these questions. He stepped back and walked five metres to see the message on the garden fence.

"Shit, he'll go nuts on this," was all that came out. Because he had spoken, an audio guy tried to place a microphone in front of his face. In the huddle that followed the various crews rushing forward the microphone hit George on the chin and so he reacted in the most natural way for him.

"Fuck off, you bastards. Hopkins will kill you bastards if you don't go away," and he lashed out with fist and boot. Two reporters went down, and all the others backed off and made a three-metre circle around him. The circle moved as George, now in a state of anxious regret over his actions and words, slowly and hesitantly backed to the gate and entered the driveway, securing the gate behind him. As he walked up to the house, they all rushed back to the vans, and you could hear the whoops of joy when they realised that they had it all captured on video. Within minutes, this video, edited with bleeps, was on every national breakfast news programme.

George entered the house distressed and could not believe that his boss was in the back finishing breakfast and listening to the radio completely unaware of everything that had gone on outside.

"Morning, George. Late again, I see."

"Mr Hopkins, the press, they are all outside… it's crazy."

"What do you mean? Who's outside?" He saw the fear on George's face and crossed to the front of the house. A glance through the living room window saw a phalanx of news reporters and cameras all looking up at him. He backed off, pulling the net curtains together. Again, all captured on video.

"What in God's name is going on? George, what's down there?"

"Mr Hopkins, someone has painted graffiti on your garden fence."

"So, what does it say?"

"Oh God, I can't remember. Something about you being a gangster and a bad neighbour. I don't remember it all."

"It's on the news, come see," shouted Hopkins' wife from the kitchen.

Hopkins walked into the room and leaned on the counter as he squinted to see the morning news special on an old, small colour television. At the sight of George's words being bleeped as he lashed out at the reporters, the significance of the moment started to come home to him.

"George, you stupid bastard, you cannot attack the press and you certainly cannot mention my name. Get away from me or I will do something that you won't forget in a hurry."

Hopkins' wife put an arm around the stricken lad and walked him into another room before returning to her husband as he paced up and down. He desperately wanted to look again from the window but didn't want to appear gazing from the curtains again.

"I'll have to go out and talk to them. Just have to."

Five minutes later, in full diplomatic mode and wearing slippers and cardigan to try and appear the retired gentleman, Hopkins walked out of the front door and waved to the press as he slowly ambled down the driveway towards them.

"My goodness, what is all this fuss?" he asked with an innocent smile as he met them at the gate.

"Are you Mr Hopkins? Are you a gangster? Who wrote the message on the fence?"

"What message?"

Shutting the gate behind him, he edged through the press to see the fence.

"Oh, my Lord, why would someone do that?" he bemused aloud. "You know, I bet it is those silly kids, they were throwing sticks up to try and hit a squirrel that they saw up a tree in the garden and I came out and shouted at them. Told them I would call the police if they didn't stop. They called me names and ran off. That was a few days ago. It is the only thing I can think of," he said out loud for them all to hear. "It will have to be painted over. I'll go and arrange that now. Thank you, please, out of my way." And he headed back to his gate again like a somewhat doddery old fellow.

The press was just not going to accept that, and the questions came back fast and loud.

"Perhaps it wasn't a squirrel, Mr Hopkins. Others have called you a gangster before, haven't they?"

Hopkins spun around, no longer the confused old fellow.

"Who said that what the hell are you suggesting? You think it's true? Get the hell out of my way."

"Didn't Roland Johns claim you were a gangster? Do you think he did it?"

"Mr Johns was touring London's East End, when he saw me talking to some old work colleagues. He got confused and the police took him away. For God's sake, I am a retired man. Now you lot go away before I get the police to move you." With that, a clearly frustrated Hopkins pushed his gate and securing it behind him, walked back to the house without responding to any more queries or even looking over his shoulder to give them a picture. Once inside the house he sat down and scowled loudly to no one in particular as he collected his thoughts.

After reflecting for a moment, he picked up the phone and made a call.

"I don't fucking care. That fence must be painted before the end of this morning. Don't disappoint me." He hung up. His second phone call was a little bit more controlled. "No, I cannot come. You saw the news, didn't you? If I come, they might follow. So, listen up, we'll do it as a teleconference call. Yes, you get everyone there and I'll call in. Have you got a speaker phone? Good. Don't worry, give me a little time and I'll sort it out. I'll call at three o'clock, bye."

He sat back and pondered the situation. He was not convinced that that guy, Roland Johns, had done it. If he was going to do something like this, why do it on his garden fence? Johns would have done it in the city or on the internet with that crazy website he had set up. Johns would not come in the middle of the night and paint on his fence, he was not the sort of person who would have asked someone else to do it. So, who was it? Who was trying to bring attention to him?

Chapter 25

They Took Him

That question that Hopkins was wrestling with was also being pondered by all who had seen any of the news reports, and many had seen them. Roly was bemused. Gareth rang and asked him what he thought and when he arrived at The Water's Edge he gave Chrissie and Jamie the same answer to the same question but without the pleasantries he had spoken with Gareth.

"How should I know what's going on or who did it? That guy is a gangster and God knows how many people he has had an impact on, but I was here in Cranport with all of you so don't think I have any answers. God only knows why I ever got involved before but I'm not now."

He walked away from them all and entered an office. He tried to sit down and do some work. He even went as far as to pick up some office papers but when he found himself re-reading the same sentence three times without any meaning, he put them down and walked back out to Chrissie and Jamie.

"I'm sorry, you two are the last people I should shout at and be grumpy with. Look, this is as much a surprise to me as it is to you. It has nothing to do with me so why don't we just get on with this work as there is still so much to do." He hugged them both together and walked back to the office hoping to be more in control.

The day was uneventful until around lunchtime when journalists appeared outside with requests to interview Roly. At first, this was declined but when they stayed and even broadcast from outside without him, Roly decided that a short, simple interview might put an end to it.

Gareth advised him on who best to invite and then went outside to bring them in.

"Nothing fancy or over the top please," stated Roly as he sat them down with a simple video camera and presenter, "and five minutes maximum," as he tried to establish control.

The presenter started, "I'm at The Water's Edge in Roland Johns' office. Today, we have all seen the graffiti messages painted on a man's house in Basildon where he has been portrayed as a gangster. So, Roland Johns, is Mr Hopkins a gangster? After all, the newspapers reported that you called him that just a few weeks ago."

"These two incidents are not related. Yes, I had some words with this man in London, but I had nothing to do with this painting on his fence last night. I was here."

"Let me repeat my question to you, Mr Johns, is this man a gangster?"

Roland had so wanted to control what he said and how he said it. He wanted to simply clear himself from being associated with this graffiti prank, but he failed.

"Look, this man in my view is an evil person. He treats people as prey, he controls others by fear and pain, and he makes money from crime taking advantage of the weak and needy. What would you call that?"

"If you're right, Mr Johns, I would call that a gangster."

"So would I, but let me repeat what I said earlier, I had nothing to do with this fence painting. God only knows how many people this fellow has had dealings with, so why don't you check with them and see if they did it."

The lunchtime news got worse for Hopkins. There was Roly's face in the camera and the words echoed out.

"Look, this man in my view is an evil person. He treats people as prey, he controls others by fear and pain, and he makes money from crime by taking advantage of the weak and needy."

Hopkins appeared to be in control but as he put down his teacup there was a bang on the table, and he looked crazily at his hand that now held just the cup handle. He sat down to think and prepare for his three o'clock phone call. He knew that if he appeared out of control, he would appear weak. He had no intention of that happening.

***

At 3pm, several characters were sat in a room at the back of the pub waiting for the phone to ring. They had all seen the news reports, they were all confused. Some were wondering how it would end for Hopkins; all were wondering how it would end for them. The phone rang. It was picked up and put on a speaker cradle.

"Are you all there?" echoed the harsh voice of Hopkins.

"Yes, boss. How are you?"

"I'm sure you have all seen the news this morning." Several of them nodded. After a pause, Hopkins continued. "Look, this is just a crazy one-off. The press is already thinning out outside and in a few days it will all be behind us. We must ensure that we do nothing that will keep this nonsense going. As soon as there is another national story of interest, they will be off. So, I want you all to just take it easy."

One of the men spoke, "Boss, do you know who the hell did this?"

"Not at present, but we will."

"Did you hear what that guy down south said?"

"Yeah, but I don't think it was him. Yet, we don't need him speaking out anymore. This hero," said with a sneering voice, "is the type of person who can keep it in the news. We've got to find a way to keep him quiet."

"So, what do you want us to do, Boss?"

"As I said, nothing at the moment. Don't stick together. The last thing we need is for the television to be broadcasting outside the pub counting you guys in and out. Take a few days' holiday. Spend some time with your wives or tarts. Keep your heads down and you'll be contacted when I need you. Mind you if you hear anything or find out anything be sure to keep me informed. OK, your holidays have started. Get out and take it easy. We will be back into business shortly. Take care and bye."

The phone went dead, and they all looked at each other. It didn't seem that straightforward to them, but it was Hopkins' problem, not theirs.

"Fuck it, I'm going to Newbury Races, anyone coming?" asked one older fellow. Some did but some didn't. They split up and moved on.

The youngest there had been Terry and ever since he had replaced Ronnie in the group he had been treated as an outsider. He attended meetings and he got involved in more activities, but they didn't treat him as an equal. Terry felt it, his lads felt it, the group knew it. For quite a while now, Terry had been exercising his small brain to try and find a way to establish himself. He wanted to be recognised, not as an equal but far higher than that. Ronnie had been viewed as the eventual successor to Hopkins. Terry wanted that role for himself. He walked into the bar and strolled across to one of his lads.

"Get everyone back to the house. We have some things to sort out. See you in an hour." He then walked out to his car still in deep thought.

In the shabby house they sat around waiting for Terry to speak.

"The boss is in trouble, you've all seen the news. Well, we are going to sort it out for him and if we do it right, he will be well pleased."

They all looked at him in bemusement. "What's wrong with the boss?" asked one.

"Don't you bastards ever watch the news or read the newspapers?"

His comments received simply more bemusement.

"Shit," he continued, "someone is trying to get at the boss. Someone painted a message on his garden fence saying he was a gangster. Another guy was interviewed on television and said the boss was an evil man and a gangster. All this is causing a lot of attention that we don't need. So, we are going to help fix it."

"How? Who are these people?" asked one of his more lucid lads.

"Who the hell knows who painted the fence, but the other guy is from down south. If we can find his address, we can pop down and pay him a visit. We need his name and town. I think his name is Roland Johns, but we need to check. OK, let's get on the web and check out the BBC and whatever else we can."

It took less than thirty minutes on his iPhone for

Terry to have not only the name of Roland Johns and the town of Cranport but also the name of his hotel The Waters Edge. That was enough. Terry spoke again.

"OK, by tomorrow morning four of us will be there. Meet me here at 2am and don't be late. Bring some sandwiches and a drink but no booze. Now, go get some sleep, we might be up all night."

***

While all this was going on, for Roly things seemed to be calming down. The journalists had all left, Chrissie or Jamie had been around to ask questions about normal work issues and as the end of the workday approached, he sought them out.

"I thought I would head off back to the flat. Anyone want to come along?"

"Sorry, Roly. Derek is already back at our place, and he is preparing something for dinner."

"Ah, Roly," answered Chrissie. "Mum and Dad are out tonight so I have no babysitter and I cannot bring Stevie. On school nights he needs an early night. Just take it easy and I'll see you here tomorrow."

"Ah, tomorrow," interjected Jamie. "I need someone here early with me. We have furniture being delivered first thing. A big delivery."

"OK, an early night for me then, but I will be in tomorrow at what time, Jamie?"

"Eight at the latest."

"Done," said Roly and then made his way back to his flat.

In the middle of the night, Terry and his lads drove down

the motorway all looking with high frequency as the GPS noted the reducing mileage to Cranport. As the day's light started, they entered the town and followed the GPS to the harbour and the parking lot of the hotel. It was empty and they parked up at the back corner. It took five minutes for them to pull out some bags from the back and inevitably two of them had to piddle in the hedge but then they sat down to wait.

"Listen up," said Terry. "That website said that he worked here each day. The hotel isn't open yet, but he is organising it all. So, we wait here until he arrives and then we take him. If we get questioned, we are just visiting the seaside and slept in the car overnight because we'd been drinking. Got it?"

They all nodded and slumped into their car seats and waited. It was over two hours later before Jamie arrived. He drove straight into the carpark but parked up to the right of the hotel entrance and as he was getting out, in came Roly. They waved and Roly parked next to him. Only when they were together walking towards the hotel entrance did they notice the three men approaching and a car following slowly behind.

Assuming that these were all to do with the imminent delivery, they waved and waited at the door. It happened so quickly. Roly stepped forward to greet the front man when a smaller man at his side stepped past him and punched Jamie in the face. The only sound was the crunch of the fist against Jamie's face but that sound alone was enough for Roly to spin around in horror and shock. Then came an equally powerful blow into the side of Roly's back. It took all the wind out of his body and his knees simply crumpled. As he started to fall, he was grabbed from under his arms and the car doors opened.

Roly was thrown in with a thug at each side of him and then the car accelerated away.

Jamie lay unconscious on the floor, and it was several minutes later before a passer-by on their way to work looked over and saw him. It was several more minutes before the police and ambulance arrived. It was even longer before Jamie woke up in the hospital. Even in severe pain from a broken nose, damaged teeth and split, bloody lips, Jamie screamed for the attention of the police.

"They got him, they got him."

The bemused police looked to the doctors to calm down the patient. Jamie refused to allow it. He got them to call Chrissie before slumping back on the gurney and waiting in agony.

By this time, the gang and their captive were already halfway back up the motorway. Roly had tried to struggle but each move brought him another punch and more pain. So, he sat in fear and waited.

"OK, listen up. Time to call the boss. No speaking when I'm on the phone."

Terry picked up his mobile and speed dialled Hopkins. It was answered on the second ring.

"Boss, I got him."

Hopkins listened and in puzzlement answered. "Who have you got?"

"That Roland Johns guy. The guy that said all those things about you on the news yesterday."

"What? How? Are you fucking crazy?"

This was not the response that Terry was expecting and now somewhat troubled he tried to explain.

"But, boss, you said yesterday that we had to find a way to get this guy. So, I did. I looked him up on the internet and me and the lads went down and got him. He's here in the car now."

"I told you all to take a holiday. Oh my God, who the hell do you think they are going to suspect when this gets out? Where are you going?"

"Where do you want me to take him, boss?"

"Jesus, you idiot. Do you want to bring him here so he can whitewash the fence?"

Terry was actually thinking about this option when Hopkins continued: "You fucking fool, you can't return him now so just take him to your house. What time will you get there?"

"About eleven-thirty."

"I will be there at twelve. Now listen to me, you goon. Drive sensibly. Get there, get inside and stay out of view until I arrive. Do nothing more. Do you understand me?"

Terry was in the middle of answering yes when the line went dead. Stuck in rush hour traffic, moving at a slow but regular pace, all of them with high anxiety stared dumbly ahead. Now the anxiety that Roly felt was almost matched by the others.

Chrissie rushed into the hospital demanding to see Jamie. He was curled up and his face was crumpled and still bleeding. Chrissie cried out and delicately cradled his head in her arms. In a mix of jumbled sounds Jamie looked into her eyes and spoke, "They got him, they got Roly. Oh, Chrissie, what are we going to do?"

"I saw his car in the car park. How many were there?"

"Three and a driver"

"Let me get the police here."

Chrissie rushed out, grabbed a constable by the arm

and dragged him into Jamie's cubicle.

"Officer, listen to him. Someone has kidnapped Roland Johns. You've got to put a search out for him."

The policeman looked confused but recognised the urgency.

"Who's kidnapped who?" he asked as he pulled out his pen and notepad.

"Jamie, did you see them?" asked Chrissie.

"Three or four thugs."

"Have you seen them before? Do you know who they are?"

Jamie shook his head at the constable.

"What car were they in... did you get any details? Colour? Model? Any part of the registration?" To all these questions Jamie simply shook his head and sobbed in Chrissie's arms.

"I'll call it in to the office, Miss, but without any details I don't know what we can do?"

They were left sobbing as the police officer left to radio in the incident, and as the doctor entered the room, Chrissie said, "Jamie, leave it with me now. We'll do something I promise you, but now you have to let the doctor mend your pretty face. Just relax, I'll be back in a short time, I promise."

As she left the hospital car park heading to the hotel, she wrestled with what she could do. As the hopelessness overwhelmed her, she drove with heaving shoulders, sobs and tears rolling down her face.

"They took him, they took him," she repeated to herself.

Chapter 26

How Lucky Can You Be

Chrissie entered the hotel and there in the front of the car park were two large delivery trucks. Her dad and Derek were trying to organise them. She called them over and walked to the general office area. Gareth was making coffee. Chrissie had stopped crying but still clearly shaken she called them together and explained.

"What can we do? The police said they had nothing to work on, but this is just like what they did when they drove away with that kid. Can't we get them to put a block on the roads to London?"

"We need to raise this as a big news item, let me make some calls." Gareth left and started calling on his mobile.

Derek wanted to go to the hospital and Trev said he would take him, but they were pulled back to everyday life by a delivery man shouting over.

"So where do you want this stuff?"

Chrissie looked at the other two and shrugged. "Just put it in piles in the reception area."

Gareth returned. "I have contacted all the news people I know, and they are going to be running notices on the TV, on their websites and on newspaper headlines. What else can we do?"

As the sobs returned, Chrissie shook her head, "I don't know, I just don't know."

"Well, we must stay here in case the reporters, or the police arrive."

They were soon joined by Trev and Margie, and they spent the next several hours just waiting. Yet what Gareth had done was to prove vital.

***

The car was now off the motorway, and they were now winding through the streets of London and all beginning to feel more at ease, except for Roly.

Bob and Mary were heading home after their weekly supermarket shop. He walked with a walking stick in his right hand while Mary walked with one in her left hand. This was so convenient because each other hand held the edge of the handle of their new shopping trolley. It was a gift from their daughter, and it had made a significant improvement when shopping. Mary talked and Bob listened. Whatever was the subject of Mary's conversation it received the same nodded response from Bob. Bob's main attention was not the conversation but rather the wobbly front wheel of the trolley. If either his or Mary's pressure on the edges of the handle were not equal the trolley would shoot off to the left or right. God forbid if the small wheels got caught in any pavement crack. As the trolley threatened once again to surge to the left, Bob pulled up slightly on his side to re-establish it straight ahead. This delicate task made him unaware of the approaching car. As they moved forward there was a large beep from a car horn, and they had to stop fast as a car pulled off the road onto a driveway into a dark, dreary house.

"He almost hit us. What was all that about?" said Bob.

Mary had only slightly paused on whatever she was

talking about before she continued straight on. As they walked Bob glowered, looking through the broken front hedgerow he saw some young men get out of the car. What really got his attention was that one of the men seemed to stumble only for another to grab him and slap him across the head at the same time.

"Did you see that?"

"Did I see what?" asked Mary slightly annoyed to be interrupted.

"He hit that other man on the head."

"Well, it's got nothing to do with us. Now come on, almost home and a nice cup of tea is waiting."

On they plodded. Minutes later with the shopping all put away they sat down with their cups of tea. Time to read the paper, thought Bob and just a little while before the one o'clock news.

Terry rang the boss to say they had arrived and was pleased to end another sharp, unpleasant call. He waited and shared his anxiety with his lads. Roly was hunched up in the corner of the room on a hard chair that had seen better days. As he huddled down, he tried desperately to herd his body pain into one particular area. It did not matter which area, but he felt that he could control it more effectively from one place rather than allowing waves of pain to swarm over his entire body. It was the only way he could stop it overwhelming him.

Constantly looking through the front window, Terry announced, "He's here."

Everyone, except Roly, jumped to attention as Terry walked to the door and opened it. George had driven his boss on their thirty-minute journey. In that time not a single word had passed between them. The atmosphere in the car was chilling and every few minutes George would glance at his boss in the interior mirror hoping to see if he had calmed down.

"Stay in the car and just wait," he said.

Hopkins strode up to the front door and ignoring the welcoming smile from Terry, simply barged past him into the room. Ignoring the others, he walked over to Roly and sat down in front of him on an old armchair.

"You are one crazy bastard. Why did you go on television and say those things?"

Roly looked up and for the first time felt some sort of energy run through his veins.

"Good morning, Mr Gangster. Now we have an interesting situation, don't we? However, let me answer your question. I did not go on television. They came to me. They asked me a question and I gave them an honest answer. That is what's confusing you, the very idea that a question deserves an honest answer. Now with me missing, who do you think they are going to put their next set of questions to?"

Hopkins shook his head and glanced over with disgust at Terry, who was standing there.

"You stupid bastard, he is right about that point."

"Hey, boss, he can't talk anymore if we finish him. Why don't I..."

As he spoke Terry removed a pistol from a bag and waved it in Roly's direction. Hopkins, with a speedy reaction far beyond expectation for an old man, reached up and slapped his hand away.

"Get the fuck out of here, get back. When you don't think you are stupid, when you do think you are worse. Let me think this out. You and the lads get in the bedroom. Now. I'll call you when I want you."

They all moved sullenly into the bedroom and when the door shut, Hopkins and Roly could hear them whispering.

"Talking about stupidity, can I ask you a question?"

Hopkins looked over and half-smiled before he responded.

"You got a question, go for it."

"You are a truly evil man but not an unintelligent one. What I don't understand is why an intelligent person would choose to live like this."

Hopkins sighed and leant back in the armchair. He paused for a time as he thought about how to answer the question. He certainly was not going to justify himself to Roly or indeed to another person, but he felt a yearning to explain.

"You see me as an old, intelligent man. Would you, I wonder, have recognised that intelligence if I was young, inexperienced, poor and from a low, working-class family? No one chooses the situation they are born into. As you grow up your world widens. First, it is your immediate family and house, then it is your school and local area and then as you approach adulthood you become aware of the broader world. All along that journey you start to understand the rules. You cannot argue against what your parents say. Then you have to do what the teachers say. You have to fit in with what your friends want to do. Then suddenly, you are thrown out into this wide, wide world and told to get a job. A job, as what? Go to a factory and be treated as an adult schoolkid, God knows you cannot get an office job because you're from the poor side of town. University? That was full of all those characters in the books you read in the town library but not real. Not for you. So quickly you start to understand. If you cannot live the life you want by the rules then obviously, those rules don't apply to you."

Quite a long speech and it seemed to change the relationship between Roly and Hopkins.

"So, you just set up your own rules?" asked Roly.

"Yes."

"But not on your own."

"No, there were and there are many who want to live by different rules. I just made sure that they lived by mine. If they didn't want too much, they got it. If they wanted more, they often got a surprise."

Suddenly, a car horn started to beep loudly and then stopped suddenly. Hopkins got up and walked to the front window and even the lads in the bedroom started to come out.

"Would you believe it," said Hopkins and he slowly walked back to his armchair. "Fuck, it's the police, my God, they're everywhere, and they're armed." "What are we going to do?" asked Terry.

"Just sit down you fool, it's over. Don't make it worse."

But Hopkins' words did not have an effect on the young lads. They all ran to the back door and as they tried to exit, they were met by a myriad of armed officers.

Roly and Hopkins sat staring at each other, listening to the shuffling and squeals outside. Soon it was quiet.

"Time to go, I suppose." Hopkins stood in the middle of the room. Roly stood clumsily and took a step. He half-stumbled and Hopkins put his arm under his and held him steady.

"Thanks," mumbled Roly.

"Well, you know me, I like to help the weak and feeble."

They opened the front door and in front of them was their waiting reception.

Within minutes, Hopkins, Terry, and the lads were all whisked off in police vans. One Police Inspector stood by Roly.

"Are you hurt? Do you need to go to hospital?"

"No, bruised a bit but I just want to go home. You know, they have a gun, a pistol."

The Inspector waved his hands and spoke with one of his men, "Make sure you find their gun."

He turned back to Roly who had a more critical question to ask.

"How did you find me?"

The Police Inspector pointed to Bob standing over the far side of the street.

"An honest citizen saw you being taken into the house and when he heard it on the lunchtime news, he called us."

"My God," sighed Roly. "How lucky can you be?"

Chapter 27

Epilogue

Weeks later, after the trials, after the news frenzy, after Jamie's face recovery, life returned to what they all hoped would be normal.

Chrissie had started to move beyond following Roly everywhere, from room to room, just to make sure he was fine. If Derek and Jamie had some short words, Derek would kiss Jamie on the small scar the side of his nose and tell him that he still loved him, and The Water's Edge started a live trial with three selected families for a week.

The gun had proved critical. The police were able to link it to the murders of Ronnie and Jules. Hopkins and his gang of lads were now going away for a very long time. No doubt, Hopkins had left an empty seat that someone would fill but this was an ending for Roly.

Mid-afternoon, Roly strolled across the reception and headed for the ice-cream hut in the corner. The sun streamed in as he sat on the open bench with ice-cream in hand and looking out over the shore. He heard a slight commotion over one side and saw a young mother struggling to control an energetic three-year-old. The child broke free and ran over to Roly.

"Mr. Mr. Buy me an ice cream, please?"

The mother ran over and clearly embarrassed, apologised. "I'm sorry, sir. I'm truly sorry. I told her that I had no money for ice-cream, but she just wouldn't listen." She tried to grab the child as Roly responded.

"No need to apologise. You see here in this place ice creams are free. Let me get you both one." He continued to talk as he stepped over to the ice cream hut and took two ice creams from Derek and handed them over.

"The Water's Edge is a place to help those who through no fault of their own have fallen on hard times. Just remember, you do not need to apologise, we are all trying to get by as best we can."

The mother leaned over and kissed him on the cheek and whispered, "Thank you."

As they walked away, Roly sat back and smiled as he heard his inner voice speak to himself, "All my life I seem to have been looking for something, but I never knew what. Sometimes it seemed so elusive I stopped searching, but I always knew there was something missing. Now there is nothing missing."

The End

Milton Keynes UK
Ingram Content Group UK Ltd.
UKHW020213141023
430514UK00009B/84

9 781835 630037